By VICTORIA MILNE

PURPLE METHOD
Purple Method

Published by DREAMSPINNER PRESS
www.dreamspinnerpress.com

PURPLE
METHOD

VICTORIA MILNE

Published by

DREAMSPINNER PRESS

5032 Capital Circle SW, Suite 2, PMB# 279, Tallahassee, FL 32305-7886 USA
www.dreamspinnerpress.com

Purple Method
© 2019 Victoria Milne

Cover Art
© 2019 Garrett Leigh
http://www.blackjazzdesign.com/
Cover content is for illustrative purposes only and any person depicted on the cover is a model.

Trade Paperback ISBN: 978-1-64405-342-3
Digital ISBN: 978-1-64405-341-6
Library of Congress Control Number: 2019900690
Trade Paperback published July 2019
v. 1.0

Printed in the United States of America
(∞)
This paper meets the requirements of
ANSI/NISO Z39.48-1992 (Permanence of Paper).

For Maria

ACKNOWLEDGMENTS

A MASSIVE thank-you to my family and friends for their continual support, understanding, and patience throughout this journey. I couldn't have done it without you.

Maria—thank you for helping me realize that Max needed his own story. Purple Method wouldn't exist if it wasn't for you.

A special thank-you to my wonderful beta readers Jane A. and George Loveland.

Thank you to everyone at Havant and District Writers' Circle for their generous and supportive feedback that has helped me to grow as a writer and to make Purple Method better.

And finally, to everyone who has helped me with my writing since I began in 2012, thank you so much. Max was one of the very first characters I wrote seven years ago, and after a very steep learning curve, I'm excited to be able to say that his story is finally ready to tell….

PROLOGUE

MAX DIAZ'S legs were trembling so hard, he was amazed they were still holding him up. As he waited at the edge of the stage, hidden out of sight, his throat grew tight, and he dreaded the moment he'd be expected to perform. He didn't think he could speak right now, let alone sing the complicated vocals.

After years of Max pleading with his brother to let him join the band, Tony had finally relented. He suspected Tony had done it to ease the blow of their dad leaving them. It was just the two of them against the rest of the world.

But that didn't change the fact that Max was now the lead singer of an actual band. He still couldn't believe it. Couldn't believe they'd trusted him with the responsibility of fronting them when they were all so talented.

The venue was small, but right now, the stage looked huge. There had to be at least twenty people watching them. Twenty people who would witness his epic failure if he didn't pull his shit together.

Tony, Lee, and Kyle—his bandmates—were preparing the equipment, like Max had seen them do countless times before when he'd been to their gigs. Next time he'd help out, but right now he wasn't complaining that they were leaving him alone. Kyle was testing the microphones, Tony was moving one of the drums, and Lee was tuning his bass guitar. It wouldn't be long now.

Max's legs were numb as the trembling crept through his body all the way to his fingertips, and his head swam as queasiness threatened.

"Max, breathe," Tony said.

Opening his eyes, Max gasped a breath and tried to focus on his brother.

"You've got this."

"But what if I don't—"

"You do. Just pretend we're back home in the garage. You're ready. Do you think I'd let you onstage with us if you weren't?"

Max scrubbed his hands over his eyes. That was true. "But what if I let you down? What if I screw up?"

Pulling him into a hug, Tony said, "Focus on the music and you'll be fine. If you're thinking about screwing up, then you will. Don't think about that."

"Ready?" Lee asked.

Tony patted Max on the back and released him.

"Yeah. Let's do this," Max said, and prayed Tony was right.

While the others took their places onstage, Max turned his thoughts to their chaotic band practices. Was it helping? He wasn't sure. If anything, he was more nervous.

Oh God. The queasiness worsened, and Max knew he couldn't hold it in this time. He made a dash for the restrooms out back, barely making it in time. When he returned to the stage, Tony and Lee were playing the intro on loop, and all three of them were glaring at him.

Max grabbed the microphone and gripped it as hard as he could, terrified it would slip through his fingers as he stepped onto the stage. He closed his eyes and focused on Tony's deafening drumbeat, and then on Lee's bass guitar, the deep notes thundering through his body, dissipating the tingling in his limbs. By the time Kyle's guitar joined the mix, Max's nerves were giving way—transforming into the familiar charged excitement music always brought him.

Bringing the microphone to his lips and taking a deep breath, Max opened his eyes. Their audience looked interested, but they weren't leaping about yet. As Max sang the first lines of "Scream My Name," a couple of people whistled and nodded their approval.

He could do this. He totally could. And if he had the chance to perform like this for the rest of his life, he'd die happy.

Grinning, Max raised his arms in the air, and he swore that by the end of their set he'd have them all screaming for Purple Method.

CHAPTER ONE

Max
Four years later

"FUCKING CANCEL it, then, Lee," Tony screamed. "We may as well not bother playing tonight if you're gonna make us start with that piece-of-shit song."

Max winced as his brother slammed Lee's bedroom door and stood in front of it, his arms folded, glaring at the two of them as they sat on Lee's bed. Great. If only he'd left to go unpack like he'd meant to five minutes ago rather than coming in here to talk to Lee about some new pictures on social media from their gig last night. Now he was trapped in the middle of their shouting match—again.

Lee stood, and Max turned to look at him. His eyes had narrowed and his jaw was clenched as he thundered across to Tony, his long black hair flowing in a wave behind him. It was a world away from only moments ago when Max had been relaxing with a beer and enjoying being back home after months of touring.

Lee stopped inches from Tony, squaring up to him. "Just 'cause you didn't write it, doesn't automatically make 'Solitude' no good."

It was the same old argument every time. Max didn't feel guilty for not taking his brother's side. Not one bit. Tony was infuriating these days. It seemed like everything had to be done his way or it wasn't good enough. Max wished Tony would open up to him, but it felt as though each day they drifted further apart.

Tony stepped closer to Lee so they were nose-to-nose. The fact that he looked as though he was enjoying the confrontation was making Lee even angrier—Max could tell by the flush to the side of Lee's neck.

"We play 'Bind Me' first, or I don't get onstage tonight."

"What, and disappoint all your adoring fans?" Lee taunted as they began to circle each other. He snorted a laugh. "I could replace you like that." Lee snapped his fingers in Tony's face. "You think I don't have ten drummers knocking on my door, wanting to take your place in Purple Method?"

Max shifted so he was leaning forward, ready to get the hell out of there the second he got the chance. He didn't have to wait long. Lee and Tony stepped closer to the bed, leaving just enough space for Max to squeeze past. He took his chance and breathed a sigh of relief as he slammed the door on them.

"Try it. I dare you." Not even the closed door was enough to shut them out. "You know as well as I do none of them can play like me. We start with 'Bind—'"

He had to get out of there. Max opened the front door and walked out into the sweltering midafternoon heat.

As HE sloped into the shade of the juniper tree that obscured the entrance to the townhouse he'd been to countless times before, Max wondered what Pete would say when he showed up unannounced like this—if he'd be surprised. He took a drag from his cigarette and then exhaled the tension that had been intensifying all afternoon.

Traffic crawled past along the dusty street as shoppers headed away from downtown Elfinbrook's air-conditioned mall. It was almost tempting to seek sanctuary there from the blistering northwest Nevada sun… almost.

Max leaned back against the coiled bark of the tree and kicked at the dirt as he took another drag from his cigarette and half closed his eyes. A loose chunk of rubber from his New Rock boot caught on the metal gate to his left, and he jerked it free with a sharp tug, causing the gate to judder back against the crumbling wall with a clank.

"Kiai!"

His heart leaped and thundered in his chest. What the hell was that? Rescuing the squashed cigarette from between his lips, he molded it back into shape and searched for the source of the sound, squinting against the sharp rays of the sun.

"Kiai!"

There it was again. Max glanced around, half expecting a band of stampeding ninjas to be headed right for him, but the sidewalk was deserted. His gaze rested on the dance academy opposite, where a banner advertising Bernstein's School of Martial Arts was plastered across the lower half of the building; that was new. When had that changed? Six months on the road felt more like years, so much had altered.

He took another look at the banner and shuddered as he relit his cigarette. Getting beaten around the ring at ninja school was not something he'd be trying anytime soon; getting knocked out by a softball when he was a kid had been enough to put him off sport forever.

As he rested his head back against the tree, a lime-green-and-black Kawasaki motorcycle, not dissimilar to his own Yamaha, pulled away from the traffic and rumbled to a halt in front of the school in a flurry of dust. The tall rider swung his muscular leg across the bike to dismount. Long board shorts clung to his ass and his thighs, and a black tank top emblazoned with a scarlet eagle rippled as a slight breeze caught the material.

Max's mouth was suddenly dry. Fuck, that guy was hot. Maybe trying ninja school wouldn't be such a bad idea after all. As the guy turned to face away, he removed his helmet, revealing short blond hair, then shrugged a duffel bag from his shoulders, his tanned triceps flexing under the strain—

"Late, as usual."

Fuck! Spinning around, Max crushed his glowing cigarette against the mailbox and clenched it into his fist, his chest hammering. His vocal coach's lips contorted into a smile as Pete tamed his long dark dreadlocks into a thick rubber band while propping the front door open with his foot. "How was the tour?"

Max huffed out a breath. "Usual chaos."

"Glad to hear it."

Discreetly flicking the stub into Pete's garbage can, Max shoved his hands into the pockets of the black cargo pants he always wore and wandered up the path, pretending to ignore the hovering yellow jackets and hoping they'd extend him the same courtesy. After jogging up the last steps to the townhouse, Max pulled his friend into a hug, avoiding the long silver spikes protruding from Pete's face, and resisted the urge to point out that it was impossible to be late if Pete hadn't been expecting him. He hadn't even known he was coming here himself until an hour ago.

Pete patted him on the back and took a step away to hold Max at arm's length and look him up and down. His scrutiny was unnerving. "You've lost weight. You been eating properly?"

Max shrugged. "Kinda." If you counted beer as food.

"Struggled without a kitchen, huh?"

"Yeah, I guess." Max shoved past him, paused, and then looked back at Pete. "You got time for a quick singing lesson?"

"I thought you had a gig tonight?"

"I don't have to be there until six thirty, so I've got a while." Until the biggest gig of his life, here in his hometown, with practically everyone he knew going. He took a shaky breath and hoped Pete didn't notice.

"In that case, step into my office."

Freshly sprayed wood polish almost masked the lingering scents of engine oil and cat litter as Max headed along the hall toward Pete's studio. The studio was Max's dream room, crammed full of musical instruments, but in a professional way—not like his makeshift garage-cum-studio back home. Quality guitars lined the walls, amplifiers were piled high, and a ton of recording equipment was stowed in a booth in one corner. It was also properly soundproofed so neighbors didn't come knocking on Pete's door, complaining about the noise and ruining a perfectly good recording session at three in the morning. Not that he was jealous of that… much.

After scooping up two disgruntled cats that were feigning sleep on the Steinway piano, Pete tucked one under each arm and deposited them outside the room. One of the cats fluffed up its fur and gave them a bitter look that vowed revenge.

"Have you kept up with the singing exercises I gave you?" Pete asked as he closed the door.

"As often as I could." Sitting at the eight-piece Pearl drum kit, Max tapped out a gentle rhythm.

"That's a *no*, then, I take it?"

"I had to share a room with my brother while we were away. I couldn't do them in front of him. Apparently music lessons are a waste of time. He reckons my voice is good enough as it is."

"Noticed any improvement?" Pete asked and sat at the piano, playing a melody in perfect time to Max's beats.

"With Tony?"

"With your voice, not your brother." Pete chuckled. "And I don't see the big deal in telling him. He won't care. He supports you more than you know."

"Are you kidding? I'd never hear the end of it. He's never had to take a music lesson in his life."

"Perhaps it's time he did, get rid of some of those bad habits. Have you warmed up your voice?"

"Didn't get a chance. Why do you think I'm here, boss?" Max gave him a cheeky, hopeful grin. Pete would bail him out; he always had.

As Purple Method's lead singer, Max would be first in the firing line if anything went wrong, and he wasn't about to be the one who messed up because he hadn't prepared.

"And yet you've been smoking," Pete said. "Don't try to deny it, you stink of it." Max rolled his eyes dramatically, and Pete pointed at him, never losing his melody. "The second it affects your voice, you're quitting." It was an argument they'd had more times than Max cared to remember, and it always ended in a deadlock. It was tough being blond, tanned, and in a heavy metal band. To be taken seriously Max had to compensate for it somehow, and he drew the line at dyeing his hair black. He was sure Pete knew he would never jeopardize his voice… not really. "We'll start with a triad." Pete played a short sequence of notes, singing, "Ma."

Max's drumsticks clattered to the ground, and he sat up straighter on his stool. After taking a low breath, he copied Pete's vocals and then continued up the scale as Pete replayed the sequence a little higher each time.

As Max reached the top notes of the mezzo-soprano range, his vocal cords tightened, and it was a real effort to project the full sound. Fuck. Had Pete noticed? He did his best to conceal his struggle, but Pete stopped playing and rested his hands on his thighs.

"You've been straining your voice to be heard above everyone else, your cords are tight and dehydrated, and now you can't sing at the very top of your range. It's getting worse each time you sing, isn't it?"

Max shrugged. There was no point in denying anything. "We had gigs almost every day for six months. It's fine if I don't sing for a couple of days."

"Max, we've been through this." Pete sighed. "You need to do a sound check before each gig to make sure you don't get drowned out by the others, and you need to do the exercises I gave you, they'll help protect your voice, and start using your steam inhaler every day. If you don't look after your voice, the problems are only going to get worse. Then you really will have to give up smoking if you want to continue singing."

"I know. It'll be easier now we're home, anyway."

"You've been getting a sore throat as well, haven't you?"

Max scowled. All he'd done was sing a few notes; how the hell could Pete tell all that?

Pete lifted his fingers back to the piano keys. "You're a bit breathy. Bring the sound forward and tilt your larynx to give more protection."

"Breathiness sounds sexy."

"Breathiness makes you sound like an amateur, and you won't sound sexy if you lose your voice. I've taught you better than this. Come on, Max, remind me how good you are."

Playing a low note on the piano, Pete began another scale, and Max tried his hardest to sing to the standards Pete expected. It was tough after such a long break from his lessons, but with Pete shouting reminders every so often, by the time they'd finished the warmup, Max knew he was going to be okay for the gig that evening.

From the final scale, Pete drifted into a tune Max recognized intimately: "Someplace to Hide," a song Max had written for Purple Method. In fact, he'd composed it in this very room before their tour.

Picking up the drumsticks, Max tapped out the slow-yet-complex rhythm, adding stronger beats leading into the vocals. Putting every effort he could muster into his voice as he sang, he tried to show his mentor he could sing as well as Pete expected after all the free training he'd given him. Pete finally nodded his approval, and Max relaxed with each subsequent breath he took.

With his brother's effortless talent on drums and the other guys in the band never seeming to work at their craft either, he felt like the dunce of the group—like he had to prove himself and play catch-up. It didn't help that at twenty he was also the youngest by a couple of years. Tony had even had to get him a fake ID so they could play in bars and clubs. It was mortifying.

"How about some of your pancakes as payment?" Pete asked later as they finished up their session and emerged to grab a well-earned beer.

"Sure, why not." Max was starving, and performing on an empty stomach was no fun. He gathered the ingredients from Pete's kitchen cupboards and started on the mixture.

Pete sat at the oak dining table, clearing some of the motorcycle parts to the floor. "I'm impressed. Despite picking up a few bad habits, your voice is getting stronger in the midrange. Have the others noticed?"

"Na, they don't care so long as I don't mess up."

"I'm surprised they haven't. The change is pretty obvious." Pete stroked one of his cats as it picked its way through the hunks of metal and sidled along the table toward him.

Max poured the thick batter into the sizzling pan, tilting it to spread the mixture. "Tony was the one who messed up most. He got slaughtered before the Seattle gig and fell off his stool during one of his solos."

Pete snorted with laughter. "Yeah, I saw the pictures on the internet."

Max checked the pancake and flipped it in the air, then caught it with expert precision back in the pan.

"He only has a couple of beers before each gig now. Makes up for it afterward, though." Max waited a minute and then tipped the pancake onto a plate, sliding it in front of Pete, who pulled it from the cat's reach as it hooked its claw and tried to swipe it from the plate.

"I don't doubt it," Pete said. "How're things going with Zoe and Lisa? I bet they're glad you're home."

The habitual weight in Max's stomach grew heavier at the reminder. "Same, I guess. It's a casual thing." He turned his back to Pete and poured more batter into the pan. Now that he'd returned to Elfinbrook, there was no way he could avoid seeing his girlfriends. He hated having to pretend, but with three of them in the relationship, it was easier than when he'd tried having one girlfriend. The girls weren't so demanding of him because they also had each other. It meant if he didn't see them for a while, they didn't seem to notice as much. It went against everything he believed a relationship should be, but he couldn't see any other way to hide his sexuality. What had seemed like the perfect facade had become something he dreaded, but he had to continue—everything depended on it.

"Lucky thing. They're both gorgeous. I'd want to make it a bit less casual if I were you."

Max winked at Pete. "Maybe I'll change my mind once I'm old like you. For now an open relationship suits me just fine."

Out of everyone, Pete had come closest to guessing he was gay, and yet still didn't seem to have a clue. Pete was like a surrogate dad to them. It was better to live a lie than to risk being disowned by him and Tony—better than facing a future alone.

"Yeah, funny. Forty's not old."

"If you say so, old man." Max grinned at him. "By the way, we're opening for Vanquished Villains in a couple of weeks. I've asked Angelo to put you on the guest list again."

"Thanks, bud." Pete shoveled a forkful of pancake into his mouth. "Wouldn't miss it. I'm surprised Villains are still playing. Didn't their bassist overdose last month?"

"Yeah, he did. As far as I know, they managed to get someone to cover."

"Sad, isn't it." Pete shook his head. "He was only twenty-seven. Have you decided what you're opening with yet?"

"Don't you start," Max groaned. "When I left the house earlier, Tony and Lee were arguing about what we're opening with tonight, let alone in two weeks. Tony's trying to coerce him into using one of his songs, but Lee's not having it, as usual. Me and Kyle still never get a say."

Max left a pancake cooking in the pan and joined Pete at the table, inhaling the citrus aroma of a fresh lime before squeezing its juice over his pancake and savoring the sweet, sour mouthful. He knew he shouldn't be eating citrus and batter before a gig, but after his session with Pete, he knew his voice would be fine.

"It doesn't matter if they never use any of your songs to open," Pete said. "You can outdo Tony's drums with your vocals on any of the songs... if you want to, that is?"

Max laughed. Sometimes Pete laid it on thick. Who was he kidding? He'd never be in Tony's league, not in ten lifetimes.

"I'm serious, you need to quit putting yourself down. You're as good a musician, if not better, than any of the others; you need a bit more confidence in yourself, that's all."

Max finished his pancake and got up to check the one in the pan. "You're biased, boss."

"Okay, maybe a little." He lifted his fork and waved it at him. "But that doesn't change anything. You're my star student."

"Your other students are still in high school. I'd be offended if I wasn't."

"Shut up." Pete smiled and rubbed the cat's belly. "Hadn't you better get going? It's nearly six thirty."

"Fuck." How had it gotten so late so fast? Max tried to grab the pancake out of the pan and cursed again when it burned his fingers. "You're coming along tonight, right?"

"Yeah, in a bit. I'm meeting a friend there at seven thirty. Rick's new in town, so I thought I'd bring him along and introduce him to everyone. Is it okay if he comes to your party afterward?"

"Yeah, 'course." Max half saluted as he rushed past, swerving to avoid the corner of the table.

"Max...."

"What?" He paused, wobbling on one foot, and stared at Pete.

"Knock 'em dead like I know you can."

As Max approached the Torrens Club, he noticed that a long line of noisy Purple Method fans waited outside the huge black building on the other side of the road. It still had the painted neon images of dancers with wild tattoos, crazy hair, and outrageous piercings that had been there when Max was a kid.

Panting from his mad dash downtown, Max ducked behind an industrial trash can and crouched out of sight while he caught his breath, wafting the bottom of his T-shirt to cool down and wishing he'd ridden his motorcycle to Pete's instead of walking.

What was Angelo playing at? Everyone should've been inside by now. How was he going to sneak past to the back entrance? He couldn't be late for this gig; he just couldn't. Lee really was going to kill him this time.

He peered around the edge of the can. Tonight's crowd would be the biggest Max had ever played for, even with only half the tickets sold. It was terrifying, and there was no way he could get past without risking being seen. His other option was to go around the block and approach from the opposite direction, but that would take ages. He took out his cell from his pants pocket—6:45. Fuck.

Staring back at the Torrens Club, Max bounced on his toes until Angelo opened the doors and people began to disappear into the venue. If he waited a few minutes, they'd all be inside and he'd have more of a chance of sneaking past unnoticed. It'd be quicker than going all the way around the block. He gazed at the dusty sidewalk and scratched a picture of a treble clef in the dirt with his finger while he waited for the fans' excited chatter to fade.

Max's cell vibrated, and he glanced at the screen. It was Kyle, Purple Method's lead guitarist. Thank God it wasn't Lee or Tony. "Hey, what's up?"

"Where the fuck are you?" Kyle hissed.

"I can't get near the building. There're too many people outside."

"Max, seriously, do yourself a favor and get your ass here now." The faint drone of Lee's voice in the background grew louder. "I gotta go," Kyle whispered and hung up.

It became a no-brainer: face the wrath of Tony and Lee or risk getting mobbed by a dwindling number of fans who may or may not recognize him. Taking a deep breath, Max squeezed his eyes shut for a second and then sprinted across the street toward the back of the club. Nobody had been looking his way until he whizzed past, trying to look inconspicuous, but suddenly it felt like all eyes were on him. A few people pointed, and Max swore he heard someone shriek his name, but luckily none of them thought to pursue him.

Rounding the corner of the building, he spied their tour bus, which was a converted ambulance that he'd painted black with Purple Method in huge lilac letters along the sides. The ambulance doors were still open. That was a good sign; it meant his friends hadn't finished setting up yet. If he grabbed some equipment, perhaps he could convince them he'd been there all along.

"Max!" Kyle came out of the club and rummaged in the back of the ambulance. "Thank fuck for that. Here, grab these, will you?" He threw a coil of leads at Max, who scrabbled to catch them and failed. He managed to retrieve them from the ground before Kyle noticed. "Where have you been? Tony and Lee have been going crazy."

"They were doing that way before I left, and that had nothing to do with me."

"I can't believe how many people are here tonight."

"Yeah, it's gonna be great." Max grinned. A fan shrieking at him had been an instant ego boost. If he'd thought to record it, he could've put it on instant playback the next time nerves got the better of him. He felt like he could take on the world right now and kick its ass. "What're we opening with?"

Kyle grimaced. "'Bind Me.'"

Surprise, surprise. "Tony won, then. Figures."

"Yeah, those two need to sort it out. Seriously, they squabble like a couple of kids lately."

"Why do you think I left them to it," Max said as they made their way into the stuffy building, along the bright corridor, past an office and their dressing room. The door was wide-open, and the room was already full of Purple Method's usual chaotic mess.

They turned a corner, and the massive stage was right in front of them. Max gulped. They were really doing this. All his newfound confidence evaporated in an instant.

From the wings, the excited chatter of their most eager fans convening in front of the stage was terrifying, mostly because of the level of noise and therefore the sheer number of people who had to be out there. He pictured them clinging to the steel barriers and glaring at anyone who dared challenge for their spot. He knew the deal, and he always got the best spot, right in the middle—the best place from which to admire and study his favorite singers. It also meant that as soon as the mosh pit fired up, he was there at its core.

There was nothing Max loved more than live music. Thunderous beats reverberating through his body, exhilarating to the extreme, and only released by either throwing himself around in an aggressive mosh pit or by the most mind-blowing sex he could imagine. Max tried not to imagine it as his thoughts teetered on betrayal. His cheeks burned as he dropped the leads in a heap next to a stack of amplifiers.

"What the hell, Max?" his brother's voice boomed nearby, and Max leaped in the air, cringing, and turned to face him. Tony marched up to him. "Do you have any idea how worried I've been?"

"Worried? Are you kidding? You really think I'm gonna hang around and listen to you and Lee screaming at each other again?"

Tony was about to argue back but seemed to think better of it. He lifted a bottle of beer to his lips and took a long drink. "Just let me know when you go out, yeah?"

"I'm twenty, not ten. I'm not gonna tell you every time I leave the house. You're being ridiculous."

Lee rounded the corner and stormed up to them.

Tony winked at Max. "Uh-oh." He took another sip of beer.

"How many times, Tony?" Lee threw his hands up in the air. "No drinking before gigs, okay? I swear I waste my breath. I thought we agreed after last time—"

"It's one, Lee. Lighten up."

"I'll lighten up the day I can guarantee you're not going to ruin a gig by falling off your damn stool."

"Ouch." Tony gave Max a sidelong grin. "That was below the belt, even for you."

Lee shook his head and glared at Max. Oh man, so much for Tony distracting Lee from the inevitable lecture he deserved. Max braced himself. "And you. Don't even get me started. You may be our singer, but that doesn't mean your lazy ass can't give the rest of us a hand setting up the equipment. You wander in here, late, expecting the rest of us to take up your slack, again. Despite your delusions, we're not your servants. Don't think I won't replace you if you don't pull your weight."

"Whoa, don't you dare joke about that," Tony warned, taking a step closer. "My little brother leaves the band, I go too; you got that?"

"You think that's a deterrent?"

"That's enough!" Max shouted. If they didn't pull together, there was no way they'd be able to get up on that stage and nail it the way he knew they could. "Tonight is our chance to show how awesome we've become. Don't risk blowing it for all of us because of some stupid argument. I'm sorry I was late, okay, Lee?"

Tony bear-hugged Max and squeezed the breath from him. "Aw, check out my little brother, all grown-up and wise and stuff. I raised you well, little bro."

"Jesus." Lee shook his head. "That's one dysfunctional family right there."

"Come on." Tony waved Lee over and dragged him into a group hug. "Show us the love."

"You're crazy, you know that?"

Tony noisily kissed the top of Lee's head, and Max snickered at the look of disgust on Lee's face.

"That's sweet, guys, but we've got a gig to do," Kyle called out.

Max pushed away from them, grabbed Kyle's guitar from the stand, and tuned it for him while the others finished up sorting out the leads and testing microphones. It was something they should've done before their audience arrived, and maybe even left time for a sound check, but judging by the heckling that was going on, it was no bad thing to build up anticipation further by giving fans a glimpse pre-set.

With all the guitars tuned, Max dusted off an old amp and hauled himself onto it, enjoying the bustle of last-minute preparations. The anticipation had been part of the thrill for him since he was a kid, watching his dad onstage. If he'd told their dad about tonight, Max was sure he'd have been excited for them—or at least that's what he said to himself.

Max shrugged out of his leather jacket and lifted the bottom of his T-shirt to wipe beads of sweat from his brow, grateful that he could blame his current state on the failed air-conditioning and pretend it wasn't the profuse panic taking over his body. Tonight couldn't be the night he screwed up—not here. Max gulped as the queasiness worsened, and he tried to concentrate on the soothing rumble of Lee's bass guitar as he warmed up. How had performing for hundreds of people ever felt like a good idea?

"You okay?" Tony crouched in front of Max, placing a bucket on the ground and flicking his long blond hair over his shoulder as he peered up at him.

Max scowled, and the bucket rattled as he kicked it.

"Just as I thought." Tony smirked, stood, and called out, "We're ready to go, guys."

The words Max despised. Nausea overwhelmed him, and he reached for the bucket, taking an expert aim to a chorus of jeering. He snatched the tissues and breath mint Tony handed him and scrubbed his mouth.

Lee patted Max on the back. "Let's make this the best one yet."

"I hate you all."

How the hell had his unfortunate habit become their good omen?

CHAPTER TWO

Rick

STARING FOR longer than was probably polite at the immaculate makeup of the goth who walked past him to join the line to get into the Torrens Club, Rick smoothed down his navy T-shirt and hoped he didn't stand out too much.

He relaxed a little when he spotted Pete approaching and waved.

"Hey, Rick." Pete smiled a little too wide.

"What?" Rick glanced down at his new stylishly ripped jeans and pristine red sneakers, and back up at Pete. "You knew before you invited me that I'm no metalhead. Don't act all surprised that I'm not dressed like the living dead."

"Hey, I didn't say a word. You look great. Very… um, smart. It's not obligatory to wear black, you know. I told you that the other day."

"I know." Rick grimaced. "But I can feel people staring."

Pete laughed. "Ignore them."

They walked past the line and over to the main doors, where Pete got them in on the guest list. It seemed he knew everyone in town. "What time is Purple Method due onstage? How long have we got?"

"Dunno. Depends what time Max got here in the end; he was running late. That guy is incapable of being on time for anything. Doors opened early, though, and they don't have any openers, so it could be anytime now."

Rick's breath hitched at the mention of the guy he'd been crushing on ever since Pete showed him a clip of Max onstage a couple of months back. The guy had the most incredible voice he'd ever heard—smooth and effortless, but with a sexy, gravelly tone when he hit the lowest notes that sent tingles straight to Rick's balls, guaranteed every time. Add to that the countless pictures of Max on social media, half-naked and clearly sleeping with the majority of Purple Method's fans, and that made the anticipation of meeting him all the more exciting. The guy was sexy as hell.

Rick steadied his voice. "You've spoken to Max?"

"Yeah." Pete held the door to the main hall open, and Rick walked past him into the huge, noisy room that was buzzing with excitement. People rushed about the stage, and Rick craned his neck to see if any of them were Max, but Pete grabbed his arm and pulled him toward the bar at the back. "Can you believe they only got home off tour this afternoon? He popped in earlier to say hi and didn't leave my place till six thirty."

His stomach sank. What was going on with him? He should *not* be that disappointed. "I just missed him, huh?" If only he'd left his martial arts school a few minutes earlier….

"You'll meet them all soon enough. Beer?"

"Yeah, thanks. I haven't had one in ages."

"You're kiddin'?" Pete looked horrified.

"I've got that mixed martial arts competition over at Leatherton coming up. Been training hard for that with the MMA guys. We've got a good chance of placing high."

"I didn't think you were competing at the moment."

"I had someone drop out of the heavyweight class. Figured it would be easier to compete than find someone else at this late stage." He hadn't been disappointed at the prospect. The lure of competition had always been hard to resist, and there was nothing quite like getting in the ring. Besides, he couldn't risk missing out on an opportunity for his MMA team to be seen, not when some of the top clubs were going to be at the event—taking notes on up-and-coming trainers. His career was everything to him and always came first.

"Pete." A bartender with intense dark eyes and an easy smile leaned across and shook Pete's hand, his sun-kissed hair falling across his face. "Thought I might see you here tonight. Your boys have got this place buzzin'."

"Sure have. If there's one thing they're good at, it's getting the party going."

The bartender laughed. "Never a truer word spoken." He gave Rick an appreciative smile. "Who's your friend?"

"Angelo, this is Rick. He's new in town."

"I guessed as much. That's not a face I'd forget. What can I get you guys?"

"Couple of beers, thanks."

"You've been working here a while, then?" Rick said.

Angelo scraped his hair behind his ear as he poured their drinks. "Yeah, I've been running the place for a few years now."

"Angelo, the pump's stopped working again," a bartender yelled.

He placed their drinks on the bar. "I'll catch you guys later," he said, waving his hand when Pete tried to hand him a twenty-dollar bill. "On the house."

Rick sipped his cool beer and watched Angelo, who looked back and grinned when he caught him looking.

Pete sighed and shook his head. "I love Angelo, but he's the biggest flirt, sorry. Ignore him. He's harmless enough."

"It's fine. I don't mind. To be honest, it's kinda nice to get some attention. I didn't expect it tonight."

"There aren't many guys in here who are gay or bi, so you probably made his night."

Rick snorted a laugh. "Half the guys in here are wearing makeup and... is that a guy wearing a corset and skirt over there?" Wow, that wasn't something you saw every day. He carried the look off better than any of the girls.

"What, Dave? Yeah, his girlfriend loves it. She's the one in the Bayonetta cosplay outfit."

Rick stared at Dave in amazement. "He's straight?"

Pete shrugged. "Yeah, like I said, not many in here like that. Angelo's the exception rather than the norm. But he's discreet, usually, believe it or not."

"So Angelo's the only one here tonight?" Rick asked, pushing a little to see if Pete would divulge Max's orientation.

"Uh, let's see." Pete scanned the room. "You could try Joe." Pete pointed to a petite guy with spiky black hair and the tightest PVC pants Rick had ever seen. "He's been known to hang out with Angelo quite a bit. Then there's Colin over there. He's the only one who I could say for sure is gay."

Rick glanced at Colin. He had lank, waist-length black hair, a tall sturdy build, and looked to be in his midthirties. Several pairs of handcuffs dangled from his belt, and Rick shivered. Definitely not his type. "That's everyone?"

"'Fraid so. Sorry, bud. Not something you wanna broadcast around here, as a rule. Colin and a few others from here got beat up pretty bad some years back for being gay. Couple of them didn't make it. They never did catch whoever did it. It hit the community hard, and we never really recovered." Pete nodded toward the stage as the lights turned out and the crowd cheered and whistled. "Looks like they've finally got themselves organized."

Taking a sip of his beer, Rick fixed his gaze on the stage, and he and Pete took a few steps closer to it in the darkness. The enthusiasm of the crowd was intoxicating, and Rick felt a jittery excitement.

Suddenly, the stage burst to life with pillars of billowing smoke and rainbows of distorted flashing lights. Purple Method exploded into the dynamic guitar riffs and heavy drums of what Rick recognized to be "Bind Me." Max raced across the stage as the crowd's cheering grew louder, and to his surprise, as Max raised his arms in the air, Rick found himself copying, along with most of Purple Method's other fans. He was totally fangirling, but right now he didn't care at all.

Max brought his microphone to his lips and paused as the chanting of his name increased to a deafening level. Rick had known Max was popular, judging by what he'd seen on social media, but this was insane. As Max brought his cupped hand to the side of his head, a girl next to Rick let out a piercing shriek, and Rick laughed, rubbing his violated ear as Max began to growl the low notes of the first verse. The power of Max's voice thudded through him, and Rick gasped as the vibrations settled in his thickening cock.

"What do you think?" Pete shouted at him as Kyle, the guitarist, joined Max at center stage to sing, creating intricate harmonies that complemented the heavy guitars and potent bass lines.

"They're better live. They're incredible."

Pete nodded. "That they are, but don't tell them I said so."

Rick laughed again and turned his attention back to the stage.

Purple Method's songs got louder and louder, and more intense if the mosh pit was anything to go by. Max was egging them on, leaning over the edge of the stage and spinning his index fingers in circles. Whatever he was trying to do, it seemed to be working. Practically the whole room was joining in, and the mosh pit grew more violent every time Max did it. Rick was tempted to join in, but with an important fight coming up, the last thing he needed was to show up with a black eye— not that he couldn't hold his own in a mosh pit, he was sure of that. He wasn't used to them was all.

"Here we go," Pete shouted.

"What's that?"

Pete pointed at Tony as the other musicians put down their instruments. Max even disappeared off the stage. Rick turned his attention to Pete, who said, "This song, 'Zombie Zoo,' has the longest drum solo I've heard in my life."

Tony launched into the spotlight, showcasing his effortless skill and flamboyant tricks. "He's pretty good, though," Rick said.

"Yeah, he is. Don't get me wrong, I love the guy. His heart's in the right place, but he does have a tendency to go overboard. You want another drink?"

"Sure. I'll get them."

When he returned from the bar, the deep rhythmic thud of Tony's bass drum slowed, and Rick took a sip of his beer, watching as Max sauntered across the stage and inched his way to the front as Tony stopped. Soft lighting highlighted the crowd, most still jumping around and cheering, and Max closed his eyes and shook his head.

"Come on, Max," Pete said under his breath but loud enough for Rick to hear.

"Is he okay?"

"Yeah, he's fine. He told me he's been practicing this speech all week." Pete grimaced. "This isn't his favorite part. He worries he'll say something inappropriate, or that he'll go blank. Lee helped him write this one so he wouldn't say anything stupid."

"Oh." Max didn't come across as lacking in confidence; he hid it well. "Come on, you can do it," Rick whispered.

Max lifted the microphone, opened his eyes, and began to speak, telling the fans how awesome they were and how great it was to be back home in Elfinbrook. He was scanning the crowd, every so often grinning at people, who Rick guessed must be his friends. Max eventually looked in their direction, and Pete gave Max the thumbs-up. Willing Max to notice him, Rick kept his eyes fixed on him. He didn't have to wait long. Their eyes locked, and his breath caught, and he gave Max a warm smile. Max held his gaze for a long moment until Rick swore Max's cheeks colored, but then he looked away to the farthest point possible. That was weird.

For the rest of the gig, Rick kept his eyes on Max, and Max didn't look his way again. Damn it. Had he blown his chances already? Maybe he should have dressed head to toe in black like 90 percent of the people there. Maybe that would've given him a fighting chance with Max.

Purple Method finished their final encore, "Glimmers of Insanity," and trooped off the stage as the crowd cheered, whistled, and stamped their feet, demanding more. Rick joined in.

"They've gotta be happy with that," Pete said as the lights came back on and background music played—a song Rick didn't recognize. Purple Method was the only heavy metal band he listened to, and that was only because of Max. "They could do with a hand packing up. If we help, they might even give us a lift back to their place for the party. You coming?"

"Sure, sounds like fun." Finally, his chance to speak to Max.

They elbowed their way toward the entrance foyer, where a slim girl with a platinum blonde bob with nuclear-pink streaks was selling Purple Method T-shirts, CDs—for those who still played them—and vinyl.

"I'm just gonna check she's okay." Pete headed toward the girl, and Rick followed. "Need a hand, Sian, or have you got this under control?"

"Pete!" Sian rushed around the table and gave Pete a hug. "I didn't think you'd made it."

"Yeah, we were at the back."

"By the bar, no doubt." She laughed, giving Rick a sidelong glance. "I had to stay with the gear but managed to get to the mosh pit a couple of times."

"Sian is Kyle's girlfriend," Pete said. "Sian, this is Rick."

"Nice to meet you," Sian said. "Are you coming to the party?"

"If that's okay?"

"Sure. I think most people here are gonna try to make it. Should be a blast."

Hordes more people pushed through the doors and headed straight for the table. "Catch you later," she said and returned to her post.

They watched for a moment as she sold piles of merchandise.

Pete snorted. "She's fine. Come on; let's give them a hand loading up."

After leading them around to the back of the building, Pete stopped by a black ambulance that was shuddering, and loud bangs and crashes came from inside. Rick shook his head and laughed. When he'd seen a picture of this on the internet, he'd thought it was a joke, but no, they really did haul their equipment in that thing.

Pete lifted a guitar case off the ground that had "Max—hands off" painted on it in huge letters, and he approached the back of the ambulance.

"Great job tonight. Do you believe me now?"

"Maybe." Max's face peered out the back.

Rick took a step closer, his heart thudding, and Max froze.

"I brought some extra muscle to help out," Pete said and patted Rick on the shoulder. Max eyed Rick and looked back at Pete. "Rick moved to Elfinbrook some months back while you were away."

"Hi," Rick said awkwardly as Max snatched the guitar case from Pete and busied himself stowing it. "Pete's right, you were awesome tonight. I particularly enjoyed your speech."

Rick lifted a large amplifier and handed it up to Max. "Thanks," Max mumbled. Were his teeth gritted? Did the guy hate him already? So much for making a good first impression. He let go of the amplifier as Max took it and cursed as it crashed to the ambulance floor.

"Oh here, let me give you a hand." Rick jumped up into the ambulance. "Where do you want it?"

Max pointed to a corner at the back and pressed his finger to his mouth.

"Rick, why don't you stay here and help Max out?" Pete said. "There's loads more heavy stuff to come."

"Gee, thanks, Pete. I can handle it, you know," Max said.

"I know, but the quicker we get done here, the quicker we can all get to your party." Pete patted the side of the ambulance and disappeared into the club.

Again, Max eyed Rick. "I'm stronger than I look, you know."

What a strange thing to say. If Max hated him, then surely he wouldn't care what Rick thought about his strength. Perhaps he'd read this all wrong.

"You don't have to explain. It's okay. You've been leaping around the stage for hours. I'm surprised you've got any energy left at all."

"I've got plenty of energy." Had Max's cheeks flushed? It was hard to tell for certain as Max turned away from him.

"I'm sure you have." Rick raised an eyebrow and smiled. Maybe he had a chance after all. He reached out to touch Max's arm, his skin hot and smooth beneath Rick's fingers. Max glanced around at him, eyes wide. "You must get this a lot, so I understand if you say no, but would you like to—"

"I'm straight." Max avoided looking Rick in the eyes as he pulled his arm away.

"You are?" His stomach sank, and he forced himself to smile as he shook his head. Man, had he read this wrong. "Sorry. Guess I should have checked first before blurting it out."

"Don't worry about it."

"Pete's been telling me my gaydar needs fixing—"

"Pete knows? About you liking guys?"

"Yeah."

"And he's okay with it?"

"Of course. Why wouldn't he be?"

"But… Pete's not gay."

Rick studied Max. For someone who was straight, he sure was concerned about what Pete thought about it. He'd never understood straight-guy thinking and how much they seemed to panic if anyone suggested they might like guys.

Tony and Kyle appeared with some more equipment, dumped it outside the ambulance, and disappeared back inside without so much as a word.

"Have you always known you wanted to be a singer?" Rick asked as he hopped out and handed the equipment up to Max. Perhaps they could at least be friends.

Max seemed relieved at the change of topic. "I guess. Tony's always played drums, and Dad played guitar, so singing was the obvious choice."

"Like a family band or something. That's awesome. Your dad must be proud of you."

"Why'd you move to Elfinbrook?"

"My folks live here. They own the dance studio on Wardell Street, opposite Pete's house. Do you know it?"

"I've seen it."

"I finished up training as a chiropractor over in Leatherton a couple of months ago, and I've moved back with them for a bit while I figure out my next move. It's weird being back. I've been in Leatherton for nine years—"

"God, Lee's a slave driver," Tony grumbled as he hefted another drum case into the ambulance. "Why he couldn't let us do this tomorrow, I don't know."

"He saw the amount of beer we got for the party," Kyle said as he joined them. "Don't think any of us are going to be in a fit state to do anything tomorrow." Kyle yawned.

"Did Sian get back home okay to start letting everyone in?" Max asked.

"She messaged me a couple of minutes back," Kyle said. "She's nearly sold all the gear, so Jade's giving her a lift."

"You all live together?" Rick asked.

"Guys, this is Rick, friend of Pete's."

Rick gave a little wave.

"Hey," Kyle said.

"Yeah, we do," Tony said. "Lee and Kyle moved in three years ago, and Sian, what, a year back maybe?"

"Yeah, something like that." Max nodded toward the club. "Is there much left in there?"

"Na, a few odd bits," Tony said. "If you want a shower, you'd better go do it now. Your bag's in the dressing room."

"Thanks." Max leaped out of the ambulance and turned to look at Rick. "Don't let anyone mess up my system. They forget we all need a place to sit."

"Hey," Tony said. "That shit was fun. What part of sitting on top of the amps as we drove back to the motel wasn't fun?"

"The part where I fell on my ass and nearly got crushed. That part," Max said, clearly trying not to laugh. "I'll be back in a bit."

Rick was careful to follow his instructions, and it wasn't long before Max reappeared with dripping hair and dressed in fresh black cargo pants, a tight black T-shirt, and chunky, buckled boots. He was a walking wet dream—a straight wet dream. Rick sighed. Just his luck.

"Come on, Max, we've got a party to get to," Lee called out from the driver's seat as they all took their spots.

The ambulance choked to life. From where Rick was sitting, near the front behind Lee, he could only see Pete opposite him. Kyle was someplace toward the back, and Tony sat up front with Lee.

"Fuck me, I have a seat," Max said, and Rick craned his neck to watch him clamber into the back and sit in the one clear space. He gave Rick a small smile as he did so, but then curled up, rested his head on one of Tony's drums, and closed his eyes.

Rick ignored the excited banter going on around him, choosing instead to watch Max sleep. Max looked so vulnerable, so different from how he'd been onstage.

It turned out that Purple Method didn't live far from the Torrens Club. The ambulance soon braked hard, rattling, and came to an abrupt halt. Max unlocked the back doors and jumped out. The noise coming from outside almost matched what they'd left at the venue. By the time Rick had scrambled out, Max was nowhere to be seen. A multitude of cars and motorcycles surrounded what looked like a three-floor townhouse on a slight hill, with the open front door on the middle level and steps leading up to it. Hordes of people wearing Purple Method T-shirts headed right for them, and loud rock music blared from the house.

"Looks like Sian's done a good job," Kyle said as she waved and hurried over.

"Yeah, it was a great idea getting her to let people in." Tony patted him on the back. "Don't want to upset the neighbors by having everyone hanging around outside."

Rick gaped at him. Tony was serious. Surely the number of vehicles surrounding their place, not to mention the volume of their music, should have also been a concern to him. They must be the worst neighbors ever. He was thankful he lived in a quiet cul-de-sac across town.

"I can't believe their folks let them do this," Rick said in a low voice to Pete.

Pete laughed, but there was a sadness to it. "Na, it's just them. Their mom left when they were small, and their dad fucked off to Florida four years back, left them to it once Tony hit eighteen."

"Are you serious?" Rick's jaw dropped a little farther. Had their dad seriously left them the house? And when Max would've only been sixteen. That couldn't have been easy for them. "They're all on their own here?"

"Yeah, it's become the ultimate party house. Come on." He beckoned Rick to follow as he headed toward the steps. "Should be a good night."

Rick followed him into the drab hallway. The wallpaper looked as though it had been peeling for decades, but he guessed it made sense that with parties like this, it was a waste of time fixing it. A track of scuffed floorboards led first to a staircase that went upstairs, and at the end of the hall was another staircase that led down to the basement. There was a lot of muffled laughter coming from downstairs.

"Pete, where's the bathroom?"

"There's a half bath downstairs, but you're best off going to the bathroom upstairs. It'll be quieter. They won't mind."

"Okay, where shall I meet you?"

"I'll be down in the kitchen," Pete said. "That's where they've stashed the drinks."

Rick climbed the staircase and stopped as he reached the top to peer into the doorway to his right. The door was ajar, and even with that small glimpse, he could see that the room was a complete mess. He pressed the door and it swung open. Max was lying on a large bed in the center with his arm draped across his face and a tequila bottle on the black pillow next to him. Great, of all the doors he could've picked. He hoped Max didn't think he was stalking him. Max dropped his arm to his chest and stared at Rick, letting out a disgruntled huff before allowing his head to fall back and staring at the whirring ceiling fan.

"Uh, sorry. I was looking for the bathroom."

"End of the hall."

"Thanks." Rick turned to leave.

"It's not usually like this."

"Excuse me?" He looked back at Max.

"My bedroom. It's not usually in this state." Max shifted so he was sitting up with his back against the wall. "I didn't get a chance to unpack."

Rick leaned against the doorjamb and scanned the disaster zone that was Max's bedroom. There were black clothes scattered everywhere, the Indian-style rugs barely visible beneath. Haphazard stacks of old vinyl lined the wall under the window at the front of the house, and to Rick's left was a desk piled high with notebooks. "You've been away a long time. It takes a while to get settled."

"I guess."

"It must feel good to be back in your own bed."

"I'll have to let you know about that. Haven't slept in it yet." Max opened the tequila bottle and took a drink. "Want some?" He held out the bottle, and more than anything, Rick wanted to take it, but touching that would have him passed out before midnight—not a good look.

"Thanks, but I'm okay."

"Suit yourself." Max took another drink and sighed, slouching down and closing his eyes for a long moment.

Rick took that as his cue to leave. When he walked past on his way back from the bathroom, Max's door was closed and he was nowhere to be seen. There was a keypad on the door—that had to be a wise move when it looked like they had all-night parties every day of the week. Rick followed the ear-blasting music down to the kitchen, where it was impossible to hear himself think, let alone talk to anyone, and yet a large group huddled in there seemed to manage by shouting at one another.

Tony was sitting on the kitchen table in the center of the smoke-hazed room, relaying what sounded like one of their tour anecdotes. There was an old washtub under the kitchen table that was filled with ice and bottles of beer, and spirits and soda were crammed onto the counters. These guys knew how to throw a party. Rick ducked to grab a beer and twisted off the cap.

There was a doorway leading off the kitchen, where people were streaming from, and with no sign of Pete in the kitchen, Rick made his way in there to look for him. He found himself in a large, crowded lounge. But there was still no sign of Pete. He was beginning to wish he'd made an effort to dress in black. He was getting some disapproving looks from the metalheads and goths, and he was pretty sure he was being discussed by a few of them.

It was a little unsettling being there and not knowing anyone—feeling like a complete outsider. If this was going to become a habit, he was going to have to invest in a pair of black jeans, and maybe he could wear his biker boots and leather jacket next time. At least that way he wouldn't completely stand out. He tried to shrink into a corner, which was difficult at six foot two, and sipped at his beer.

Rick heard Max before he saw him, even above the music. When Max poked his head into the lounge and did a quick scan, Rick expected him to leave or to speak to someone else, but after pausing for a moment, Max walked right up to him. His stomach was doing little flips, and Rick sighed, trying his best to ignore it.

"Having fun?" Max asked as he approached. His tequila bottle was half-empty already, and yet he didn't appear to be affected by it.

"Yeah, I don't know where Pete got to." Rick took a swig of his beer.

"Best not to ask," Max said. "Ready for something stronger?" He tried to hand him the tequila bottle again.

"No, I'm good. Thanks, though. I'm not a big drinker."

Max huffed a laugh.

"Alien concept?"

"What gave you that idea?" Max took another gulp of his drink. Something seemed to catch his eye, and he waved. "Jade, over here." As Rick looked toward the door to the kitchen, he groaned. This could not be happening. "Jade, this is—"

"Rick?" Jade looked at him in surprise. "What are you doing here?"

"You two know each other?"

"Um, yeah, kind of," Rick said, recalling their occasional hookups. "Small world, huh?"

"Yeah, wow." Jade snaked her slender arm around Max's waist. "I guess you must've finished studying now?"

"Yeah, just finished. You?"

"Last year. I'm working here in Elfinbrook now."

"How do you two know each other?" Max asked, frowning.

"College over in Leatherton when I was doing my hairdressing course," Jade said. "Our classes were in the same building."

"Right."

"Oh, and we went out a couple of times."

Rick cringed. *Thanks, Jade.*

Max's expression froze for a second. "What?"

"Yeah, nothing serious, though, right, Rick? Don't worry, sweetie, I think we got it out of our systems. I'm all yours when you decide to give me a chance."

"I thought—"

"I've got a thing for blonds." Jade laughed and ruffled her hand through Max's hair. "Although this one keeps turning me down and pretending he's not interested."

"You're my best friend's sister. There's no way I'm going there. Do you know how much stick Sian would give me?"

"One day you'll give in to my charms," Jade said and hugged him. "Make sure you drink plenty, sweetie. You deserve it after putting up with that lot on tour. See you around, Rick."

"Yeah, bye, Jade."

"You and Jade, huh?" Max said finally.

"She's a sweet girl."

"What happened to you liking guys?"

"I like guys too. I'm bi."

"Right."

Rick tried to hold back a smile and failed. "Is that a problem?"

"I have no reason to care who you sleep with."

Rick took a swig of beer, giving him the courage he needed to push a little more. "Pete was right about you."

"How's that?" Max frowned.

Their eyes locked, and despite his effort to ignore it, a spark of desire rocketed through him. Rick grinned. "That you have a sexy ass."

Max rolled his eyes and glanced around nervously. "He did not say that. That's totally gross. Pete's like family."

Rick waited until Max looked at him again. "No, you're right. Doesn't make it any less true, though."

"Are you always like this?"

"Like what?"

Max tugged at the label on his bottle. "Confident, I guess."

"Life's too short, right?"

"Right. Listen, I have to go see if my girlfriends are here yet."

"Sure, I'll see you later."

Damn it, he should have known that was pushing too hard. And that Max would be in some sort of relationship. Flirting with Max was definitely out of the question; he knew that now. He just hoped he'd get a chance to see Max again later, that it hadn't destroyed any chances of friendship with him.

CHAPTER THREE

Max

MAX HAD no intention of trying to find Zoe and Lisa; in fact, they were the last people he wanted to see. He shimmied through the crowded kitchen, jogged upstairs, and pushed open the flimsy back door to the yard.

Sandy, barren flowerbeds and overgrown hardy bushes followed the perimeter of the yard, and numerous abandoned chairs blocked the end of the long pathway that led to the garage and the large barbecue smoker beyond that. Like Pete, neither Max nor his housemates had discovered a love of gardening.

Slumping on a weathered chair, Max lit a cigarette and inhaled. He swung the half-empty tequila bottle between his legs, and the swell of golden liquid sloshed against the glass. It was peaceful out there on his own—despite the booming music and occasional shriek coming from the house. A rare cool breeze blew strands of hair across his face, and he scraped it from his eyes as he contemplated the shitstorm that was his life. Pushing Rick away was like a reflex, a survival instinct; yet each time he had turned him down, another small piece inside of him had fallen away into a chasm, leaving him even hollower than before.

The back door creaked open, and the other members of Purple Method and Sian emerged. Max took another drag from his cigarette and idly looked up at them.

"It's getting too crowded in there," Lee said. "Thought we'd hang in the garage for a bit. Coming?"

Max hauled himself out of the yard chair and waited as Tony fiddled with the stubborn garage door lock. It clicked open, and his brother barged his shoulder into the door, which was thick from soundproofing. Kyle flicked on the light, and their small group piled in.

Tony's drum kit lay in abandoned pieces near the entrance, a pile of guitar cases and the smaller amplifiers had been dumped farther back, and a huge tangle of leads lurked in a dark corner. Max guiltily remembered that he hadn't hung about and given them a hand to unload the ambulance, but Lee didn't seem to care now he had a strong drink in his hand.

They clambered over the obstacles, and Kyle slammed the door shut behind them.

"Someone help me get this lot sorted." Tony lit a joint and grabbed the biggest drum case.

They all pitched in, and when everything was set up, Tony sat at his drum kit at the far end of the garage and played along with the heavy music thundering from the stereo, which was perched on an empty beer crate. Max lounged on a large, stained beanbag, swigging his tequila. With any luck, he'd be able to hide out there all night.

"You okay, babe?" Sian asked as she came over to sit next to Max on the beanbag. "You don't seem quite yourself."

Max gave her a slight smile. "Yeah, guess I'm a bit worn out from the early start this morning."

"Kyle's been flagging too." She curled her legs behind her and accepted the joint from Lee. "He'd better sort it out. I haven't seen him in two weeks since I came to your gig. He's not getting to sleep early tonight."

"I didn't need to know that." It was bad enough that he could hear them in the bedroom beneath his. They weren't quiet at the best of times.

Sian chuckled. "I saw Lisa earlier, and she said she hasn't seen you since before you went away. I didn't realize it had been so long."

"I wanted to focus on the tour, you know?"

"What's going on, babe? You not into her anymore? You never said anything."

"It's fine. Just haven't bumped into her or Zoe yet."

"You're avoiding them, you mean."

"Fuck off, why would I avoid them?"

Sian scrunched up her face. "I don't know, but something's going on with you."

"I'm tired, like I told you already."

The door to the garage quivered and then flew open. A metalhead peered inside. "We were wondering where you guys got to. Mind if we come in?"

"Sure, come sit down," Lee shouted at them. "And shut the door."

Max groaned as a stream of people followed the guy in. They all found places to sit and chattered among themselves, occasionally striking up a conversation, when they dared, with the members of Purple Method. Luckily no one tried to talk to him.

"This party's going lame," Tony called out.

"We could play a drinking game?" Max suggested.

"Or spin the bottle?" said a pretty girl who Max recognized from the front row of the audience at the gig.

"I'm liking your idea," Tony said, and she turned her attentions to him.

Max took a long drink of tequila and tossed the bottle into the center.

"Usual rules?" Tony asked, leaving his drum kit and joining them, sitting next to the girl.

"Of course," Kyle said.

"And they are?" someone asked.

Tony and the girl suddenly stood. She giggled as he grabbed her hand, and they headed toward the door. "Don't mind us," he said as they left.

Kyle sighed and shook his head. "Mixed partners only. And if you don't use tongues, it doesn't count, and you have to do it again. Ready?"

Everyone nodded. Kyle spun, and the bottle rested pointing at Sian.

"That was convenient." Max laughed. "You sure you didn't fix that?"

"Shut up, it's your bottle," Sian said, giving him a nudge as she leaned forward to kiss her boyfriend.

Max watched with vague interest as the game unfolded, smoking the joint and relaxing back.

The door shuddered and flew open again. Cooler air dissipated the hazy smoke, and Pete, Rick, Jade, Angelo, Joe, and several other people Max vaguely knew, bundled in.

"So this is where the real party is. Might've guessed," Pete slurred. He wobbled, and Rick helped him find a beanbag before he fell over. Great; so much for hiding out for a while.

"Brandon, you're holding the game up," Lee said to a guy with a blue mohawk and thick black eyeliner. "Go ahead and spin."

"Awesome," Angelo said. "Can we join in?"

"Wouldn't have thought it would be your thing," Max said, tugging at the loose piece of rubber on his boot. He hated behaving like this, but ribbing Angelo about his sexuality was an easy way to detract from his own.

"Ugh, you're not using those same stupid rules as last time, are you? Don't you think it's about time you stopped being so narrow-minded?"

"Hey! I'm not narrow-minded."

"Prove it," Angelo challenged.

"I'm not playing if we're dropping the mixed-couple rule," Brandon said. "There's no way I'm kissing a guy. It's disgusting."

"This is stupid—" Kyle said.

"Okay, let's get this sorted," Lee said. "Anyone who doesn't want to play with the new rules—"

"Babe," Sian whispered, and Max turned his attention to her. "You know how you were saying you needed new boots? I was thinking of going downtown on Monday. Kyle's going fishing with Lee up at Marigold Lake. I reckon it's an excuse to avoid coming shopping, but still." She sighed. "Will you take me?"

"Yeah, sure. Like you said, I could use some new boots." He twanged the loose rubber. "We could make an afternoon of it."

"And go for a drink afterward?"

"Sounds like a plan."

"Everyone ready?" Lee asked as Kyle, Brandon, and a few others exited the garage.

Angelo spun the bottle, and Sian chattered about their shopping trip. Max nodded in all the right places, stealing glances at Rick, who was busy looking after Pete. It was unusual for Pete to be so drunk this early.

He began to wish he hadn't donated his tequila bottle to the game. A small amount of drink sloshed inside, tormenting him each time the bottle spun. He hadn't thought to bring any more alcohol out there with him.

Instead he took some tobacco out of one of his pockets and busied himself rolling another joint. The other one was taking far too long to come back around.

Max relaxed back with his eyes closed, smoking, when he noticed the room had quieted.

"This is going to be so hot," Angelo said.

Max lazily opened his eyes. Everyone was staring at him. *What the fuck?* His gaze darted, and in the center of the room his treacherous bottle pointed at him. Rick shuffled forward. Panic erupted within him, and Max stared at the bottle for a long moment and then up at Rick. No way. This could not be happening.

"No skipping the tongues," Angelo said.

"Spin it again," Max said, his voice trembling. "I'm not doing it."

"It's not optional," Joe said. "You agreed to play the game. You don't get to pick and choose."

Angelo hunched forward and smiled. "Why are you acting like it's such a big deal? It's just a kiss."

"I'll take your place if you want?" Jade offered.

"Yeah, okay."

"Grow a pair and get on with it," Angelo said. Then he raised an eyebrow. "You never know, you might like it."

Oh God. Max looked Rick in the eyes and felt queasy. What would everyone say if he went through with it? Would they guess the secret he'd been hiding his entire life? Blood drained from his limbs and they tingled as the panic took hold, and he began to feel faint.

"You don't have to do it if you don't want to," Rick said.

Max glanced around. Everyone was watching him… judging him. The longer he left it, the more unbearable it got. If only he could get up and walk out, but that would make it one hundred times worse.

This was not how he'd imagined his first kiss with a guy. It was, without a doubt, his worst nightmare, and yet the one thing he craved more than anything.

"I'll do it." He barely recognized his voice as the words left his lips.

"Are you sure?" Rick asked, concern etched on his face.

No. Max took a shaky breath and nodded. Rick closed the gap between them, and Max glanced back at Sian, hoping for sympathy, or support, but all he saw was her giggling at his predicament.

With a glare, he handed Sian his joint, and upon turning back, Max found himself inches away from Rick. His body trembled as he closed his eyes. A man was about to kiss him. Oh God. If anyone questioned his sexuality based on tonight, he could always blame it on peer pressure, not the fact that he wanted this man to kiss him more than he'd ever wanted any woman.

He couldn't believe he was doing this—and with an audience. Max wanted to both savor this moment forever and scramble away before it was too late to undo it… but this could be the only chance he got. There was no way he could allow himself to kiss a man again.

The instant the heat of Rick's lips touched his, there was no denying he was kissing a man—the sandpaper roughness of his skin, the heady musk of aftershave, and the strength of Rick's forearm as it pressed against his back, encouraging him closer.

Max's stomach twisted in desperate need as he kissed Rick, his anxieties almost forgotten. How was that even possible? Rick tilted his head, and Max parted his lips, keeping them firm but soft enough to allow Rick's tongue to slip past them. Max was helpless in his response as Rick's tongue dipped into his mouth. His lips were like velvet, and he tasted of Max's favorite beer. It was intoxicating.

He gave in to the urge to explore Rick's mouth, and their tongues twirled. Rick moaned against his lips, and Max's cock jolted at the sound. He lurched away, suddenly hyperaware of their audience, guilt and fear smothering him as the enormity of what he'd done in front of them took hold.

"That was more like it." Angelo chuckled. "Didn't know you had it in you, Max. I take it all back."

Max slumped against the beanbag, struggling to breathe as his eyes locked with Rick's. Had he felt it too?

"Come on, Max, don't keep us waiting." Lee pointed at the bottle.

In a daze, Max spun, did what he had to do, and made a swift exit, mumbling about getting more tequila.

Puffs of smoke escaped as Max stumbled outside and around the corner of the garage, away from curious eyes. The cooler air stripped any remaining control he had over his legs, and he slid to the ground with his back resting against the wall, a lifetime of suppressed emotions escaping in an uncontrollable flood. He brought his hands to his damp face and pressed against them as more tears escaped.

How could everything go so wrong so fast? When he'd woken up that morning and driven the final stretch from their gig the previous night, he'd been excited about getting home after such a long time away. But now all he wanted was to run away and never come back.

The garage door slammed closed, and Rick's tall form emerged. He was tense—Max could tell that without even seeing his face.

Shrinking into the shadows, Max wiped his eyes and tried to suppress his tears, praying he wouldn't be seen. Rick scanned the yard and then turned to look behind him. Seeing Max, his eyes narrowed, and he marched up to him.

"You didn't need to lie to me, you know." Crouching in front of him, Rick's face softened. "But I get why you did."

Max clenched his fists and stared at his boots. They were falling apart. He really did need a new pair. "It was a game," he mumbled.

"A game?" Rick reached out to touch Max's cheek, but Max swiped his hand away. "If it was just a game, why are you so upset?"

"Leave me alone," Max whispered, his eyes fixed on his boots.

Rick ignored him and lowered his body so he was sitting next to Max, their backs leaning against the side of the garage.

Why couldn't he do as Max had asked and leave him alone? There wasn't anything that could be said to fix this. All it could do was make it worse.

In a matter of hours, Rick had figured out the secret Max had kept his whole life. How was it possible for everything to have crumbled apart with one look from this man?

"Talk to me, Max. You can trust me, you know."

Max stole a glance at him.

"Well, you don't know you can because we just met, but… you can, okay?"

Max scrubbed his hands across his face. A part of him wanted to talk, but the thought of it terrified him. If he said it aloud, there would be no taking it back. It would be real. A sob escaped, and he clapped his hand over his mouth as tears once again began to fall.

Rick didn't say another word. He reached across and put his arm around Max's shoulders. The warmth of his touch and weight of his arm was a comfort, and Max leaned closer, his thoughts racing out of control.

If any of his friends found out, he'd be kicked out of the band for sure. Image was everything in their world, and having a gay front man wasn't the image of a successful heavy metal band. Hell, he even knew of one guy in a band similar to theirs who'd committed suicide by taking an overdose because the media had found out he was gay. Max had worked hard on his music his entire life, and because of Rick, he'd likely end up homeless and busking on a sidewalk someplace if his true feelings ever got out.

"I'd lose everything," Max said, and pressed his damp cheek against Rick's strong shoulder.

"You can't hide who you are forever, Max."

"Wanna bet?" Max glanced up at him, and Rick smiled.

"Well, for what it's worth, I'm glad I got to kiss you."

"You are?" Max dried his eyes with the palm of his hand and leaned back so he could look at Rick properly.

"Yeah." Rick stared at him, and Max held his gaze, his heart beating fast. "And you should stop looking at me like that if you don't want it to happen again."

Max's stomach somersaulted. He'd already kissed him once that evening. Would it be so bad if it happened again while nobody was watching? Rick leaned closer, close enough that his breath caressed Max's jaw.

"Last chance to stop me," he whispered and reached up to stroke Max's cheek.

His skin tingled under Rick's touch, and he was helpless to resist— he didn't want to resist, not this time.

Rick rubbed his thumb across Max's lips, never breaking eye contact. Closing the final distance, he replaced his thumb with his lips and snaked his arm around Max's back, pulling him closer until their bodies touched. This time there was no holding back.

The second Rick's soft, warm lips pressed against his, Max opened to him, every touch burned to memory, stored away forever for all the lonely nights he was destined to have for the rest of his life. Rick's tongue was strong as they battled, both wanting more and doing whatever they could to get it. His slight stubble grazed Max's skin, and he welcomed the new sensation. Rick probed his mouth hard until Max found himself struggling to breathe, but instead of drawing away, he pressed their bodies closer.

Rick pulled away, and Max groaned. Was it over already?

"You enjoyed kissing me." Rick reached up and stroked Max's jaw. "Didn't you?"

"Maybe," Max whispered, the words barely leaving his lips. "But this can never happen again."

Rick pressed his lips to Max's ear and whispered, "I don't believe you."

THE NEXT morning Max's head felt as though it was going to explode as he jolted into a heavy consciousness. Nauseous waves rose from his chest and threatened to burn his parched throat, a feeling that had become all too familiar over the past months.

Cautiously he sat up, then rubbed his forehead as his vision stabilized.

The familiar sight of his bedroom after so long away made him smile. The two naked women sleeping on either side of him, however, were not a welcome sight. It looked as though Zoe and Lisa had found him after all. A ripped condom foil lay on the bed, the unused condom next to it. He scrambled over Zoe, slithering off the bed and groaning as he attempted to haul on his pants, which had been in a crumpled heap on the floor.

Max stumbled along the hallway to the bathroom and reached it in time to throw up into the toilet. He felt more human until he looked in the mirror and saw the dark circles beneath his eyes, a stark contrast to his currently pale skin. It was nothing a cup of strong coffee or ten wouldn't fix. He stripped, lingering under a steaming hot shower and brushing his teeth twice before staggering down the two flights of stairs to the kitchen, stepping over several sleeping bodies along the way.

"You're up early," Pete said. "It's only three in the afternoon."

Max grunted and headed past him to the coffeepot, which had seen better days, weaving his hand between the empty bottles to switch it on.

"You stayed?" It was unusual for Pete to crash over. Max slumped on one of the kitchen chairs and, after clearing a space, rested his elbows on the table.

"No. Rick and I shared a cab at around four. Apparently the party was still in full swing, though." Pete chuckled. "Don't you remember?"

Max frowned. Last night was hazy. He didn't remember much beyond…. Max froze as the memory of kissing Rick returned, and he looked up at Pete. Did he know? Oh fuck. "I don't remember a lot after getting back here from the gig."

"Wow, you did hit it hard. I thought as much. I have to admit the last part of the evening is a bit vague for me too."

Pete took Max's giant-sized skull-and-crossbones hangover mug from the cupboard and filled it with strong coffee and several sugars. He poured another for himself and joined Max at the table.

"Thanks." Max slurped the hot caffeine goodness and tried to ignore his tongue burning.

"I figured you guys could use a hand clearing up after the party." Pete gestured at the trash bag that was already bursting with bottles.

"You don't have to do that. We can take care of it."

"Max, when I came over to keep an eye on things while you were away, the house was an absolute disaster. I would've expected you to at least have attempted to clear up a bit before going away for six months. Especially after the party you had the night before."

"We were running late." Max snorted a laugh at the memory. None of them had given a thought to clearing up before leaving. Pete was right. Max loved having parties, but they were a pain in the ass the next day when they were left with all the mess. "I'll give you a hand once I've had a couple more of these." Max lifted his hangover mug and gulped the coffee down.

Hearing light footsteps on the stairs, Max glanced up. Oh no. He grimaced as his girlfriend grabbed a coffee and kissed Max on the temple before joining them at the table.

"Hey, Zoe," Pete said. "Great party last night. I bet you were glad to see this one." He ruffled Max's hair.

"Yeah," Zoe said. "Are you okay?" She studied Max.

"Sure. Why wouldn't I be?"

"It's just…." Zoe looked at Pete. "Never mind."

"Either of you want waffles?" Pete asked. "I brought some over. Figured you hadn't had a chance to get groceries yet."

"That'd be great."

Pete got up and went about fixing their breakfast.

Zoe leaned closer to Max and whispered, "Was everything okay last night?"

"How do you mean?"

Zoe blushed. "Well… you know…. How much do you remember?"

"Not a lot. I was blasted."

"But you couldn't… you know…." Zoe glanced at Pete again, but he wasn't paying them any attention.

"Zoe, I was really drunk. What do you want me to say?"

"Nothing, I—"

"What? What are you suggesting exactly?" Max hissed. He knew where this was heading, what she was referring to. He'd found a way to avoid having sex with her and Lisa, and she didn't like it. He'd never let that happen before with them, had always been so careful. He couldn't let this fall apart, not now. He stroked her cheek and said, "I drank my bodyweight in tequila last night. I'm not superhuman, you know."

Zoe gave him a relieved smile. "Yeah, I know. Sorry. I missed you, that's all." She hugged him close and rested her head on his shoulder.

"Here you go." Pete slid plates of waffles and crispy bacon across the table toward them.

"Thanks, Pete," Max said as his stomach growled.

"These look delicious," Zoe said. "I don't get how you're single, Pete."

"Yeah, well, if you know anyone"—Pete joined them—"feel free to give them my number. It's probably about time I started dating again."

"Mm, I'll think about it."

Loud crashing reverberated from upstairs.

"I'll fix Tony a plate," Pete said and had it ready on the table by the time Tony jumped down the last few steps into the kitchen.

"How is everyone this fine morning?"

Zoe shook her head. "It's three in the afternoon."

Tony sat next to Max and tucked into the waffles. "You didn't make these, did you? Wouldn't have thought you'd feel up to it after last night." Tony chuckled and pulled out his cell phone. "I got some great footage of you." He thrust his cell into Max's face. It was a video of Max, naked and dancing on the kitchen table. "What's it worth for me to not put this on the internet?"

Max's cheeks burned. "You wouldn't dare."

"Na, maybe not." Tony flicked through his cell some more. "But this one's fair game." Tony showed them a picture of Max, still naked, passed out, and being carried upstairs by Rick in a fireman's lift.

"Oh God. You've got to be kidding me."

Tony let out a huge belly laugh. "Zoe and Lisa tried and failed to carry you up, didn't you, darlin', but you're a heavy lump when you're passed out, and I sure as hell wasn't going to do it while you had no clothes on. Luckily, Rick offered, otherwise you'd have been sleeping here on the kitchen table. I got the perfect caption too—"

"Tony," Pete said, "remember we talked about the line that shouldn't ever be crossed? Posting naked pictures of your brother on the internet is about as far across the wrong side of the line as it gets."

Tony sighed and chuckled, giving Max a squeeze before turning his attention back to his food. "You're too easy to fuck with. As if I would." He glanced up. "Maybe—"

"How would you like it if Max crept into your bedroom, took a picture of you before you'd had a chance to shower, and—"

"He wouldn't dare. That would be a terrible thing to do." Tony draped his arm over Max's shoulders.

"Try me." Max took a sip of coffee and shrugged Tony's arm off. "And I'd make sure all your fancy creams and hair products were in the shot as well… and your straighteners with the skulls on them."

Tony gasped. "He doesn't stick on this side of that fucking line you're always harping on about, Pete. See what I have to put up with?" Tony gently swatted Max around the head. Max ducked, and wished he hadn't as his head began to swim.

Pete took their plates and loaded them into the dishwasher. "You both do what you like, but don't say I didn't warn you."

Zoe snickered. "You have straighteners with skulls on them? That's so cute."

"Shut it, you." Tony reached around Max and playfully punched her arm. "Sian got them for me last Thanksgiving as a joke."

"Yeah," Max said, "but he's been using them ever since. Haven't you noticed how silky smooth his hair is now?" Tony glared at him.

The front door slammed, and Lee's whistling traveled down to the kitchen.

"What's that tune?" Pete stood with his head tipped to one side as he listened. "I recognize it but can't for the life of me think what it is."

"It's Defeated Nightmare's new one."

"Mm." Pete hummed the tune. "Yeah, that's it. Thanks, Tony."

"Hi, everyone," Lee said as he wandered into the kitchen, his arms loaded with groceries. Pete cleared a space for him next to the refrigerator, and Lee put his bags down before stacking his groceries into his cupboards. They all fended for themselves, although Max often decided to cook for all of them. "Finally up, then?"

Tony winked at him. "You must have been getting up about when the rest of us turned in."

"Fuck off, Tony. Not all of us need as much beauty sleep as you."

"Oh, I wasn't sleeping." Tony grinned at him.

Lee shook his head, putting the last few groceries away and mumbling, "Of course you weren't. Why do you think I got the hell up?"

Max chuckled. Lee had the room beneath Tony, and he did feel sorry for him. Lee was always complaining about the noise.

"Lee, do you want some waffles? I think there's enough left," Pete said.

"Yeah, that'd be nice. Thanks." Lee sat at the table, and Max got up to make himself another coffee. "How are you feeling today, Max?"

"Why does everybody keep on asking me that? I'm fine."

"Freaked out yet?"

"Freaked out about what?" Zoe asked Lee.

"You haven't said anything?" Lee asked Max, who caught his eye for a second before turning back to his coffee. He'd forgotten Lee had witnessed him kissing Rick.

"Said anything about what?" Zoe asked again.

Max knew he had to make a decision right then. Should he claim that the alcohol had wiped his memory of the kiss, or should he own it and brush it off as if it was no big deal? He wanted to brush it off, knew that was the best thing to do, but….

"Said anything about what, Lee?" Max raked his fingers through his hair. "What did I do this time? My memory's pretty much blank from when we got back after the gig. I hit the tequila as soon as we got home." He clenched his hands around his mug to stop them from shaking while he waited for this to play out.

Lee studied him for a moment. "You kind of got bullied into playing a game and you freaked out straight after."

"What game?" Zoe asked.

"Spin the bottle," Lee said and squinted at them. "You really haven't heard? I guess the game didn't last long—"

"What? What happened, Lee? Spit it the fuck out," Tony said.

"It's okay," Zoe whispered in Max's ear. "You don't need to worry. It's not like we're exclusive. I won't be upset."

Lee laughed. "Let's just say Max fell victim to a temporary change in the rules last night. You should've walked out. That's what I would've done."

For a moment Max forgot that he'd pretended to forget. He gathered his thoughts again just in time. "What the hell are you talking about?" Tony and Pete watched him with their mouths gaped in surprise. "What rule change?"

"You fucking kissed some guy, Max," Lee said.

"No." Max went cold as Lee's words hit him. He tried to shrug it off, but Zoe was looking thoughtful. "I was fucking drunk," Max screamed.

Tony glanced at Pete and then put a careful hand on Max's arm. "It's okay, Max." He glared at Lee and the others. "Let's just drop it, all right?"

Max grabbed his skull-and-crossbones mug and made for the stairs. He made it halfway to his bedroom before he realized Lisa was still in his bed. Fucking great.

He turned around, headed for the door, and went out into the yard to sit around the back of the garage by his smoker, where he'd kissed Rick for the second time.

As soon as he reached the spot, his legs gave way, and he sank to the ground in a flood of tears. This really was his worst nightmare. A part of him had hoped that if everyone found out, it wouldn't be a big deal, that they would all accept it and tell him it was okay if he was gay, but no.

"Max," Zoe said as she approached. "I'm sorry, okay?"

Max raised his head a fraction before staring at the ground.

Zoe sighed and flopped down next to him, tucking her long black hair behind her ear. "I missed you while you were away, and I guess I panicked when you seemed so distant last night. I never meant to doubt... you know."

Well, now he felt like an asshole. He'd been so wrapped up in his own problems that he'd not considered any feelings Zoe or Lisa may have. "I'm sorry too." Max took a deep breath and put his arm around her and hugged her close. "How's Lisa? Is she okay?"

Zoe kissed Max's neck and stroked her fingers along his collarbone. "Yeah, I think so. I haven't spoken to her yet this afternoon, but we talked a bit last night after you passed out."

"Talked?" Max raised an eyebrow, and she laughed.

"Okay, you got me. Let's just say last night wasn't a total disaster." Zoe sighed. "It's weird, isn't it?"

"What's that?"

"Well, nobody cares that Lisa and I had sex last night, but as soon as anyone suggests two guys sleeping together, or kissing even, it's a big drama."

"I guess."

"I hate all these double-standards; it doesn't make any sense."

Max snorted a laugh. "Yeah... it doesn't bother you, what I did, then?"

Zoe rested her arm across his shoulders. "I can't see the big deal. Love is love, right?"

"It's not like I wanted to do it, you get that, though, don't you?" Max chewed his lower lip, terrified that if he agreed with her about the whole "love is love" thing, she'd see right through him.

"Yeah," Zoe said softly, "I got that." Max rested his head on her shoulder, and they sat in silence for a few moments. "We should go back inside. Pete's got everyone clearing up, and they'll never forgive us if we don't help."

"Okay." Max huffed and staggered to his feet, holding out his hand to help Zoe up.

Under Pete's instruction, Zoe, Max, and Sian, who was now up, headed out to the garage with trash bags to begin the cleanup operation. It didn't take as long as Max had expected, and a couple of hours later they were done.

After everyone went home, Max went out to stock up on groceries, and then headed up to his now-empty bedroom with the burritos he'd made. It was still a mess, as the cleanup operation hadn't stretched as far as upstairs.

Max sighed and shuffled onto his bed, leaning back against the wall as he ate his meal. He paused between mouthfuls, the sudden silence after the chaos and constant noise during the tour agitating him. He thought he'd have welcomed it, but instead it felt as though something was missing, and it made him feel empty. Weird. Max finished his meal, put his plate down on the comforter, and stared at his bedside table. It was crammed with empty bottles and snack wrappers. The rest of the house looked great now, and it further highlighted the state of his bedroom.

With a sudden burst of energy and the need to do *something*, Max climbed off the bed and began to tidy his room. As he placed the last bottles in the trash, a single piece of ripped paper tucked between them caught his eye. He frowned as he retrieved it. There was a cell number written on it and beneath the number "Call me" and a smiley face.

His fingers trembled. Was this a joke? It was exactly the kind of thing his friends would find amusing. But what if it wasn't? What if he was holding Rick's actual number?

Max knew Rick had been in his bedroom after he'd carried him upstairs. His cheeks burned at the memory of Tony's photograph. If Rick had wanted Max to contact him, it would have been the perfect opportunity to leave his number discreetly. Hell, there wasn't even a name on the paper, which meant it probably was him…. Max sank to the floor and stared at the number.

Should he call it? The thought terrified him.

CHAPTER FOUR

Rick

"MORNING, LOVE." Rick's mom looked up from where she was preparing food in the kitchen. He'd slept in that morning, which was unusual for him. It was nearly midday. "This arrived this morning." She handed him a letter and went back to chopping an onion. "Do you want some lunch?"

The logo on the envelope was of the MMA gym in Vegas that he'd been waiting to hear from. His fingers trembled as he opened it.

"Rick."

"Huh?" He looked up.

His mom smiled. "Lunch, love?"

"Um, yeah, thanks." He walked through to the lounge and finished ripping it open. It didn't take long to scan the contents of the letter.

Thank you for your interest in applying for the trainer position. We have decided to proceed with another candidate.

He let out the breath he didn't realize he'd been holding and fell back onto the couch, his arm dropping next to him as he released the paper. That had been the final top-level MMA club he'd tried. How was it that with his fifteen years' experience in martial arts, and now as a certified chiropractor, he was still unable to get his foot in the door as a mixed martial arts trainer? It was frustrating beyond belief.

Setting up a top-level MMA club took a huge amount of investment, and he didn't have that kind of money. He'd had to make do with a minimal amount of second-hand equipment and hiring space from his parents at a discounted rate to have his own club at all. It would take years to build it up enough to be taken seriously, and after all the years of training it felt like he'd already waited a lifetime. His current setup was only ever meant to be temporary.

"Any luck?"

Rick removed his arm from where it was covering his eyes and looked at his mom. She meant well, but he had zero privacy living with his parents again.

"No."

"And that was the last one?" She handed him a plate of sandwiches.

He nodded.

"Well, love, maybe it wasn't meant to be. I think it's time you got a proper job as a chiropractor, don't you? All that training…." She tutted and shook her head. "I spoke to Mr. Sanders, you know, at Elfinbrook Chiropractic, and he has an opening coming up in September for a junior chiropractor—"

Rick stood, his frustration building. "Mom, no. I can take care of this myself, okay? I don't need your help. I'm twenty-seven, for God's sake; I can do this on my own. You knew I didn't want to work in a regular chiropractic clinic before I even started my training. We discussed it, remember?"

His mom held up her hands and gave him that annoying, dismissive look that she'd last used when he'd told her he was going to give up dance and focus on martial arts. It was her way of saying "You do what you want and see if I care," and it made him angry because he knew full well that she expected to get her way this time—expected him to let her interfere.

His dad walked in and pursed his lips. "It's okay to be frustrated, but there's no need to take it out on your mom."

"Sorry, Mom." Rick sighed and slumped back on the couch. "It's just so annoying. I can't seem to catch a break here."

His dad sat next to him and patted his knee. "I'm a firm believer that it simply means something better is around the corner."

"But the best MMA clubs are in Vegas. I've tried all of them now." Rick caught his dad giving his mom *that look*, which was never a good sign. "What? What is it?"

"Not all the best MMA clubs are in Vegas."

"What are you talking about?"

"Dietmar's coming to visit in a few weeks' time. I finally managed to persuade him to take a vacation. I know his nightclubs are important and take a lot of work. But even he needs to take a break."

"Yeah, so?"

"Do you remember his partner, Neil?"

"Sure I do." Neil was the one who'd gotten him interested in martial arts in the first place. When he was twelve and they were visiting with Neil and Dietmar in London, Neil had taken him along to his kickboxing club. He'd been hooked ever since.

"Well, Neil opened up an MMA gym in London last year." He frowned. "I'm sure I mentioned it to you at the time…. Oh well, anyway, I could put in a good word for you, see if he has something."

Rick snorted a laugh. "I can't move to London."

"He's right. Jakob, don't put such silly ideas in the boy's head. London's too far away."

His dad shrugged. "Just saying, Lily, that it would be a good way for him to get some proper experience. Even if it's only for a short while."

"Rick's fighters have competed under his training," his mom said, "and I don't see how exactly the same in London could benefit him. It wouldn't even be his own club."

"Neil's fighters compete globally." His dad glanced at him. "Rick's been doing the local circuit with his fighters."

Rick sat up straighter, his thoughts racing. Perhaps his dad was right. Maybe that would be a way in, to prove himself on the global rather than the local scene.

"Do it, talk to Neil. See if he has something."

"Are you trying to push them all away?" His mom shook her head, a hint of tears in her eyes. "First Isla moves to Vegas, and now you're convincing our son to move to another country."

"Mom, it would be temporary. Besides, we don't even know if Neil has anything yet. Like I said, all the best clubs are in Vegas, so it wouldn't be permanent." It would simply be a way to get his foot in the door to the job he'd dreamed of since he was a teenager.

"Are you ready, Rick?" Isla, his twin sister, asked as she rummaged through her handbag. She was only visiting with them for a couple of days, so he wanted to make the most of their limited time together. Unfortunately, that meant going shopping with her.

"Yeah." Rick hauled himself to his feet. "Let me just eat lunch quickly." He had a lot to think about. A walk around the stores with Isla to find a wedding present for her friend would help to clear his head.

"WHERE DO you want to go next?" Rick asked Isla as they strolled through downtown Elfinbrook in the fierce afternoon sun.

Isla sighed. "The department store, I guess. Doesn't look like we're going to have much luck with the boutiques."

"That'll teach you to leave it until the last minute."

"They had a short engagement, it's not my fault. I was working."

"Maybe you should wait until you're back in Vegas, get something there? A pair of jazzy Elvis wedding dolls or something?"

"Rick, it's not funny," she whined. "Gracie's wedding is this weekend. I have to get something now or I'm in trouble." Rick grinned, and she thumped him. "Stop it. I am getting more organized, I swear." She grabbed his arm and dragged him toward the mall. "Help me out here. The sooner we get done, the sooner you can treat me to ice cream."

Rick raised an eyebrow and allowed himself to be dragged. "I'm treating you?"

"Yeah, 'cause you're so happy to see me," she said as they entered the air-conditioned mall.

To their right was an alternative clothing store with neon lights flashing and electronica music blaring from the dark tunnel of steps leading to the hidden store beneath. The window of the music store to their left was filled with an array of shiny electric guitars on sale, and Rick paused to look at them.

"Ever considered learning a musical instrument, Isla?"

She stopped and stared at him. Then she burst out laughing.

Rick folded his arms. "What?"

"Are you serious?" Isla joined him at the store window. "One kiss with a musician and suddenly you're dreaming about being a rock star? What happened to not wanting a relationship 'cause you're focusing on your career? You have got it bad."

"Have not." How did she always manage to do that, to embarrass him over nothing? True, he'd enjoyed the party on Friday night and meeting Max, but it was one night, one kiss—okay, two, but he hadn't shared everything with Isla. Max was so far in the closet it would be almost impossible to pry him free and explore anything more between them, no matter how good it had been. Max had even orchestrated a fake casual relationship to stop people from questioning his sexuality. He'd never seen anyone go that far to hide it. It was so frustrating. "I should have known you'd make a big deal out of it. You'd think I'd have the sense by now not to tell you anything."

"Aw, don't be like that." Isla grabbed him around the waist and hugged him. "I believe you that... what was his name again?"

"Max."

"That Max didn't mean anything, or at least I would if you didn't keep bringing it up." Isla glanced at the alternative clothing store. "Maybe you could invest in a funky black T-shirt or some luminous chaps to entice him."

Rick swatted at her head, but she ducked out of the way, laughing. "You're too easy."

They reached the department store, which spanned three levels, and stopped by the store plan to figure out which sections to visit.

"What kind of thing were you planning to get Gracie, anyway?"

"I don't know." Isla sighed and pointed to the fine-china section. "There ought to be something in there, right?"

Fine china, really? "This is the last time I come shopping with you."

"Stop sulking and maybe I'll spring for the ice cream... or perhaps one of those sexy guitars." Isla began to play air guitar, and Rick scowled at her.

The elevator dinged as they reached the third floor, and Isla and Rick stepped out, scanning the floor to get their bearings.

"Fine china, this way," Isla said, pointing straight ahead, and Rick followed her.

As they approached the vast section of gleaming plates and cups, Rick spotted a bench by the entrance. "I'll wait here. Come get me once you're done."

"Suit yourself."

Rick sat down and watched his sister disappear before closing his eyes.

A loud voice cut through the quiet. "If it wasn't for you, we'd all be in the fucking bar by now. If I'd thought it would've taken this long, I never would've come." Rick's eyes flew open. The voice sounded familiar, but he couldn't quite place it.

He stood and looked to the far end, where Tony and Sian were apparently arguing over a set of plates. Rick blinked. If they were there, then maybe.... He glanced around, searching, hoping. He took a few steps closer, and a smile crept onto his face.

Sure enough, Max was with them, over by the china cups, his golden hair falling forward to conceal his face as he rolled a gaudy teacup between his palms, studying it closely. He looked so out of place in his well-loved leather jacket and decrepit boots that Rick almost let out a laugh.

Max placed the teacup back and picked up another, his cute face contorting with disgust as he gingerly put it back before moving on to the next one. This time Rick did chuckle.

What was it about this guy that had him so intrigued? Apart from his unbelievably sexy ass and haunting green eyes. From the first time he'd laid eyes on him when Pete had shown him Max's picture and suggested Rick come to the Purple Method gig, Rick had known Max would be impossible to resist—that he'd be an irresistible distraction.

Rick stalked toward him, careful not to let either Max or his friends see him. He stopped close enough to feel the heat from Max's lithe body inches away, close enough to reach out and caress him. Instead he chose to lean forward and whisper in Max's ear, "I never pictured you for a fine china kind of guy."

Max froze, his body rigid. The teacup slipped from his fingers, and before Rick could reach forward and grab it, the cup shattered into tiny pieces on the floor.

At the sound of china smashing, Sian and Tony whirled around. Rick waved, and Sian grinned at him. Max didn't move.

"Hey, Rick," Tony called out. He waved two different plates in the air. "You been breaking all your china too?" Sian elbowed him in the ribs, but he seemed to be expecting it and didn't flinch. "Who knew it could take so long to choose a fucking plate, huh?"

Max's back brushed against Rick as he crouched down and began to gather the broken china.

"Hi, Tony, Sian. How's it going? Didn't expect to see you in here," Rick called back to them. He crouched next to Max. "It's good to see you again," he murmured and smiled as their eyes connected. "Are you okay?" Still Max didn't reply, so Rick grasped Max's clammy hand and examined it, but Max pulled away. "You didn't hurt yourself, did you?"

"I'm okay." Max turned his attention back to the broken china, gathering it from the floor tiles.

Max wasn't exactly giving him anything to work with, but he also hadn't told Rick to leave him alone. That had to be a good sign. "Here, let me take it. It was my fault. I'll pay for it."

They both stood, and Rick reached forward, careful to make sure their hands touched. Max flinched away and looked at something over Rick's shoulder. For a split second, Rick could have sworn Max looked jealous, but the emotion was gone as quickly as it had appeared.

"No, it's okay. I've got it." Max grimaced as Rick caught a waft of his sister's perfume and felt her arms around his waist.

"Max, this is my sister, Isla."

"Hi," Isla said.

Max's expression lightened and he glanced between them. "Your sister?"

"Hold on... Max?" Isla said, letting go and taking a step forward. Oh no, this was never going to be good. Why the hell had he said anything to Isla about Friday? "The Max? From the band?"

"Uh, I guess." Max glanced around.

Rick's cheeks burned. So much for playing it cool. This was humiliating.

"From what I hear, you were very good on Friday."

"Uh, thanks."

"Really good, in fact. Isn't that right, Rick?"

Rick elbowed her, hard. "It was a fun night, yeah."

"Finally," Tony said, shoving the box of plates he was carrying at Sian as they approached, "we can get the hell out of here. Bar next?"

"Black Ivy, remember?" Max said. "I have to get some new boots."

"Is that the alternative clothing store we passed on the way in?" Isla asked.

"Yeah, that's it," Sian said. "We were going to stop in there and then grab a drink. Would you like to join us?"

Isla groaned. "But I still have to get a wedding gift for my friend."

"Did you see the display over there?" Sian indicated the far corner. "They've got a whole summer-wedding theme going on."

"No, I didn't." Isla's face brightened, and she and Sian went over to investigate.

"I have to go pay for this," Max said and started toward the cash register.

Rick made to follow him, but Tony grabbed his arm and held him back. That was odd. "This is the last place I expected to bump into you guys," Rick said to him.

"Her fault." He pointed at Sian.

"Couldn't you and Max have waited in the music store?"

Tony took a step back and studied Rick for a moment. "Don't get any ideas about my brother."

"Ideas?"

Tony leaned in, and as Max approached, he said in a low voice, "He's not gay and never will be. He's in a heavy metal band, not some camp boy band. That should have been enough of a clue for you."

Rick stared at him in disbelief.

"Ready for Black Ivy?" Tony said to Max as he drew near enough to hear them.

"Sure. They said not to worry about the cup. Looks like we're all going, so we should wait for them." Max turned and waved toward Isla and Sian, who were chattering away as they paid for their goods.

"Awesome," Tony said, his brow creased.

TONY'S WORDS had stung, and as Rick followed the others down the steps into Black Ivy, part of him wanted to walk away right then. The other part, however, the fighter in him, wanted Max more than ever, wanted to help him reach a point where he could tell everyone the truth and not have to hide who he was anymore.

Everyone had dispersed into the store, and Rick paused for a moment to take it all in. Hard-core dance music blared, deafening him. There were black cages on either side of the entrance, containing mannequins dressed as androgynous dancers in skimpy clubwear. They had futuristic-looking goggles on their heads next to their huge, brightly colored dreadlocks, and the most incredible makeup. Wow! What was this place? It was like nothing he had ever seen before.

Rick looked down; his white T-shirt was glowing. The store was bathed in black light, giving the entire place an odd look. Tall glass cases were interspersed between the racks of mostly black clothing, and they contained all kinds of bizarre-looking things, from delicate metal contraptions that would not have looked out of place on a cyborg—but were some kind of club accessory—to huge, odd-looking dildos, and some of the most extreme bondage gear he'd ever seen. He was hot, too hot, and swallowed down his panic. Where had the others gotten to?

"Need any help?" a petite, immaculate store assistant with bloodred hair asked him.

What was it Max had said earlier? "Um, yeah. My friends were looking for footwear?"

"Through there." The assistant pointed with long black nails toward a curtained-off area near a staircase at the other end of the floor.

"Thanks."

Rick weaved his way toward the curtain and was relieved to find Max and Sian in the cornered-off space, which was filled with some of the oddest-looking boots and stilettos he'd ever seen, but also some of the coolest.

"What do you think of these?" Sian asked Rick, holding up a pair of chunky New Rock boots with metal plates on the front and a platform sole.

"For you or for him?" Rick nodded at Max, who was stretching up, scrabbling to reach another pair of boots from a high shelf. Rick walked over and grabbed the boots, then handed them to Max.

"Him," Sian said.

"Thanks," Max said to Rick. "These are better, though, don't you think?"

Max had chosen a knee-length boot, which had a flat, chunky sole, silver scalelike leather sections up the front, and five huge metallic buckles at the sides. They looked incredible.

"Those"—Rick pointed at Max's choice—"definitely those."

Sian sighed. "You won't even be able to see them beneath your pants."

"But I'll know they're there."

"You'll be far too hot in them."

"Don't care. These are awesome."

"Suit yourself." Sian shrugged. "Don't come moaning to me if your feet get all sweaty."

"Eew, they won't," Max said, and Rick laughed. "They're cool, though, right?" Max asked Sian, his eyes dancing with excitement.

The curtain pushed open, and Tony and Isla walked through, both of them carrying Black Ivy bags.

"What did you get?" Rick asked Isla.

"Just a top to wear out clubbing."

"I got some DVDs," Tony said.

"Oh yeah," Isla said, "which ones?"

Sian groaned. "We learned long ago never to ask that."

Tony held up one of the DVDs triumphantly. "Animated superhero porn."

"Thanks for that," Max grumbled and shoved past Rick as he went to pay for his boots. "I have enough nightmares about him sleeping in the room opposite me without actually knowing what he's jacking off to."

"Come on, guys," Sian said, "sounds to me like we could all use a drink."

THE BAR adjoining the Torrens Club was quiet, but then it was Monday afternoon. Rick didn't usually go into bars during the week, but if it meant he got to spend some more time with Max, then he'd go with it for now. As they walked in, Angelo was polishing glasses behind the bar, and he returned Rick's smile. They'd spent a lot of time chatting at the party, and Rick had enjoyed his company. Even though he'd told Angelo he wasn't looking for anything at the moment, that hadn't stopped Angelo's flirting. But like Pete had said, he was harmless enough.

"Let's go by the window," Sian said, and pulled out a chair to put her box of china onto before taking the seat next to it. "It's too hot to sit outside."

Rick was about to sit next to Max, but Tony frowned at him, and he thought better of it. He'd bide his time and keep Tony sweet for now. Instead he held out the chair next to Max for Isla and scanned the bar.

There was an occasional *chitck* from the pool table, which was partially hidden behind a partition, where two guys were playing with limited success, judging by the white ball rolling across the floor toward him. The only other customers were a group of students who were having a heated discussion about the merits of artificial intelligence versus the human brain, and they had claimed a large table by the restrooms near the end of the bar.

"Hey, guys," Angelo said, and Rick turned to watch him approach. "Beers all round, or are you hitting the hard stuff?"

"Beers?" Tony said, and Rick looked across the table at him and nodded.

"I'll have tequila as well," Max said, fumbling with a coaster.

"Sure, be right back." Angelo's warm fingers brushed the back of Rick's neck, and he shivered. The guy was relentless.

"Everything still okay for the Villains gig?" Tony asked.

"Yeah," Angelo called over as he prepared their tray of drinks. "I spoke to Lee earlier and settled the details. You guys need to be set up by five."

"Still think they should be opening for us," Tony said in a quieter voice, out of earshot of Angelo.

"They've sold way more records than us," Max said.

Tony scowled at him. "Honestly, Max, whose side are you on?"

"You don't think that gives them the right to headline?" Rick asked. "You can't argue with relative sales figures."

"No?" Tony said. "And what about image, stage presence, and pure fucking talent? You don't know what the hell you're talking about. You're not even a metalhead."

Rick clenched his fists under the table and forced himself to remain calm.

"Tony!" Sian gasped. "Be nice. What's Rick ever done to you?"

Angelo wisely stayed out of it, delivering the drinks without a word and then heading straight back behind the bar.

"Anyone want to play pool?" Max downed his tequila and grabbed his beer. "I think the table's free now."

That was a good idea, the perfect excuse to get away from Tony. "Sure, I'll play," Rick said to no one in particular and followed Max.

Out of sight of the others, Rick slid his arm around Max's waist, and Max flinched at the contact. Rick gave him a brief squeeze and whispered in his ear, "It doesn't bother you that I'm not a metalhead, does it?"

Max spun around to face him. "I'm playing with you?" The corner of Rick's mouth twitched, and Max sighed. "You know what I meant."

"Think you can handle it?"

Max's cheeks colored, and he drained his beer. "Yeah, I can handle it. Can you?"

Was Max flirting with him? Rick grinned. It seemed Max had found courage from someplace, perhaps from that beer. "I've been playing for years. I'm sure I can hold my own. What about you? Much experience?"

"At pool?"

Rick winked at him and set up the balls. "If you like."

"I'm fucking fantastic." Max placed the white ball on the table, bent over, and took a few practice thrusts with his cue. "At pool."

"Are you now?"

God, Max was sexy. It was all Rick could do to not walk up behind and push him against the table, thrust up against that tight ass—he'd seen Max naked at the party, and the image flashed into his head. If he wasn't careful, his desire would be all too visible. He took a breath and walked closer to the table and set up the colored balls, ignoring the flutter of excitement that rippled through his body.

"Ready?" Max asked as Rick removed the triangle.

Rick nodded and Max pulled the cue back, steadied it on the bridge of his hand, and made a powerful break. The balls scattered, and two fell into the pockets.

"Nice." Rick nodded. "Like your style."

"Thanks." Max assessed the balls and got into position for his next shot.

"Cleaned up after the party yet?" Rick had been wondering whether Max had found the piece of paper with his number on it that he'd left on his bedside table—wondering whether he was deliberately not contacting him.

He frowned and glanced at Rick. "Yeah, why?"

"Find anything interesting?"

Max froze, and Rick walked around the table until he was standing right next to him. As Max bent over to line up his next shot, Rick leaned closer to him. "You found it… didn't you?"

Max took the shot and missed. His face was flushed as he stood.

"You weren't tempted… not even a bit? Should I be hurt?" Rick tried to keep his tone teasing, but he was desperate to know.

"I get numbers thrown at me all the time. How was I supposed to know it was yours?"

Rick chuckled, his heart sinking a little. He knew that was likely to be the truth, but hearing it aloud didn't do much for his ego. "That told me." He reached out and rested his hand on Max's shoulder. It was worth at least one last attempt. "Do you still have it?"

"What does it matter?"

Rick let go and moved around the table to take his shot, hope niggling at him. Perhaps a softer approach would work better. "You don't think we could be friends?"

"Friends?"

"You didn't think I listened before when you told me—" Movement caught his eye, and Rick nodded toward his sister as she approached. "Hey, Isla. You okay? Sorry for abandoning you."

"That's okay. Who's winning?"

"Max."

Isla sighed and perched on the edge of a table. "So unfair. Rick always beats me. You must be really good."

"He is." Rick waggled his eyebrows at Max and potted two balls in quick succession, then a third. He wasn't going to let Max beat him for long.

"You never told me you were this good," Max groaned.

"Actually, I believe I did."

"Give him a proper chance before you kick his ass," Isla warned her brother. "I got a text from Mom. She and Dad are going to meet us for dinner over at the steak house on Park Avenue. We need to leave in a minute."

"Already?"

"Yeah, they've asked Logan to cover the evening class."

"That's at the dance school, right?" Max asked.

"Yeah," Isla said. "I'm amazed they got someone to cover. It's totally unlike them. They're more obsessed with dance than I am."

"You're a dancer?" Max asked.

"Yeah. I'm doing a show on the Vegas strip at the moment."

"Which is why she doesn't visit often enough." Rick gave his sister a friendly shove. "Or so she says."

"You're just jealous you're not onstage too."

"The last thing I want is to be a dancer. I had enough of that growing up, thank you very much."

"At least I don't crack bones for a living. That's totally gross."

Max's jaw dropped. "You can dance?"

Oh great. He'd been hoping to keep that a secret for a little longer.

"Mom was devastated when he went down the martial arts route instead. Rick, come on," Isla whined. "We need to go."

He sighed. "Sorry, Max."

"For what?"

Rick potted all his remaining balls, plus the black. No way was he going to let Max win. Besides, a rematch would be a good excuse to meet up… if Max ever decided to call him. "For that."

"Oh."

"I'll go get my bag," Isla said and left them to it.

Rick grabbed Max's arm, pulling him out of sight of prying eyes. There was no telling when he'd get a chance to bump into him again without looking like a stalker. This was his last opportunity to convince Max that calling his number would be the best thing he ever did.

"Listen," Rick said. It was time to lay it on the line. "You know I want you. I've made no secret of that. But I know this isn't easy for you, so I'm going to say this: if you decide to keep my number, we can be friends. No pressure for anything more, I promise." He leaned closer and whispered, "However, if you do want more, you only have to say the word."

Had that worked? Max looked more shocked than thoughtful.

Rick took a deep breath; the suspense was killing him. "Think about it." Walking away, he said quietly and more seriously, "But don't make me wait forever if that is what you want, okay?"

THE LAST MMA student left, and Rick locked the door behind them. It was Tuesday. Accounts day. Something he despised, but was unfortunately unavoidable if he wanted to run his own business. He did need some new boxing gloves, though… maybe the accounts could wait a few minutes more. They wouldn't take him that long. He sat at his desk and logged into his computer, wondering whether to go with Everlast or Venum.

There was a knock at the door, followed by the door handle rattling. Rick sighed. So much for having some time-out this evening. He unlocked the door, and his eyebrows rose when he saw who it was.

"Tony! What are you doing here?"

"Hey. Do you want to grab a beer?"

Rick gaped at him. Didn't the guy hate him? "Why?" Rick shook his head. "Sorry, didn't mean to be rude…. It's just. Well. The impression you gave me yesterday was that—"

"One beer? Please?"

Rick sighed, curiosity getting the better of him. "Sure. Why not. But I'll be having soda. I've got a competition this weekend."

"That's fine." Tony smiled. "Torrens Bar?"

"Give me a sec to lock up."

TONY CHOSE a booth that was tucked away toward the back, near the pool table. Rock music played in the background, and the bar was mostly empty, although it was starting to fill up.

"So, what's this all about?" Rick asked after they'd sat in silence for what felt like ages.

Taking a gulp of his beer and then sighing, Tony said, "I know you think I'm some kind of asshole for the way I behaved yesterday. Just know that it's nothing personal."

"Okay," Rick said slowly. "Don't worry about it."

Tony looked up with a defiant expression. "But I wasn't kidding when I told you to stay away from Max."

"It's up to him who he spends time with. He's not a kid—"

"You're not getting it." Tony growled with frustration. "Stay the fuck away from him. Why is that so hard?"

"Maybe I don't want to stay away from him. You can't stop me."

"Rick, don't do this. Please." Were there tears in Tony's eyes?

Rick frowned. "What is this all about? Why is this so important to you?" Did Tony seriously think Rick would be such a bad influence on Max? Had he even seen Max's social media? This didn't make any sense.

Tony swiped at his cell phone. Then he slid it across the table to Rick. Warily, Rick picked it up. On the screen was a news article about

Vanquished Villains. He recognized the name of the band from the posters plastered over the walls of the Torrens Bar, advertising their gig at the club the following week. Its members looked like they'd stepped out of a horror movie.

"Read it," Tony said.

As Rick scanned the article, Tony's behavior suddenly made sense. Vanquished Villains' bassist had taken an overdose after coming out. He'd been twenty-seven. Apparently he'd gone into a deep depression after negative press coverage about his sexuality. Rick lowered the cell phone and passed it back to Tony.

"That's the third this year," Tony said. "There was a suicide and another overdose. They weren't in the media as a result of their sexuality, but I've spoken to the bands and know for a fact that they were. This can't happen to Max. I can't lose him." The fear in Tony's eyes shocked Rick.

"You know?"

Tony nodded. "Not for sure until the party, but I've suspected for a while."

"You need to tell him that you know."

"It's better this way. I don't understand it, but I wouldn't have a problem with it—it's everyone else…." Tony covered his face with his hands, bringing them to rest over his mouth. "It's my job to protect him, and he's not strong enough for this shit." Tony threw his cell phone across the table. "It's not safe for him. You need to help me protect him. If he ended up like that"—he pointed at his cell phone—"it would be your fault for not putting a stop to whatever it is that's going on between you."

"Do you realize what you're asking?" Rick was aghast.

"It's the only way."

Rick shook his head. "By forcing him to suppress this, you're only making it worse."

"What else can I do?" There really were tears in Tony's eyes now.

"We can protect him from the media. You, me, your friends—"

"But what if we can't?" Tony whispered. "Don't let this happen, Rick, please. I'm begging you." He glanced around, downed the rest of his beer, stood, and walked out.

Rick swirled his soda around the glass, barely seeing it. Why did his heart feel so heavy? He'd never before felt the intense connection he had with Max. And until now he'd liked it that way. It had made it easy to focus on his career—

"You okay?" Angelo asked, his easy smile infectious despite Rick's heavy mood. "Do you want to come sit at the bar? We can chat while I'm working. Unless you'd rather stay here on your own?"

With a sigh, Rick shuffled out of the booth. "Yeah, that'd be good." He stared at his soda. "Could I get a beer instead?"

"Sure. Come on over."

Two beers later, Rick was more relaxed and was actually beginning to enjoy his evening. Angelo was good company and a good distraction, and to his surprise they laughed a lot. After his third beer, his inhibitions were falling away, and Angelo's flirting was starting to appeal. After his fourth, Rick found he was flirting back.

Maybe this was the best way to get over his feelings for Max. If he hooked up with Angelo, then maybe he wouldn't want Max so much. It had been a while since he'd hooked up with anyone, after all. Tony was right. He'd never forgive himself if something happened to Max and he was to blame. But it would be ridiculous of him to turn down offers of sex for the rest of his life in the hope that one day Max's situation would change.

"You've stolen my spot, and there're no other stools left." Rick jumped at Angelo's warm breath ghosting along his neck, then leaned back until he was resting against him.

"Aren't you supposed to be working?"

"Not anymore. Emily's closing up for me tonight." Angelo dropped his arms over Rick's shoulders. "You smell good." He pressed his lips to Rick's neck, and Rick groaned.

Rick grasped Angelo's arm and pulled him around until they were facing each other. It was nice to have that kind of easy flirtatious contact from someone who wanted him. He raised an eyebrow and smirked. "I was told you were discreet."

"Hmm, I guess they weren't looking so closely." Angelo whispered, "You're still in my spot."

"What are you going to do about it?"

"I think a blowjob ought to do it. What do you reckon?"

"I reckon you're trying to take advantage of me while I'm drunk."

"Would that be so terrible?" Angelo waggled his eyebrows.

Rick was seriously tempted. Perhaps it would help take his mind off Max, help him to move on. Angelo was watching him with hooded eyes. Surely he wasn't expecting him to drop to his knees in the crowded bar. The thought of it made his cock stiffen.

Angelo gyrated against him, and Rick groaned. "What if I say no?"

"You won't."

"You sure about that?"

"Yeah, I'm sure." Angelo nipped at Rick's neck, making him shiver.

"What if I don't like you like that?"

Rick felt Angelo's lips smile against his neck as Angelo pressed their cocks together. Angelo was as turned on as he was. "I think we need to take this someplace quieter, don't you?"

Stroking his fingers along Angelo's jaw, Rick sighed, giving in to the desire building in his groin. "Where did you have in mind?"

"Follow me." Angelo unpeeled himself from Rick and made his way toward the door beside the bar, swiped his card to unlock it, and waved Rick through. The door slammed shut behind them.

Angelo grabbed Rick's hand, pulling him into a crushing kiss. Rick reached down and squeezed Angelo's cock as he forced his tongue deeper into the man's mouth, desperate for release as he thrust against him. But Angelo pushed him away, panting as they separated. "We do this here and the whole bar will see us if Emily comes through that door. We'll go to my apartment."

That wasn't what Rick had in mind. This was only supposed to be a quick one-time hookup. He frowned. "I'm not leaving the bar for this."

"You don't have to." Angelo started to walk down the long corridor, dodging crates of beer and other supplies. "My apartment came with the job. I live right here—one of the perks of being in charge."

Several twists and turns later, Angelo stopped at another door, swiped his card, and led Rick up a narrow staircase into his apartment. It had a gothic feel to it, with black candleholders on the gray walls and a large unmade bed to his left with black sheets. To his right, opposite the bed, were a tiny kitchen area and a single door that Rick assumed must lead to the bathroom. Angelo walked over to the far wall and pulled back the floor-to-ceiling heavy velvet curtains. The empty

Torrens Club was revealed below, and Rick took a step to the side, closer to the curtains.

"Don't worry. If anyone's down there, they can't see us." Angelo tapped the window. "It's one-way glass. Pretty cool, huh."

"Yeah, it is."

Angelo moved in front of him and dropped to his knees. Refocusing on the man before him, the niggling doubt Rick had about going through with this dissipated as Angelo took him into his mouth.

CHAPTER FIVE

Max

THE DAY of the Vanquished Villains gig came around all too quickly, and on Thursday afternoon, Max found himself hauling equipment from the garage all the way to the ambulance. In the stifling heat, it felt as though he'd run a marathon by the time they were done.

Max lifted his T-shirt to wipe the sweat from his face. He couldn't wait until they made it big and were able to pay people to lug all this around for them.

"Are we heading over now, or stopping for a beer first?" Tony asked as Lee slammed the garage door closed. "Or waiting and having a beer when we get there?"

Lee's eyes narrowed. "I hope you're joking."

"Lighten up, Lee. We've got hours yet."

"Yeah, and we've also got the sound check to do as well."

Max had finally had the courage to arrange it. Pete was even coming down to give them a hand.

Tony waved his arm. "Count me out. I don't need to practice."

"Tony, either we all do it, or it's not worth doing," Lee said. "And it's not about practicing. It's about making sure we sound the best we can. As a band."

"Turn the drums up loud, and then we're guaranteed to sound perfect."

"Quit bickering," Kyle said. "Don't want Max here disappearing on us again."

"Fuck off. I'm here, aren't I?"

Kyle's pupils were larger than they should have been out there in the bright sunlight. He'd have to keep an eye on him. Despite Kyle taking pills every so often, he usually kept it together. He reckoned they helped him chill out and forget how shitty his life got sometimes. Max had never done anything stronger than weed, and that was all the chilled-out buzz he'd ever wanted.

"Torrens Club first," Lee said. "We'll unload, get ourselves cleaned up, and then do the sound check. Pete's meeting us there at four, and Villains isn't due until five. But we have to be out of their way by then."

"Such a pile of shit that we don't even get the dressing room," Tony said as he clambered into the back of the ambulance.

"Start taking this seriously and someday we will," Lee said.

IT DIDN'T take them long to unload at the Torrens Club. Max made sure he got to the showers in the dressing room first, as they only had use of it for a couple of hours, and then found a quiet corner of the club—upstairs in the balcony bar—to finish warming up his voice. He could see the stage through the glass windows, and when his bandmates convened at their usual table at the edge of the dance floor, he went down to join them.

"Angelo ordered us takeout," Tony said and grabbed a large slice of meat-covered pizza. He sat down, took out a Dr Pepper bottle, and sipped from it.

Max went to his duffel, grabbed the tub of chicken salad he'd made, and sat down to eat.

Tony peered over his shoulder at the contents. "It weirds me out when you do this."

"It's chicken salad. It's perfectly healthy."

"It's weird. Why can't you eat normally like the rest of us?" Tony shoved another slice of pizza into his mouth, leaned back in his chair, and licked his lips. "What's not to like about cheese, meat, and bread?"

Max ignored Tony's ribbing and was halfway through his lunch when the club doors swung open. Was it four already? He glanced at the clock above the bar, and when he looked back and saw who had arrived, he choked on a piece of chicken.

Rick walked in, wearing dark aviator sunglasses and a black shirt, which had so few buttons done up that it did little to conceal his bare chest. The contrast with his short blond hair and tanned skin was unbelievably seductive. Max's eyes watered, and he coughed as Lee patted him on the back.

"Hey, Rick," Angelo called out and left the bar area to greet him.

"Hi, how's it going?" Rick removed his glasses and hooked them on the front pocket of his jeans.

Max watched in horror as Angelo gave Rick a hug. Okay, maybe he hadn't contacted Rick yet, but it hadn't been that long. Had he missed his chance before he'd even had an opportunity to make up his mind? Fuck.

Rick gave the rest of them a wave. "Pete went to the store. He'll be here in a minute." Rick's eyes rested on Max for a moment longer than on anyone else, but thankfully nobody seemed to notice. Maybe it wasn't too late after all. Max took his cell out from one of his pockets, and his thumb hovered over Rick's number, which he'd put in a few days ago but hadn't yet dared to use.

"No problem," Angelo said. "Why don't you come see the new lighting I was telling you about? We're testing it out tonight."

"Sure. I needed to talk to you about something anyway."

As they disappeared backstage, it was too much for Max to bear, and he sent the text: *You didn't tell me you were coming.*

He didn't have to wait long for a reply: *What? And ruin the surprise! It might've helped if you'd given me your number ;)*

Pete walked in and came over to them as Angelo and Rick reappeared. "Hi, gang," Pete said. "Ready to go?"

"Nearly." Max put the lid on his empty tub and took a bite of his apple.

"Don't you eat pizza?" Rick asked Max, glancing at the pizza boxes and back to Max's lunch.

"He's on one of his queer health kicks," Kyle said and scrunched up his nose when Max waved the apple in his face.

"Chicken salad and apples aren't odd."

"That's what I had for lunch," Rick said and then grinned. "But I've got the excuse that I'm in training. Anyone want a drink?"

"No beer until after the gig," Tony said and took a swig from his Dr Pepper bottle. "Lee's rules."

"I'll have one," Pete said. "Thanks, bud."

When they all declined his offer of alternative drinks, Max watched Rick walk to the bar, where Angelo served him. They were chatting as if they'd known each other for years. When had they become such good friends?

"What time do you go onstage?" Pete asked.

"About eight," Lee said. "Villains are on at nine. They're opening the club at ten thirty as normal."

"Guess we'd better get on with the sound check, then," Pete said, thanked Rick for the beer, and headed over to the sound booth.

Max gathered up his things and followed him.

"How's your voice today?" Pete asked.

"Good. I even ate the right things."

"About time," Pete said and chuckled. "Warmed up yet?"

"Of course."

"Ah, yes, that's right, always the professional."

"Hey, enough of the sarcasm. I do my best."

Pete gave him an affectionate nudge. "Yeah, you're a good kid."

"Kid?"

Pete's voice was serious as they reached the sound booth. "Now, listen to me. I'm going to keep the volume high for your vocals, so don't strain during the sound check. Sing however is comfortable, and I'll adjust the volume back here so you're not struggling to be heard over the rest of the band during the gig. Okay?"

"Yep, got it. Thanks, Pete. You're not going to tell the others, are you?"

"Of course not. I've got your back, don't worry."

They completed the sound check without any hiccups and finished as Vanquished Villains arrived, acting like the rock stars they believed they were.

Lee and Kyle behaved like star-struck idiots, following them around and offering to help them set up. Max thought they were an awesome band but would never admit it to their faces. After greeting them, he'd made himself scarce, going to sit with Tony, Pete, and Rick at the bar. With Lee otherwise occupied, Max ordered himself a beer.

"Could Lee crawl any further up his ass?" Tony commented as they watched Lee follow the lead singer around the stage.

A message flashed up on his phone from Zoe, and Max quickly checked it and replied. She and Lisa had gone to Vegas for a few days with some of their friends, and they'd been sharing pictures with him since they'd arrived earlier that day.

Angelo served Max his drink and snickered. "If I didn't know better, I'd think he was a loved-up groupie, not that his band was opening for them."

"He's such an ass." Tony snorted a laugh. "But I suppose he should make the most of it. It's not like they'll ever let us open for them again."

"Why's that?" Rick asked.

"Why? Because we're going to blow them out of the water. We're far better than they are. They won't know what hit them." Tony touched his glass of beer to Pete's.

"Are you keeping the same set list as last time?" Rick asked.

"We like to mix it up a bit," Max explained. "We've got so many songs to choose from that we always play a different combo. Besides, tonight we're only playing for an hour."

"Are you going to play 'Storm My Dreams'?" Rick asked. "That's my favorite."

"Yes!" Max punched the air and looked pointedly at Tony.

Rick frowned. "What? What did I say?"

Pete shook his head. "That's one of Max's songs."

"He can't have listened to everything we've done," Tony said, "or he'd never pick that one."

"I've got both your albums: *Afterthoughts and Anguish* and *Black Lipstick and Fallen Angels*."

"Ha, ha, see?" Max leaped from his seat to do a celebratory dance.

"Whatever. I'm gonna check on the instruments. You coming, Max?" Tony asked and finished his drink.

"I think I'm gonna stay here with Angelo and Rick, actually."

"You sure? I could use a hand."

"You don't usually need me to help with that."

"Yeah, but tonight's a big night."

"You managed okay last gig, and that was a big night too."

"Come on," Pete said and grabbed Tony's arm. "I'll give you a hand. We'll be fine checking them with just the two of us."

Tony huffed, and he and Pete wandered over to the stage.

"I didn't know you wrote any of the songs," Rick said.

"Yeah, some. Lee won't let me use all of them, though. Says they're not the right style for the image of our band."

"I'd like to hear them sometime."

"Well, maybe you can, now we're friends, that is."

"So, it's official, then? The text sealed it." Rick took a long drink. "I thought I'd scared you off."

"You were never going to do that," Max said quietly so Angelo couldn't hear him. "I'd like it if we were friends."

"Good to know. I'd like that too."

Then Max frowned. "What are you doing here? If you thought you'd scared me off, I mean." He wasn't sure he wanted to know the answer.

"I was at Pete's house and he was heading down here, so I came with him to keep him company. I can leave if—"

"No, stay," Max said and smiled into his drink. "I'm glad you're here."

They sat at the bar while Vanquished Villains completed their sound check, and hung out until it was time.

Angelo shouted from the other end of the bar. "Max, we're about to let the hordes in. You want to hide backstage first?"

"Yeah, suppose I should." Max slid off his stool, brushing against Rick's arm. "I'll see you later."

"Good luck."

Max joined the others backstage and went through his final preparations. Having already warmed up his voice, he did a couple of exercises to ensure his vocals were spot-on. He didn't want to let the guys down tonight when they were opening for such a popular band.

He took deep breaths to calm his nerves as the club filled to capacity. Vanquished Villains was nowhere to be seen. He guessed they weren't interested in watching Purple Method and must have shut themselves away in the dressing room.

"Max, breathe," Kyle said as he scuttled past with bottles of water, placing one at each of their spots onstage.

Crouching down with his head in his hands, Max wondered if his nerves would ever go away, and tried to convince himself that it would all be worth it once he started singing.

Tony had won the battle of first-song choice. They'd flipped a coin to decide it in the end, so they'd be opening with "No Jurisdiction." It wasn't the worst choice, he supposed. He just wished he'd been the one to write it. "Storm My Dreams" was up second, and Max smiled at the thought of Rick watching him perform his favorite song.

"Max, bucket." Lee threw one in his general direction, and it clattered in front of him.

His bandmates looked at him as he picked it up from the floor and moved it out of the way. "Sorry, guys, don't think it's gonna happen today."

"Max, not today, of all days." Kyle groaned. "We can't have bad luck, not when we're opening for Vanquish." He grabbed the bucket and held it in front of Max, shaking it as if that would help.

"Kyle, quit it. I'm fine. It will all be fine. Trust me."

"You'd better be right," he heard Lee murmur under his breath. "Everyone ready to go?"

Max grabbed his microphone and nodded.

The lights dimmed and they were off.

THE AUDIENCE was larger than it had been when they'd played there the other week. With the hall dark apart from lights dotted about from cell phones recording them, the entire club could've been filled to capacity as far as he was aware. Max raised his arms above his head as the energy of the intro to "No Jurisdiction" rumbled through his body and took hold. He felt so alive. Electric. Like he could take on the world and still have energy to spare.

As Kyle's high-pitched guitar joined in, Max paced the stage, his hands above his head, clapping, encouraging the crowd to join him. He brought the microphone to his lips and sang at a comfortable level—like Pete had told him to—and sure enough, his voice was clear above the instruments. His vocals felt effortless for the first time at a gig. It was awesome. He looked toward the bar, where he knew Pete would be standing, and Pete gave him a thumbs-up. It felt amazing knowing he was making Pete proud. He couldn't have done all this without Pete's help. He was so grateful to him.

Max bounced across to the left of the stage for the chorus. He loved the chorus of this song in particular. It had a low growly section that was fun to drop to before climbing to the top of his range. He leaned forward to tap the outstretched hands of fans in the front row and laughed when he nearly slipped off the stage to land down there with them.

It was then that he spotted Rick. He was a couple of rows back in the middle. Right where the mosh pit was starting. A space had cleared as it fired up, and people who didn't want to get caught up in it were shuffling backward out of the way. Six people began to circle the perimeter, and to Max's surprise, Rick joined them. He was clearly copying them but soon got the hang of it and was pushing and shoving back, and looked like he belonged—especially as he was wearing some black this time. As Max sang the final section of the song, Rick caught his eye. Max shook his head with a grin and turned to look at Tony as the song drew to a close.

Tony took advantage of the brief pause to wipe his face on the small towel he kept by his spare drumsticks.

"This one's called 'Storm My Dreams,'" Max growled, and Tony winked at him and smiled as he struck his bass drum with incredible speed. The crowd was screaming, and when Max spun to face the front, he caught sight of Vanquished Villains at the side of the stage, watching them. That just fueled his energy to the extreme, and seeing that a couple of people were stage diving, Max pointed toward them and raised his eyebrow at Rick.

"You?" Rick mouthed up at him. At only two rows back, Max was confident Rick would catch him.

Max nodded and ran toward the front of the stage, twisting as he leaped from it, and closing his eyes as he prayed that Rick really would catch him.

He felt a firm grip under his shoulders, breaking his fall, and then supporting him. Max opened his eyes to see Rick looking down at him, a bewildered and amused look on his face.

"I can't believe you actually went through with it," Rick shouted in Max's ear.

Max couldn't reply, instead having to sing the next verse of the song. By the time he'd come to a pause, he'd been carried away—and groped—by numerous hands. It was an effort to sing like this, but Max didn't care; it was worth it. The fans loved it, that was for sure, he thought as yet another pair of hands gripped him, seemingly reluctant to let go as he was pulled away from them. He winced as somebody's fingernails dug into his arm. He was definitely grateful for his new boots right now. It would mean no scratches on his legs, at least. As best he could, Max pointed toward the stage. He needed to get back there before the end of the song. Luckily the fans got the message and deposited him at the front. As the final bars of the song blasted out, Max scrambled up.

In the center, Kyle and Lee stood back-to-back, their faces screwed up with effort as they went straight into the heavy intro of "In These Chains." Max ran behind them and up onto the steps in front of the drum kit and leaned back, opening his mouth wide to sing the fast, complex vocals of the first song he helped to compose.

WHEN PURPLE Method filed off at the end of the final song, "Under My Skin," the entire crowd was screaming for an encore, and it took quite some time before they settled and were ready for Vanquished Villains to perform. Some of Purple Method's most loyal fans even left before the headline act, muttering that the best band had already played, Sian told them, shouting to be heard above their fans.

"That was awesome," Rick said as Max peeked out the door at the side of the stage, ready to join the party. "Even better than last time." He pulled Max to one side before anyone else recognized him. "And you were incredible."

"Thanks," Max said. "Did you like my stage dive?"

"I think you're crazy for going through with it." Rick laughed and shook his head. "But I'm impressed you can crowd surf and sing like that at the same time."

"It's my specialty. Thanks for catching me. I've been dropped a couple of times in the past, and it fucking hurts."

"Anytime." Rick looked him in the eyes and took a swig of his drink.

Oh no. He'd been spotted. A couple of people were sidling toward him, their phones out ready for pictures.

"I'll come find you in a bit. This could take a while," Max said, sighing as he braced himself for being mobbed. A disorderly line was already forming. He just hoped his bandmates would join him soon. "Don't suppose you'd mind grabbing me a beer, could you?"

"Sure. I'll take care of it," Rick said, squeezing his shoulder before being swallowed into the crowd.

Max smiled, warmth enveloping him. It was nice to have someone looking after him for a change. It was tearing him apart more than ever now, knowing it was impossible for them to be together, to be more than friends. He wished there was a way around it, but every scenario he'd run through in his head had ended in disaster.

"Max, can I get a picture?" A girl with particularly heavy makeup and a Pikachu T-shirt held up her phone and pouted as she pressed their faces together for the picture. He plastered on his best fake smile and fixed it in place for what would likely be the next hour at least.

"I'M PRETTY sure six across is *dirty*," Kyle said.

Max picked up his whisk and bowl of waffle batter and stepped closer to the doorway so he could see into the lounge. Sian was sitting cross-legged on the floor, and Kyle was lazing next to her, peering over her shoulder at the newspaper.

"Can't be, babe." Sian rattled a pen between her teeth. "'Cause nine down is *grebe*. Doesn't fit."

It was the day after the Villains gig and Max was on a high. It could not have gone any better. And it had been awesome to spend most of the day with Rick, even if he'd barely got to see him after he'd finished with their fans.

"What're you doing?" he asked.

Sian grinned and waved the newspaper in the air, barely missing Kyle's head. "Finishing Lee's crossword. Wanna help?"

"He's going to kill you. Again."

"I know." She giggled and made herself comfortable, leaning back against Kyle.

"He'll be back any minute. He said he'd be about an hour."

"Quick," she shrieked, "we've got two left. Max, 'heavily polluted or thickly accumulated filth.' Five letters beginning with g."

"Um, I don't know… grimy?"

"Ooh, yes, of course, and that makes four down limbo."

Sian leaped up, tossing the paper to the ground and raising her arms in the air. She rushed over to Max and kissed him on the cheek, then snatched the batter bowl and gave it a stir with the whisk. "Did you use buttermilk?"

"Of course."

Max followed her back into the kitchen and sat on the table, watching with a smile as she scrutinized his work. He was the one who'd taught her to cook, and now she worked in a bakery she seemed to think she was the expert.

"I found these freeze-dried raspberry pieces at the grocery store the other day. We could put them into the mix." Sian reached up to the cupboard where she kept her grocery supplies. It was crammed full. How she ever found what she was looking for was a miracle. She pulled a small packet out and tossed it to him. Reaching out to grab it, Max missed, and it smacked to the floor. "You're such a klutz." Sian chuckled as she reached down to retrieve them, then placed them into the palm of Max's hand.

"Can I try one?"

"Sure."

The raspberry pieces were tiny. Max tipped a pile of the bright red specks into his hand and then into his mouth. The sharp yet oversweet taste ricocheted, and it was all he could do to stop himself from spitting them out. Swallowing as much as he could before taking a gulp of his drink, he turned to glare at her, his eyes watering.

"No way. Absolutely no way. What the hell were you thinking? They're disgusting."

"Wanted to try something new." She shrugged. "You need to learn to be more adventurous."

"I try stuff."

"Sure you do." Sian snickered and poured the batter into the waffle maker. "Kyle, you want jelly beans on yours?" she called out.

"Yeah, course."

"Ugh, that is the worst waffle accompaniment ever. I can't believe you make that for him."

"See. Unadventurous."

Waiting until she turned to look at him, Max gave her a pointed glare. "Whatever. I'm still in charge of our competition barbecue."

"Are you kidding? With you in charge, we came sixth last year. If I was in charge, we'd win the whole competition."

"It was my idea to enter in the first place."

"I know. Only a few weeks to go. I can't wait. Did Tony tell you he managed to organize for you to play there as well? It's gonna be a busy weekend."

"What's that?" Kyle asked as he wandered into the kitchen.

"The jamboree whole-hog contest," Max said.

"Oh, that." He slid onto the table next to Max and yawned. "I don't get why you're making it out to be such a big deal. It's not like many people enter—"

"Aren't you and Tony supposed to be playing hockey this afternoon?"

"Yeah. Supposed to be." Kyle sighed. "I think he's lost motivation now there's little chance of us making the team this year, though."

"Why's that?"

"'Cause we've been away for so long. If we turn up at the rink, we've been told we can take part in the practice at least. If he can drag his lazy ass out of bed, that is."

"He's not up yet?"

"He's got some girl in there with him. You wanna wake him? 'Cause I sure as hell don't."

"Not a chance."

The smell of warm, sweet batter drifted toward them, and Max began to salivate. It wouldn't be long until they were ready. After jumping down from the table, Max pulled out a large jar of maple syrup from his cupboard. There was enough time to warm it through before the waffles were ready.

While Sian served them up, Max couldn't resist checking his cell for the thousandth time that day. There were more pictures of Vegas from Zoe and Lisa, but still no message from Rick.

Max poured warm maple syrup into each of his waffle grooves as Kyle picked out all the black, orange, and white jelly beans and created an intricate pattern with them by stuffing them into the gaps before pouring maple syrup over the top.

"That looks disgusting," Max said, looking up from his cell. He'd made several attempts to start a message to Rick, but everything he'd typed felt contrived and stupid, so he shoved his cell back into his pocket.

"That's 'cause you have zero taste."

The front door slammed.

"Must be Lee," Max said when they heard no further movement. Lee's bedroom was right by the front door, so he must have gone straight in there. "Where did you leave his crossword?"

Sian giggled and pushed her chair back with a screech. She sprinted into the lounge and brought the paper back with her, placed it on her chair, and sat on it.

"Coward," Kyle said through a mouthful of multicolored waffle.

Heavy footsteps climbed the stairs to the top floor, there were muffled voices, and then three pairs of heavier footsteps descended, the front door banged again, and then two pairs of footsteps headed their way.

"Looks like Lee deserves the bravery award for today." Sian took a sip of her juice as both Lee and Tony came into the kitchen. "We made waffles for breakfast if either of you wants any."

"No. Thanks. Can you all come into the lounge? I've got something important I need to tell you," Lee said.

"Why can't you tell us in here?" Max asked, eating another mouthful.

"Does it have to be now, Lee?" Sian asked. "I'm doing the late shift at the bakery and have to leave in a minute."

"It's a Purple Method thing."

"Okay, I guess I'll see you all later, then." Sian cleared her plate and put it in the dishwasher before heading upstairs.

"Lounge?" Lee walked through, clearly expecting them to follow, so Max shoved the last of his waffle into his mouth and got up.

Tony slumped on the sofa next to Kyle. "What the hell is all this about, Lee?"

"Chill out, Tony, it'll only take a minute." Lee scanned the room, clenching and relaxing his hands.

After sitting on the sofa next to Tony, Max rested his head on his brother's shoulder. "So, what's up?"

Tony flinched, and Max lifted his head. His brother was looking at Lee with a serious expression. "It's okay, we've already guessed—"

Lee looked puzzled. "How could you know? I just got off the phone."

"You're looking a bit puffy. I'm not surprised you're telling us now. It's not like you could hide it for much longer. You know you have our support, right?"

"Fuck you," Lee said. "This is serious."

"Spit it out, then, Lee," Kyle said.

"Right, well." Lee cleared his throat and flicked his long black hair over his shoulder, staring at Tony with a defiant smile. "I'm sure you all noticed I spent most of the night with Vanquished—"

"Traitor," Max said and grinned at him. They all loved Vanquished's music, but Lee had been the one fangirling all night.

"Yeah, whatever, Max." Lee glared at him, and Max's stomach lurched. What was going on? "I noticed you were too bigheaded to even bother watching them."

"I was spending time with our fans. I heard them."

"What the fuck, Lee?" Tony raised his voice. "Why do you give a shit whether any of us watched them or not?"

"You could learn a lot from them," Lee said.

"Bullshit! We were way more professional than them, and everyone says we were better."

"According to who? Your doting groupies? Have you asked anyone with a valid opinion?"

"What the hell's gotten into you?" Kyle shook his head in disbelief. "Why don't you want to believe we're better than them?"

"We'll never be better than Vanquished."

They all stared at him with open mouths.

"Lee…."

Lee studied his hands. "We'll never be as good as they are because you refuse to take it seriously. You're drunk or high by the time we play, you sleep with all our fans, there are more obscene pictures of you on the internet than I can quite believe, and you're rude and obnoxious when anyone tries to interview us. For fuck's sake, we're supposed to be a heavy metal band, and I'm the only one with fucking black hair. It's a total disaster waiting to happen, and to be honest with you, I'm embarrassed to call Purple Method my band. None of you make any effort to be what we need to succeed."

"Come on, Lee, that's a bit harsh, bud." The panic was clear in Kyle's voice.

"Surely we're not that bad," Max said, fighting back hot tears.

"Yes, you are!" Lee screamed and threw his hands in the air. "Why can none of you see it? I'm done with Purple Method and all the crap that goes with it. Vanquished has asked me to join them, and I've said yes."

"What?"

Everyone started talking at once, and fear shot through Max's body. How could this be happening?

"Get your things out of my house," Tony said, his voice clear above everyone else and his eyes fixed on Lee. "Now."

"Don't worry, Tony, I'm not hanging around. I've had enough of this shit." Lee turned and strode toward the stairs.

For a long moment, nobody spoke.

"Doesn't change the fact that we're far better musicians than they are," Kyle mumbled.

This wasn't right. Purple Method was Max's whole life, the reason he got out of bed each day. He marched toward the stairs. There had to be something he could say to stop Lee from leaving.

"Don't you dare," Tony said. "Didn't you hear what he just said about us?"

Shrugging, Max kept on walking. It wasn't as if they had anything more to lose. This was their band, for fuck's sake.

Lee's bedroom door was closed, so Max knocked and then entered. Lee looked up from where he was throwing his things into a suitcase and gave Max a weak smile. "Shut the door, will you?" He shoved an armload of clothes into his case. "I don't want the others in here."

"Are we really that bad?" Max perched on the corner of the bed. "Everyone was cheering so loud for us last night."

"Max, you crowd-surfed while singing and nearly lost your microphone, Tony fell off his stool halfway through one of our songs not that long ago, Kyle electrocuted himself when he spilled beer over his amp when we were in Georgia, and it's a miracle if any of you turn up at all. Shall I go on?"

"They were one-offs," Max mumbled, and Lee began counting off other incidents on his fingers until Max had to beg him to stop. It was heartbreaking listening to all the negative things he had to say about their precious band. "Okay, okay, I get your point. We can change, though. It doesn't have to be the end of Purple Method." It couldn't be. Max hunched over and rested his head in his trembling hands.

"Nobody said anything about it being the end. You can still carry on. Maybe Tony will even let you use some of the other songs you've written."

"Yeah, right. And why the hell would it be up to Tony?"

Lee stopped packing for a moment and gave Max a sorry smile. "I'll bet you anything he's down there right now taking control of Kyle… of Purple Method. If you wanted a say in how the band moves forward, I think you'll find you've missed your chance."

"But how can we even be a band without a bassist? It's not possible. It's always been the four of us—"

"I'm sorry it had to be like this."

"I don't get it. We had such a great time on tour."

Lee squeezed Max's shoulder and then went on packing. "I don't want to be in charge anymore." He zipped up his case. "I know it's under terrible circumstances with what happened with their bassist, but Vanquished has given me the opportunity of a lifetime. I'd be a douche to turn them down in favor of Purple Method."

"The others will never speak to you again, you know that, right?"

"Yeah"—Lee gave him a sad smile—"but it's time to move on, and I couldn't leave without being honest about how I'm feeling. It's been building for a while."

"For you, maybe," Max murmured. He was still numb from shock.

Lee hauled Max to his feet and stared him right in the eyes. "*You've* got the potential to take Purple Method to the very top. Don't drink yourself into oblivion and waste the opportunity to be something great, okay?"

Max nodded and hugged him. "Do you need a hand with your stuff?"

"Thanks, but Amelia's outside waiting for me."

Lee hoisted his guitar case over his shoulder, grabbed his bags, and headed toward the door. "Don't let Tony push you around, okay?"

Max wandered back down to the kitchen to find Tony and Kyle sitting around the table, clutching cans of beer.

"Has he gone?" Tony asked.

"Yeah." Opening the refrigerator with the intention of getting a beer, Max paused, thinking about what Lee had said about his drinking. Sighing, he slammed the door closed and switched the coffeepot back on instead.

"Not getting a beer?" Tony asked.

"Maybe later."

"What the hell's wrong with you? Can't you even join in a celebration anymore?"

"Celebration?"

"Yeah." Tony grinned, raised his beer, and took a long drink. Kyle avoided eye contact with him. That was odd. "We don't need Lee. In fact, we're better off without him."

"Without a bassist?" Max huffed a laugh and poured his drink, taking a sip to check the temperature. "Are you serious? How do you figure that?"

"We have a bassist."

"No, we don't."

"You play pretty well."

Max spat out his mouthful of coffee. "What? No way. There's no way I'm playing bass." Had he heard Tony correctly, or had his brother really gone nuts this time?

"If you want to stay in Purple Method, you have no choice."

"Why me? Get someone else to play it."

"You're the only one with your hands free."

"I play guitar in some of our songs. There's no way I can play two guitars at once."

"We can take them out."

"What? Why can't we get someone else to join the band to replace him?"

"No."

"Kyle could switch to bass. I play guitar better than him anyway."

"Hey!"

"Max, you're not listening. Are you in or out?"

"Out? Of Purple Method. Are you serious? You can't do that to me. To our band. There've always been four of us—"

"And for now it's the three of us. Don't you let us down here."

"I fucking hate you, Tony." Max hurled his skull-and-crossbones mug. It smashed into pieces, and a stream of black coffee splashed up the smoke-yellowed wall. He was breathing heavily, panic taking hold. Turning, he ran upstairs; he had to get away. His whole world was falling apart.

"Band practice is at six," Tony called after him.

MAX THREW himself down face-first onto his unmade bed. This was the worst day of his life, even outranking the day his dad had left. Purple

Method had been his entire world for four years, since he was sixteen. Four years of his life now wasted. As far back as he could remember, he'd done nothing but practice his music so one day he'd be good enough to perform in a band. He felt as hollow as the cavity of the acoustic guitar that rested against his bed.

Rolling onto his side, Max cursed as his cell phone dug into his leg. He pulled it out and stared at the blank screen. There was one person he wanted to call right now when his world was falling apart, and yet it felt like a ludicrous thing to do; he barely knew him. Before he could overthink it, Max dialed Rick's number. After two rings, Rick answered, and Max's stomach plummeted.

"Hey, this is a nice surprise," Rick said.

"Um, yeah, hi. How are you?"

"Yeah, good, thanks. You were lucky to catch me. I've this second finished teaching a class."

"Oh…."

"Is everything okay?"

Max took a deep breath. "Lee quit the band."

"What? You're kidding. When?"

"Just now."

"Are you okay? I mean, I'm guessing it's not going to be easy with Tony in charge of the band."

What the hell? Max's cell almost met the same fate as his hangover mug, but he stopped himself throwing it in time, clenching it in his fist and forcing it back to his ear instead. "How is it that everyone saw that coming apart from me?" This was ridiculous. Was he so blind where his brother was concerned?

"I guess he must give off that kind of vibe. Will it be easy to find another bassist?"

"Yeah, apparently. You're talking to him."

"What? You're joking. So who's going to sing?"

"He wants me to do both… or he's kicking me out of the band."

"Can you even play bass?"

"Yeah. It's not hard. I'd rather play lead guitar."

"What are you going to do?"

"What can I do? I can't leave the band. I guess I'm stuck with the most boring instrument on the planet."

"Well, that's not true."

"What do you mean?" Max shuffled up the bed so his head was resting on his pillow.

"An old friend of mine was always going on about this British band that he reckoned was incredible, but none of us had ever heard of them. He dragged me along to see them one time when they played in Leatherton. Honestly, Max, it blew my mind. The lead singer played a six-string bass like it was a regular guitar. No, better than most people can play a regular guitar. I've never seen anything like it."

Was that even possible? To play a bass like a lead guitar? "Are you kidding?"

"I'm deadly serious. The way I see it is that you have two options: drop out of Purple Method and find something else to do, or call Tony's bluff and become the best bassist out there. You write your own songs, right? So you get to dictate what you play. There's nothing stopping you writing complex bass lines."

Max bounced up from the bed and began to pace, trembling with excitement. What Rick was suggesting would be awesome beyond belief. "You really think I could do this?"

"Of course… if you want to, that is."

Max laughed. "Tony's going to be so pissed if I pull this off."

"Tell you what; I don't have another class for a couple of hours. Do you want to meet me at the mall and we can go to that music store, check out their bass guitars?"

"Yeah. Let's do it."

THIRTY MINUTES later Max arrived at the music store, and Rick was waiting for him, dressed in a black T-shirt with a red eagle on it, and jeans. It was weird meeting him like this, just the two of them. Even though he met up with other male friends all the time without thinking twice about it, he felt awkward around Rick, worried that if anyone saw them on their own, they would think they were "together." Not that they were, of course, but what if someone noticed the weird connection the two of them seemed to have?

"Ready?" Rick asked.

"To give my brother the shock of his life? Absolutely."

"Did you check out the band?"

"Yeah, you were right. I can't believe I've never seen them, but then they are a bit jazzier than I would normally listen to."

Rick held open the door to the music store, and Max walked inside the gleaming haven with shiny new instruments occupying every available space. "Think you can do it?"

"Sure. It's going to take a bit of practice, that's all. It's going to be so awesome. I've never heard a bass sound so sexy. If I can put some of that into our music—"

The store assistant looked up from behind the counter. "Hi, Max, how're things?"

"A bit crazy, to be honest, Hugh."

Hugh frowned, his trendy thick-rimmed glasses riding up his nose. "Why, what happened?"

"Lee quit."

"Fuck."

"Yeah, tell me about it."

"Is this your new guy?" Hugh nodded toward Rick.

"I wish." Rick chuckled.

Max elbowed him in the ribs, his nerves ratcheting up a notch. "He's kidding. He can't play… can you?"

"Not at the moment. Maybe one day, though," Rick said.

"Shame. Well, once you know what you're doing—"

"I can play the drums a bit. Had a couple of lessons when I was a kid until Mom decided it was too noisy and sold my kit."

Hugh closed the sheet music catalog he had open on the desk. "That's too bad."

"Yeah," Max said, "you could've taken Tony's spot, and he could've played bass instead of me."

"You're taking over from Lee?"

"Yeah, looks like it. That's why we're here. Got any sexy six strings?"

"Sure, right this way. It's a good thing you've got long fingers."

Max frowned as they followed Hugh through the store past a display of violins. "Why's that?"

"The fretboards are pretty wide. Wide enough that most people find it too much of a stretch to comfortably reach all the strings."

Max stared at his hands and wiggled his fingers.

"I think your fingers will be plenty long enough," Rick said with a grin.

Max fought the smile threatening his lips.

"So, here they are." Hugh stopped in front of a wall with about fifty bass guitars hooked to it. "We have these five in stock." He waved at a cluster of basses halfway up the wall. "But there are more online that we can order in."

"Which one do you think?" Max asked Rick as Hugh went to find some steps.

"I like the black one for you. I can picture you onstage with it."

"Can you?"

Rick's lips twitched. "Sure, it's sexier than the others."

Max checked over his shoulder, but Hugh was too close for him to risk replying the way he wanted. He was enjoying Rick's attentions—when no one else was listening.

"So, Max, which guitars do you want to look at?"

"Just the black one, I think. The others are a bit bright. It's fretless too, right? I think that would suit me better. I was going to try some slap bass."

"I hear ya." Hugh climbed the steps and hauled the bass down. "Fretless would give you more scope." Max took the guitar from him. The weight of it felt right in his hands—powerful.

He could do some serious damage with this, and mostly to Tony's ego. Hugh plugged the guitar into an amp and attached a strap, lengthening it so the bass hung low across the tops of Max's legs. "You're all set."

After checking the tuning, Max began to play "Music Is My Wonder Drug." It felt good, the deep sound reverberating through his body. He'd always loved the power of the bass, but had never given much thought to its potential as an instrument. Lee had never been adventurous when it came to his bass lines. They were heavy, that was true, but what Max had heard that afternoon had changed his perception of the instrument. It was exciting to consider where he could take this.

It was a bit of a stretch to reach all the strings, but nothing he couldn't handle. It wouldn't take him long to get used to it, of that he was sure.

"Ever tried slap bass, Hugh?"

"Slap bass? Sure. It's easy enough." Hugh grabbed a pink-and-white bass from the lower section of the wall and plugged it in. "You gotta hammer-on with your thumb." Hugh dropped his right wrist and bounced the side of his thumb against the thickest string. "And pluck with your fingers, like this." He struck up a rapid, funky rhythm with sharp lower notes followed by a higher twang, and the effect was breathtaking. "Make sure you deaden the strings on the fretboard with your left hand to control the length of the notes."

Max copied Hugh's instruction, and it wasn't long until he matched Hugh's skill. By the time he stopped playing, a small group of people had gathered, and they all clapped and cheered.

"That was awesome, man," one of the guys said before the crowd dispersed again, murmuring their agreement.

Max grinned. "I'd say it's a shame you're not available to fill Lee's spot, Hugh, but I think this is gonna be fun."

"Bass is an underrated instrument."

"I'm with you there." Max high-fived Hugh's outstretched hand.

"So, you gonna take her?"

"Yeah, definitely. How much is she?"

"This one is fifteen hundred dollars."

"Fifteen hundred?" Rick said. His horrified expression was priceless.

Max chuckled and reached up to pat him on the shoulder. "Decent instruments don't come cheap, you know."

"Can you afford it?" Rick whispered.

"We do payment plans." Hugh took the guitar from Max. "I'll get her packed up ready to go."

"Thanks, bud." Max paused for a moment, unsure of whether to share his situation with Rick, but then he shrugged. What the hell? "I have a bit saved from the tour, and I get an allowance from a savings account my dad set up for me before he left. This band is my life, Rick. It's not about whether I can justify paying out this kind of money on a guitar, but can I afford not to?"

"When you put it like that, it kind of makes sense," Rick said.

"Music is the only thing I've ever been any good at. If Purple Method doesn't work out for me, I'm going to end up busking on a street someplace to make a living, and I gotta say, that doesn't appeal. Have you seen how fucking hot it is out there today?"

Rick let out a sad laugh. "If Purple Method didn't work out, some other band would snap you up. You'd have options."

"I guess that would depend on the reason I left." Max held Rick's eye for a long moment. "Come on," he said. "Let's get out of here."

After paying for the guitar and a case, Max hauled it onto his back, threading his arms through the handles of the case. "What do you want to do now?"

"I'm teaching in about a half hour, so I have to get back to the dojo. Don't suppose you want to come and take a look? I'm pretty sure I can take you on my bike with that on your back."

"Thanks, but I have the ambulance around the corner in the Torrens Club parking lot."

"So, does that mean you want to come?"

"Will anyone else be there?"

"Probably not. Is that a problem? I'm pretty sure I can manage to keep my hands off you if that's what you're worried about?"

Heat prickled up the back of Max's neck and settled in his cheeks. "Is that a promise?"

"Yeah. Friends, right?"

Max chuckled. Like Rick believed that for a second. The tension between them was undeniable. "Okay… you win." Max shoved Rick out the mall doors and into the unbearable afternoon heat. "Show me what all the fuss is about with this ninja shit."

"IT SMELLS funny in here." Max scrunched up his nose as he followed Rick into the building. "Like sweat and cologne."

"Have you even been in a gym before?" Rick cleared some papers from the desk in the office and shoved them into the filing cabinet.

"Na, I get enough exercise onstage." Max hoisted himself up so he was sitting on the desk. There were two doors, the one they had come in, and he guessed the other must lead to the hall, as there wasn't enough room in this tiny office for kick-ass ninja moves.

"You look good on it."

"The exercise or the stage?" The words were out of his mouth before he thought to stop them, but he wasn't sure he regretted them. It was just the two of them there, after all, and somehow he felt safe, despite barely knowing Rick. It was weird.

"Both." Rick stood in front of him, and Max's pulse skyrocketed.

"Both?"

"Yeah, both." Rick reached up and tucked a strand of hair behind Max's ear, sending tingles down Max's neck, and he shivered. "You know, this is the first time I've seen you when you haven't been drinking."

"I was sober before the Vanquished gig. And at the mall."

"They don't count. I barely got to talk to you before you had a beer."

"So… what now?" Max licked his dry lips.

Rick stepped back. "Come on, I'll show you where we train."

The training hall was impressive. Along the far wall, four well-used heavy bags hung from large hooks. A set of blue mats was laid out in the middle of the hall, and cabinets lined the wall to their left. The cabinets were filled with all kinds of strange equipment that Max didn't recognize. He picked up a pair of boxing gloves and regretted it—they stank. He'd never smelled anything so bad, not even the garage the day after a heavy night of partying.

"Ugh, that's disgusting. Do people actually wear these?"

"Most have their own gloves, so it's usually the beginners who end up with these. They don't all smell so bad."

"Do I get a demonstration, then?"

"If you like. It's a bit more difficult in jeans, and I'm guessing you'd rather I didn't strip down in front of you." How the hell was he supposed to answer that? Luckily, Rick didn't seem to expect him to respond. "I'll show you one of the drills I'm going to be teaching in a minute, if you like?"

"Sure."

Max leaned back against the cabinet and watched as Rick walked away until he was halfway across the hall.

"Ready?" he asked, turning to face Max, and bringing his fists up to his jaw.

"You're not coming straight at me, are you?"

"Not scared, are you?"

Max shrugged. "I'm guessing you know what you're doing, so no, not really."

Spinning around effortlessly, Rick kicked impossibly high in the air, and then did a flurry of punches, elbow strikes, and more fancy kicks. Max's heart stopped as Rick came closer, but he wasn't sure if it was from fear of being hurt if Rick didn't stop in time, or because he looked unbelievably sexy. Mesmerized, he focused on Rick's boot as it stopped an inch from his face.

"Y-you didn't even flinch."

"I didn't?"

Rick lowered his boot, and Max stared at him, his legs quivering so much it was a miracle they were still holding him up. He couldn't quite believe what he was about to do.

Nobody had guessed there was anything going on between the two of them when they were in the music store. Would it be possible to have more with Rick under the guise of being friends without anyone guessing the true nature of what was happening between them? As long as they were careful—

"Are you okay? You've gone very pale." Rick reached forward and stroked Max's cheek. "I'm sorry. I didn't mean to scare—"

"I don't want to fight this anymore," Max whispered, staring at the ground.

"Then don't," Rick said quietly. "Don't fight it. I thought you'd blown me off—"

"Nobody can find out." Looking up at Rick, Max searched his expression for any hint that he couldn't be trusted. It was such a huge risk he was taking. "And I mean nobody. If anyone finds out, I'll deny everything, and whatever we had will be finished forever." He'd never wanted anyone as badly as he wanted Rick right now. He was aching to touch him.

If anything went wrong, he could deny it all. It had worked in the kitchen the other day, so if he had to do it once more to protect himself... he could do that... couldn't he? Max chewed on his lower lip and studied Rick.

"Can you promise me you won't even hint about this to anyone else? That you won't say a word about us to anyone?"

"I think I can do that."

"I'm serious, Rick. Promise me you won't say a word, or this is over before it even begins."

"So am I." Rick closed the distance between them. "I can do that. For now."

"What do you mean 'for now'?"

"I won't let you live a lie for the rest of your life, Max."

"The rest of my life?"

"Yeah. You can't hide who you are forever. I won't let you." Rick brushed his thumb along Max's lips, and Max's breathing quickened. "But I can promise that I'll keep your secret for as long as you need me to. To keep you safe."

"So… we're doing this?"

Rick smiled but stayed where he was. Max had expected him to make the first move to kiss him, but that was clearly not going to happen. He sucked his lower lip into his mouth, and his heart thundered in his chest. He'd kissed hundreds of girls, and even kissed Rick twice already. Why was this so hard?

Taking a deep, shaky breath, Max leaned forward and closed his eyes, his senses going into overload. Rick's musky citrus cologne and the heat from his skin as their lips touched went straight to Max's groin, and he grabbed the back of Rick's head to pull him closer. Max parted his lips, and Rick explored his mouth as their tongues dueled with more intensity than before. Rick's lips were as soft as Max remembered in his dreams, yet his tongue more experienced. All of Max's inhibitions melted away as his tongue darted deeper into Rick's mouth, the way he wished he'd been able to before. His pent-up passion mirrored and intensified as Rick returned the kiss with equal vigor.

CHAPTER SIX

Rick

As THEY kissed, Rick wondered how far Max would be comfortable taking this, but then suddenly there were voices and laughter. A door banged, and they both jumped, their teeth bashing together. That was close. Max turned away from Rick and smoothed his hair.

"It's okay. There's no way they could have seen anything," Rick said and grabbed the smelly boxing gloves from the cabinet, then thrust them at Max. "Here, hold these."

"What? Why?" Max scrunched up his nose and gingerly took them.

Rick turned to the hall door.

"Art, William, hey, guys. How's it going?"

"Hi, Rick," William said.

"Your hair is awesome, man," Max said. The tips of William's short bleached hair were multicolored. Like they'd been dipped in a paint box. William was always changing his hair, so Rick was kinda used to it.

"Thanks."

"Max here was thinking about taking up MMA," Rick said and grinned at Max, who scowled.

He was probably pushing his luck, but it would be the best cover for them spending time together if everyone thought he was giving Max martial arts lessons. Plus, if Tony was right, this would be perfect for Max right now. It would give him more confidence in his ability to protect himself, and not just physically, that was for sure. Rick had seen it time and again. It could be exactly what they both needed. It would put his mind at rest about taking things further with Max. He'd never forgive himself if something bad happened to Max as a result of them seeing each other. Plus it would be fun.

"You totally should," William said. "Best workout there is, especially if you've had a bad day. There's nothing like punching the shit out of the heavy bag. Right, Art?"

"Sparring's better."

William looked thoughtful. "Yeah, you got me there. When are you starting?"

"Um." Max glared at Rick and said through gritted teeth, "I haven't decided yet."

Okay, maybe he had overstepped. "You don't have to decide right away. Come on, I'll walk you out."

"I can't believe you went there," Max said and dumped the gloves on the desk as they walked into the office, but Rick laughed.

"You might find it fun."

"I told you, I don't do exercise."

"Shame. It'd be the perfect reason to give for us spending time together."

"The problem is that none of my friends would believe it."

"I could teach you a couple of simple moves to convince them, if that would help?" Rick shrugged. "Up to you, anyway."

"Fuck." Max banged his head against the filing cabinet. "I'm going to have to take up ninja shit. Aren't I? I have zero coordination."

Rick laughed. "I'm sure that's not true. Tell you what. Why don't you join in this class? Try it at least." Then he whispered, "If you don't enjoy it, then we can figure something else out, okay?"

"You seriously think this will be a good idea, don't you."

"What's the worst that could happen?"

"You see me make a total fool of myself."

"You won't be the only beginner in the class. Promise."

"I guess I do have some time before band practice." Max glared at him. "Don't make me regret this."

"You won't." Rick grinned. This was going to be so much fun. Showing Max how awesome martial arts was and teaching him. One thing, though…. "You'll need to borrow some board shorts and a T-shirt."

"What's wrong with what I'm wearing?"

"You're gonna get sweaty. Wouldn't you rather borrow some clothes? There are showers in the changing rooms so you can change back before you go."

Max shook his head. "I'm already regretting this."

"Come on." Rick grabbed his arm and nudged him back into the hall. "It's going to be fun. I promise."

Max didn't look convinced, but he did accept the clothing, and Rick gave him some privacy to change.

"What are we doing tonight?" William asked as Rick took his clipboard from the cabinet and ticked off William's and Art's names from his list. Most of his students paid monthly, but Rick liked to keep track of how often they were attending.

"Some kickboxing drills, and then I thought we could do some knife self-defense."

"No sparring?" Art asked.

"Not tonight. We'll do that next class. Don't worry, you'll get some more practice before your fight."

He was taking the two of them to a competition next Thursday, in a week. William was a black belt, and Art was only halfway through the grading system. It would be his first competition fight, but Rick knew he would do well. Out of all his students, Art showed the most promise of becoming a professional fighter.

Max emerged from the changing rooms and shimmied to avoid the cabinets. He looked a little fed up, and Rick hoped this hadn't been a bad idea. Max definitely looked the part now, though.

"The shorts are too big."

He tugged at the waistband. They didn't look that big. He was probably making excuses so he could change his mind.

Rick walked up to him. "You're gonna be fine. Just do as much as you can and try to enjoy it, okay? It's pretty relaxed as martial arts classes go. We work hard, but we have a laugh as well."

"Really?"

"Yeah."

The other students were arriving now, and Rick took the opportunity to introduce Max to the two newest, Nicole and Giovanni.

"Hi, guys. How are you doing?" Rick asked.

"Good, thanks, Sensei."

"Sensei?" Max said and snickered.

"Don't laugh," Rick said. "It's a sign of respect for your instructor."

Max was obviously holding in laughter. His eyes were shining and lips pursed.

Rick sighed. "It's a martial arts thing, okay? Just go with it. Please?"

Nodding, Max said, "I'll try."

"Gio, Nicole, would you mind looking out for Max? It's his first time. If you hadn't guessed that already."

"Sure," Nicole said. "We've only been coming a few weeks. It's hard, but we're totally hooked."

"The warmup's the worst," Giovanni said as he removed his sneakers and socks. "It gets better after that."

Rick put his hand on Max's shoulder. "I'm gonna go and get changed. You going to be okay?"

Max nodded. "Yeah. I think."

Gio and Nicole didn't yet have the club uniform, so it was obvious they were new to this. It would be easier for Max to bond with them if Rick was out of the way.

"We'll be starting in two minutes," Rick shouted after he'd changed.

While his students finished putting on their hand wraps and making sure their bottles of water were easy to grab at the edge of the hall, Rick ticked off names from his list. There were sixteen of them in total today.

When he took his place at the front of the hall, everyone lined up in formation. Black belts in the first row, brown belts behind them, and so on, with ungraded students right at the back. Once they were all settled, Rick brought his feet together and bowed. His students copied him. It was a tradition he kind of liked. It showed respect and got people's brains in gear, ready to start some serious training. He caught Max's eye as he finished bowing. He looked bemused. Nicole tapped his arm and indicated that Max should copy, and he seemed to reluctantly obey.

"Start running around," Rick said, and the black belts led everyone in a large circle. He connected his cell phone to the speakers and pressed Play. A high-octane dance track blared around the hall.

Once everyone was jogging around the circle, Rick darted inside and ran in the opposite direction. It gave him a chance to see how everyone was doing. To see if anyone was injured or struggling, and also to gauge how motivated they all were that day.

"When I shout out one, I want you to change direction. Two, you sprint, three, run backward, four, run forward, and five, drop to the ground and give me five push-ups."

Everyone looked to be in good shape today. Max seemed a little happier now that he was moving.

"One!" Rick pivoted and ran in the other direction.

It took a second for everyone to react, but that was normal at the beginning of the warmup.

"One!" He shouted again as soon as everyone had settled.

Their reactions were slightly faster this time. Just. He kept them running for a couple of laps before he shouted, "Three!"

This time the change was not so successful. Rick changed what the numbers stood for each lesson to keep them on their toes. After all, if their brains weren't warmed up too, they would be knocked to the canvas before they realized what was going on in a real fight.

When Rick ran past Max running backward, he had to take a second glance at him. He'd taken the instruction too literally. Rick turned so he was going the same way as everyone else, and picked up his pace to catch Max.

"Look where you're going," Rick said, trying not to laugh. Max was running backward with his eyes firmly fixed forward. It was a miracle he hadn't collided with anyone yet—or crashed into the wall. He was either fearless or had zero self-preservation. "Like this," Rick said, and looked back over his shoulder. Max copied him. "Yep, that's it."

Rick left him to it and switched so he was running in the opposite direction again.

"Four!" Rick shouted and ran forward. Most students, apart from the black belts, had forgotten what four stood for. As soon as they had sorted themselves out, Rick shouted, "Five!" and dropped to the ground for five super-fast push-ups. He was on his feet before anyone else and continued running. Max was really struggling with the push-ups. In fact, he was lying on the ground and taking a quick break. Had he attempted any at all? Rick decided to let it go this time. He didn't want to be too hard on him and put Max off coming again.

He went easy on him for the rest of the warmup, and when everyone was grabbing a drink of water once they were done, about fifteen minutes later, he realized Max didn't have any with him. Rick grabbed his bottle and went over to where he was sitting on the ground with Gio and gasping for breath.

Max narrowed his eyes. "That was brutal."

"Here, take this." Rick handed him his water. "Sip it. Don't gulp."

"It was." Giovanni nodded. "It gets easier now, though, right, Sensei?"

"Easy? You want to give me a hand with the demos?"

"No way!" Giovanni said. "I meant there's less cardio now."

"Can Max work with you when we pair up?" Rick asked him. "Nicole can work with Oli. It'll do you both good to pair up with other people for a change."

"Yes, Sensei."

"Hey, you got your gloves. That's awesome," Rick said to Giovanni, who proudly handed them over for inspection. They were black with blue flames. "These are a decent make. They should last you a good couple of years."

"Can you help me with these?" Giovanni asked and unwrapped some brand-new hand wraps.

"Sure." Rick showed him how to do the first one and watched as he did the second one himself. "Grab a pair of boxing gloves and some focus pads from the cabinet," Rick said to Max, who screwed up his nose. "The ones on the top shelf don't smell so bad. Try them first."

"Okay, guys, gather around," Rick said after putting on his boxing gloves. He beckoned to William, who put on a pair of focus pads and secured them with the Velcro fastening.

"We're going to start with a couple of kickboxing drills." He got into a fighting stance, with his left foot forward and his fists up by his jaw. "Switch kick." He paused to let William get the pads in the correct place by his right knee. "Strike with the top of your foot and land forward." He completed the move: switching his stance so his right leg was forward, and then striking the pad with his left leg before placing his foot back on the ground. "Right roundhouse." Rick put all his weight on his left foot and pivoted his heel as he brought his right leg up to strike the pad to the left of William's face. "Land forward and go straight into the left uppercut, stepping forward with your left leg. Again landing forward. Beginners up to orange belt finish with a right cross." He demonstrated and then reset to his finishing position after the uppercut. "Everyone else, carry on with a spinning elbow, striking across with your right elbow. You're aiming for your opponent's cheek with this one, and then finish with a snap kick and then a jumping snap." He completed the demonstration and repeated it three times.

Giovanni, Nicole, and Max all looked completely confused, and that really was no surprise. He knew it was a lot to take in. All the combinations had an effortless flow when you got them right, but it would take years for them to perfect them.

"Guys, come on over." Rick took off his gloves and beckoned to Oli, Nicole, Giovanni, and Max, and took them to the far end of the hall. "How are you feeling about the drill?"

"It's okay, I think," Oli said. "Can we see the footwork for the roundhouse into the uppercut again?"

"Of course. I'll take you through from the beginning. Decide who's going to pad and I'll do the drill with you."

"Shall I pad?" Max asked Giovanni.

Max seemed content to watch for now, obviously not realizing that padding was harder than it looked. If you didn't get the pads in the correct place at the right split second it was gonna hurt. A lot.

"Let's take it slowly to start," Rick said. "Max, hold the pads together so they're doubled up, by your right knee. Get your feet into fighting stance with your left foot forward, and make sure you brace yourself for the impact. Okay?"

"Got it." Max did as asked but appeared uncomfortable. It was a bit of a weird position, Rick guessed, but he'd been doing it so long that it felt natural.

"Okay. Gio and Oli, just do the first kick." He indicated for them to go ahead. Max shut his eyes as Giovanni's leg came around to strike. It was cute, but he wouldn't last two seconds if he let that become a habit. "Max, eyes open, okay?" Rick smiled at him as Max opened his eyes. He looked shell-shocked and rubbed his knee—as best he could with the pads on. "Hold your arms sturdy and it won't hurt." Max nodded, still looking slightly stunned.

He seemed to get the hang of it—so long as Giovanni didn't try to do the moves too fast. Rick left them to it to go and check on everyone else. Once he'd done a full circuit, he told everyone to switch. It would now be Max's turn to do the moves.

"How are you getting on?" he asked Max, helping him remove the pads and secure the gloves.

"He's doing great," Giovanni said and dashed across the hall to get his water bottle.

"Gio kept on missing the pads," Max said and frowned. "It fucking hurt."

"Try to gauge where he's going to strike and adjust the pads."

"But I thought they had to be in specific places for each move?"

"They do. Technically. But you and Gio are new to this, so your accuracy isn't going to be so precise as someone like, say, William, yet. It's okay to compromise a bit at this stage."

"Any final words of wisdom?" Max asked as he smacked the gloves together.

"Try to hit the pads. I don't want to have to perform CPR on Gio."

"Yeah. Funny," Max said. "You did see how high you're expecting me to kick, right? I'm not sure my leg even stretches that much."

"I guess we're about to find out," Rick said with a smirk and waggled his eyebrows. Max blushed and turned away just as Giovanni returned.

Max couldn't kick that high. Not even close. Nor could he hit the pads. Poor Giovanni would be covered in bruises tomorrow. Max hadn't been kidding about not having any coordination.

"Turn your heel toward Gio more," Rick said. He stood behind Max, who was attempting the roundhouse kick and failing miserably. Placing his hands on Max's hips, Rick tried to maneuver him into the correct position, but Max lost his balance and fell backward into him, pressing his butt right into Rick's groin. Damn, that felt good. He began to stiffen and pushed Max as he took a step away. Max was so flustered by his inability to do the kick that Rick wasn't even sure Max had noticed the contact. Or maybe he had and that was why he was so rattled.

"Try it again," Rick said, making sure to stand to one side of Max this time. It wouldn't do either of them any favors if people noticed.

Max had sort of got the idea by the time they had done a couple more drills. He was definitely improving.

"Okay, go and grab a drink if you haven't already," Rick shouted. They were about to do some knife defense and have a bit of fun at the same time. He'd created a game to test their skills, and he was looking forward to seeing it in action. But first he needed to teach them the technique.

He ran through his usual spiel about how dangerous knife attacks were and that their first form of defense should be to defuse the situation and remove themselves from it. It was too easy to get hurt when you were confronted with someone lashing out with a sharp blade.

A few years back, someone who'd attended the same martial arts school as him in Leatherton had been all too cocky when attacked by some guy with a knife. He'd thought he could easily handle it because he'd learned a couple of defense moves in class. He got slashed so badly that he'd bled out and died. It had been a harsh lesson to them all.

Rick demonstrated five different defenses from knife attacks for the blue belts and above, and sent them to the far end of the hall to practice.

"Max, can you help me show this defense technique?"

"Uh, sure. What do I have to do?"

"Pretend you're thrusting a knife at me."

Max made a fist and motioned forward with a stabbing action.

"With your right hand." Rick smirked. "I didn't realize you were left-handed."

"I'm not."

"Okay, so most people will attack with their dominant hand, and that is likely to be their right." He loved it that Max was constantly keeping him on his toes. "Try it again."

Max exaggerated the thrust with a roll of his eyes.

Rick demonstrated while talking. "Step to the side, to the left, and grab the outside of their wrist with your right hand. Goose the wrist up and twist. Max, if this gets too much at any point just tap out, okay?"

"Huh?"

"Tap my arm or leg and I'll release."

"Okay."

"Make sure you're pulling their arm while you do this. Then push your hip into their body and press down on their shoulder with your left hand. Keep the pressure on and turn your body away from them while keeping them close. With your right hand, make sure that's close to your body too so they can't stab you there. Increase the pressure on their wrist and they should drop the weapon." He released Max and gave his shoulder a quick rub. "You okay for me to show that again, faster this time?" Max nodded and thrust out his hand again. This time Rick carried out the moves swiftly, and Max groaned in surprise at the speed.

"That's what you're aiming for. Giovanni, can you take over from Max so he can watch?"

Rick had to show them quite a few more times before they felt confident with the basic moves. Leaving them to it, he checked on the other group and instructed them on the game he'd made up, and left William in charge of them.

When he returned, there was a full-scale debate going on, with Oli bent forward with his arm in the air, while pretty much everyone else gave their version of how they thought it should be done. After pairing them up and coaching them while they did it, finally they seemed to be getting it. Even Max, to his surprise.

"Okay, you've learned the moves. Let's have some fun with this now. We're going to play a game using the knife defense you've been doing. Oli, come stand over here. Max, can you put on some focus pads." He made the others stand in a semicircle, with Max at the far end, facing Oli. "Right, so I'm going to stand behind Oli. I'll point at someone at random. If you're pointed at, come at Oli as if you're carrying a knife. Oli, use the defense you've just learned, and then run to the focus pads, do a jab, cross, hook, and then run back to the center again. Got it? Take it easy with the punches, as you're not wearing gloves this time."

They were all looking at him blankly. That was not a good sign. He pointed at Nicole, and she rushed forward and thrust her fist at Oli. He managed the defense quite well. Then Oli ran to the pads, and Rick realized he hadn't told Max how to hold them. Luckily Oli showed him what to do. "Nicole, you need to go back to your spot."

"Oh, okay. I get it now," she said.

It ran smoothly after that, as each of the beginners took their turn in the middle. Then it was Max's go. He managed to defend the first attack reasonably well. Rick pointed at Oli, who came at Max's blind spot to his right.

"Oh, I forgot the punches," Max said, and darted toward his left—to Giovanni, who was holding the pads—just as Oli reached him, and Oli swiped at thin air with his make-believe knife. It was like something out of a cartoon.

Everyone laughed, and Rick shook his head in despair. This game was supposed to be easy.

"What? What's so funny, guys?" Max asked, turning to them with a bewildered look on his face.

Rick sighed. How to explain it? He almost wished he'd filmed it. Thank goodness the lesson was nearly finished.

"THAT WAS more fun than I thought it would be," Max said as he helped Rick collect up any borrowed focus pads. He'd had a shower and changed, and now it was just the two of them. "But we need to talk about your taste in music."

"What's wrong with my taste in music?"

Max screwed up his face. "All that dance music. Metal songs would work better. Get people fired up more."

Rick took the pads from Max's hands and placed them in the cabinet, then rested his hands on Max's waist. He'd locked the door, so there was no chance of anyone walking in on them this time. "Is that so?" Rick leaned down and gave Max a quick kiss on the lips. "Don't I get any points for telling you about that band with the awesome bassist?"

Max sighed and rested his head on Rick's shoulder. "Fine, you win. I owe you big-time for that."

"You don't owe me anything. I'm just glad I could help."

"You're really good at it, you know. Teaching ninja shit." Max raised his head and looked him in the eyes. "It wasn't as bad as I thought it was going to be... apart from the warmup, that is. That was far worse. That was hell."

"Hell?" Rick laughed. "You think that's bad, you should see what you have to go through to get a black belt. It's far worse than that."

"Masochist," Max said and wrapped his arms around Rick, pulling him close. It felt so comfortable to be with Max like this. To be on the receiving end of his affection. He could totally get used to this. Rick kissed the top of Max's head.

"Do you think you want to try it again?" Rick asked.

"The ninja lessons?"

"Will you quit calling it that?" Rick smiled.

"You were right; it would be a great excuse to spend time with you. I'm just not sure I can put myself through that warmup again."

"How about some private lessons, then?"

Max tilted his head and kissed Rick, and Rick opened his lips, allowing Max to deepen it. God, he felt good. "I could get on board with that," Max said.

"Would you let me take you on a date next week?"

Max froze and pulled away. "A date? What, like, out somewhere?"

He'd been ready for Max to overreact, and looped his fingers over the top of Max's cargo pants, tugging him closer. "How about next Thursday? I've got a competition fight that night. William, Art, and a guy called Rafael, who you haven't met yet, are fighting too. You could come along as part of our team. Nobody but us would have to know we were on a date, and if anyone saw you there, they'd never guess."

"Maybe." Had he nearly convinced Max? He hadn't thought it would be that easy.

"Is it a date?"

A smile crept onto Max's face. "Yeah. It's a date."

CHAPTER SEVEN

Max

AT SEVENISH, Max sauntered into the garage, armed with his shiny new bass guitar and a huge smile after his time with Rick.

"Where the fuck have you been all afternoon?" Tony shouted at him from behind the drum kit.

"I can't play without a guitar, now can I?"

"You went to Hugh's without telling us?" Kyle whined. "I needed to go."

"What for?"

"I dunno, but I'm sure I would've found something."

Between them, they'd spent a small fortune at Hugh's music store over the years.

Kyle crouched next to him and gasped as Max removed his gleaming instrument from the case. "Is that what I think it is?" He chuckled. "You're such an idiot."

"What is it?" Tony came out from behind his drum kit to take a closer look.

"She's a beast, that's what she is," Kyle said, prying the guitar from Max's hands.

"Six-string fretless." Tony shook his head and pursed his lips, obviously fighting off a smile. "You better be able to play that thing."

Taking his precious guitar back from Kyle, Max slipped the strap over his shoulders and plugged into the bass amp. It was now or never. One chance to convince Tony that taking this instrument to the next level would be the right direction for Purple Method, otherwise he'd be stuck playing monotonous riffs for the rest of his life, like most other bassists. Quickly making sure it was still in tune, Max slid his fingers up the fretboard, caressing the strings. "Insidious Girl" would be a good song to play, not only because Tony had written it but also because it had a tempo that would suit the slap-bass style without having to make drastic changes to the riff itself.

Max dropped his wrists and placed his fingers into position, took a deep breath, and played the first notes. They sounded raw and gritty, but with a funky edge to the beat. After the repetitive first bars of the song, Max bounced the side of his thumb against the lowest string, his stomach flitting as the sound rippled through his body, and then he plucked the higher note, ghosting the fretboard to deaden it, creating a crisp, clear sound before picking up the pace, his right wrist rotating, flicking back and forth as he plucked the strings and hammered-on to create a heavy, exciting rhythm.

Reaching the end of the song, Max switched to "No Jurisdiction," but instead of playing the bass line, he played the lead guitar riffs, plucking the strings to create a rumbling yet stiff style, building a unique, bass-riddled tension until he released the thunderous beats with a rapid slap-bass chorus. Smacking his palm over the strings, the instrument silenced, and Max looked up at Tony and Kyle.

"What do you think?"

"I think you're trying too hard," Tony said. "You know I wasn't actually going to kick you out of the band if you didn't play bass, right?"

"Fuck you!" Max was trembling, and he wasn't sure if it was from anger at his brother putting him through this or from excitement about what this could mean for their future. "Tell me you've heard a bass played like that before. Go on. I bet you can't. I gotta tell you, in all the music I've ever listened to, there's one band doing this, and they aren't even playing heavy metal. If we try this, we'll be the only band out there. We'll have a unique sound."

"He's right, you know," Kyle said. "And it'd be hard to copy. I don't know anyone who's trying to play a bass like a lead guitar. I bet even Vanquished don't have the skill to copy us."

"We know Lee can't play bass like that." Tony tapped his drumstick against his lip. "We've got some songwriting to get done. One thing, though."

"What's that?" Max asked. They were trying this. They were really doing it. He could barely contain his excitement.

"Turn the volume down, yeah?"

"Worried I'll be heard over your drums?"

"Drums are the backbone of any song. I don't need to tell you that. If you can't hear me, you'll be fucked, and then this will never work."

"Fuzzy logic. All that superhero porn is messing with your head." Max kneeled down and adjusted the volume on his amplifier, turning it up.

"Guys, am I gonna have to put my earplugs in again?"

"Remind me why you're in a heavy metal band, Kyle." Tony played one of his cymbals extra loud.

"Just 'cause we're a heavy metal band doesn't mean we have to be deaf by the time we're thirty."

"For fuck's sake, Kyle. Wanna borrow some superhero porn? Sounds like you need to chill out."

Kyle's face flushed. "Yeah, okay."

"Eew." Was Max going to be the only one in the house not watching that crap? "Can we focus on the music now, please?"

Tony shrugged. "Now who's using fuzzy logic? If you don't want to hear about it, don't bring it up." He sighed and shook his head. "And here I was thinking Kyle was the prude."

"I'm not a prude. Fuck off, Tony." Max grabbed the notebook from his guitar case. "You wanna hear what ideas I got for our new sound?"

"Sure, go for it."

"I've got loads more lyrics and riffs written down upstairs that would work well with this."

"Hang on," Kyle said. "If you're playing lead riffs, what am I supposed to play?"

"We both play lead riffs. We can figure out some harmonies that complement each other. It'll give us a richer sound with more depth."

Tony leaned forward, resting his arms on his drums. "I think you may have hit on something with this."

Kyle snatched the notebook from Max's hands and held it in the air. "We need to get to work."

WHEN RICK messaged him the next day and Max was having a lazy Saturday breakfast in the garden after a late night figuring out their new sound, his heart leaped into his throat as he read it.

Just been told my parents are out this evening. Do you want to come over for dinner?

Before he had a chance to overthink it, he sent back: *yes*.

And then he panicked.

The hoodie he stole from Tony was probably overkill, but as he got out of the cab that dropped him a few streets away from Rick's house, he rammed the hood over his head and was grateful for the additional disguise. Taking a drink of tequila from the hip flask he'd been sipping from during the journey across town helped calm his nerves a fraction, but he was still terrified of being recognized and people putting two and two together and guessing he and Rick were more than friends.

He'd only been to this part of town once before, and that had been with his dad and Tony to pick up a second-hand drum kit. Every house he walked past had white picket fences and expensive-looking cars parked outside. It reminded him of that movie *The Stepford Wives*, with every house immaculate and practically identical. It freaked him out a little, and he was conscious of the few people mowing their lawns staring at him as he passed.

He was beginning to think this was a bad idea.

Rick's house was in a cul-de-sac, and his front yard looked like all the others, but thankfully there were no cars parked out front. Max practically ran up the path. The front door flew open as he reached it.

"Right on time," Rick said and grinned at him. "Come on in."

Max frowned and stepped inside, then shut the door behind him. "You okay?"

"Yeah, sorry." Max shook his head. "Just a bit Stepford 'round here."

"A bit what?" Rick asked.

How could Rick have never heard of that? Rick leaned forward to kiss him, and Max immediately felt more relaxed.

"You hungry? Come on through."

He followed Rick along the light gray carpeted hall and glanced at the gold-framed pictures hanging on the walls. He spotted one of a blond-haired boy who couldn't have been more than about ten, dressed in a posh black suit with tails and clutching a massive trophy.

"Is this you?" Max laughed. He remembered Isla saying Rick had been good at dancing, but hadn't quite believed it until now. "Wow. Is that for a dancing contest?"

"Yeah." Rick had gone bright red. He walked up behind Max and slid his arms around his waist. "That was a long time ago."

"You were cute."

"Were?"

Max huffed a laugh as Rick squeezed him and rested his head on Max's shoulder, kissing his neck. "Mm, that feels good." He twisted in Rick's arms and kissed him on the lips, tentatively at first, but then Rick groaned and opened to him, kissing him hard and deep until they were both gasping for breath. Pressing his thickening cock against Rick, he could feel Rick's solid length through his jeans, and he rotated his hips to get more friction. God, that felt amazing.

Max was about to kiss him again when Rick pushed him away. "Food first. We've got all evening. My parents won't be back until about ten. No need to rush things."

"Sadist," Max mumbled, adjusting himself so he was more comfortable, and followed Rick into the kitchen—taking the opportunity to admire his tight ass. "What are we eating?"

"Steak sandwich okay?"

"Sounds good."

Max wandered up behind him and peered into the refrigerator over Rick's shoulder.

"Wow, you have the healthiest diet."

It was all salad, fresh chicken, fish, and fruit. There were no bottled sauces, no desserts—no normal stuff, apart from the four-pack of beer.

Rick took out a packet of thinly sliced rib-eye steak, a pepper, an onion, and some sliced cheese.

"You want some help?"

"No. It's okay. Drink?"

"Got any tequila?" Max grinned at him. He'd been half joking, but Rick took him seriously.

"No, sorry." Rick frowned. "I should've thought to get some. Is beer okay?"

"Beer's good." It was probably best to stick to beer for now anyway.

Rick handed him a bottle, and Max pulled out a stool from under the breakfast bar.

"I love watching other people cook."

"You do? How come?" Rick switched on the oven and put two sliced rolls underneath to broil while he chopped the onion.

Max rolled the beer bottle between his hands. "I like picking up new ideas and recipes."

"You cook?" Rick glanced at him, his eyes wide.

"Yeah." Max took a swig of beer. Rick was still cutting the onion and not looking at what he was doing. "Watch out for your—"

Rick hissed in a breath and shook his hand. "Ow, that was close."

"You okay? Did you cut yourself?"

Examining his fingers, he shook his head. "Na, I'm good. Just scraped the skin."

"Nice. That's hygienic."

"Don't worry, none of it ended up in the food. I knew I should've ordered in."

"You sure I can't help?"

"No. I got this. What made you want to start cooking?"

He seemed to be doing better with slicing the pepper, so Max looked on in amusement. He'd thought Kyle was bad in the kitchen, but even he could make a decent Philly cheesesteak. "Dad never cooked, so we always had TV dinners or takeout growing up. I kinda got fed up with it and taught myself by watching the Food Network."

"Wow."

Max shrugged. "I got half decent at it. By the time I was twelve, I was cooking for the three of us most nights."

Rick threw the onions and peppers into a skillet, started them cooking, and came over to give him a chaste kiss on the lips and run his thumb along Max's jaw. Max took a deep breath, then coughed, an acrid smell drifting in the air and filling his lungs.

"The bread!" Rick yelled and rescued the blackened rolls from the oven, dunking them in the sink with a sizzle and a tower of steam as he ran water on them. "Mom's gonna kill me." He flapped a towel in the air while he opened the back door, trying to disperse the clouds of smoke as the smoke alarm began to sound.

Max started laughing; he couldn't help it. Rick in a panic was the funniest thing ever. He was usually so cool and collected.

"It's not funny," Rick said. "I've already been banned from cooking twice since I've been back home. Oh no, not the onions as well, this can't be happening."

That made Max laugh even harder, and he almost fell off his stool.

Once Rick had cleaned up, Max made him sit down and then took over control of their dinner. Ten minutes later, they took plates of delicious Philly cheesesteaks up to Rick's bedroom to eat. Max climbed onto his bed and gazed around as he took a bite of his sandwich.

Rick's bedroom was mostly bare, the pale blue walls and gray carpet clear of any clutter. In fact, there was no clutter anywhere. A large flat-screen was opposite the bed, resting on a chest of drawers. A white wardrobe was to the left of it, and the only signs of any kind of personalization were two samurai swords lying flat in a stand and some textbooks on the shelves next to the window on Max's right.

"I had you pegged as a neat freak, but this is ridiculous."

Pursing his lips, Rick said, "I guess it doesn't feel like home anymore. I've been away for nine years. Mom redecorated right after I moved out."

"This was the room you grew up in?"

Rick nodded.

"What was it like before?"

"Posters everywhere. My mom hated it."

"Posters of who?" Max asked and took another bite of his sandwich, trying to picture a young Rick hanging out and being a kid in this clinical room.

"Um... Forrest Griffin, Urijah Faber, Gina Carano."

Max raised an eyebrow. "I have no clue who any of those people are."

"Fighters. Hot ones." He grinned, and Max rolled his eyes. "How about you? What was your room like when you were younger?"

"Homey. It hasn't changed much, to be honest."

"Any posters?"

"Not ones I'd want to display. Although I may've had one of Slash above my desk years ago. I always wanted to play guitar like him when I got older." Max sighed, putting his empty plate to one side and lying back. "It's funny how things work out. I'm not even playing guitar anymore now."

"Rick!" a woman called out. "Rick, are you home?"

"Fuck. Who the hell is that?" Max panicked, scrambling to grab the comforter, the pillow—anything.

Rick froze.

"The kitchen is an absolute disgrace. And the smell…. That's it. I won't have you cooking in this house again. I mean it this time." The voice was getting closer, fast, and Max managed to conceal his face with the pillow just in time before she entered the room. Why the fuck hadn't they closed the door? Why didn't Rick have a lock? Why had he ever agreed to this stupid idea? He should've known better than to trust they wouldn't be discovered.

"Mom, don't—"

"Oh, sorry, love. I didn't realize you had company. Your dad forgot the tickets for the ballet, so we had to come back. We can talk about the kitchen later. Enjoy your evening."

Max didn't move the pillow until the front door slammed closed. Rick breathed out heavily.

"Max, I'm so sorry. I—"

"I should go." He scrambled to get up. "This was a bad idea."

"She didn't see you. There's no way she would've known it was you. They've definitely gone now."

"No. I should…. I should go." That had been too close, and his heart was still hammering in his chest as he took the stairs two at a time.

"Max, wait." Rick rushed after him, and Max paused at the bottom of the stairs, his hood pulled up and his hand on the front door. "Can we at least say goodbye properly?" He relented, his hand dropping from the handle. Rick's arms around him were a comfort, and he hugged him tight. "I'll figure something out, okay?"

Nodding, Max tilted his head for a kiss. They definitely needed something more secure for next time. A locked door between them and the outside world at the very least.

"THAT WAS great," Tony shouted later that night as they reached the end of "Destroy the Silence." The band practices with their new sound couldn't be going any better. "'Bass-tards' next."

Max felt as though he had endless reserves of power in his voice, hitting every single note with exquisite precision and playing his monster of a bass guitar with increasing ease. It might have been nervous energy after his near miss earlier, but that didn't seem to matter. The others appeared to feed off his renewed energy, and were soon not only playing tighter than before but were also inspired to write even more new material during this session. At three in the morning, they were buzzing as they left the garage.

"I could do with a beer," Tony said and threw open the back door, heading straight down to the kitchen.

Max followed behind Kyle, trooping downstairs, and was surprised to see Zoe, Lisa, and another girl he didn't recognize sitting at the table with Sian. Panic rose inside him, but it was too late to go back up; they'd seen him and were staring right at him. It was no mistake he hadn't seen the girls since the party on the first night they were back from their tour, two weeks ago now.

They were playing cards, and judging by the tower of beer bottles in the sink, they'd been there for a while. Tony handed beers to both Kyle and Max.

"You girls made it, then." He grinned at Max. "Didn't want you to think we'd forgotten you."

"Yeah, thanks for inviting us," Lisa said and looked at Max, who busied himself opening his beer. "We know how hard you've been working with the band. It's great that you got some time tonight."

"We do?" Max did his best not to glare at Tony. What the hell gave him the right to interfere in his life like that?

"We thought we could have some fun tonight, as we haven't seen you in ages," Zoe said and put her arms around the pretty girl next to her. "This is Jasmine." The girl waved shyly at him.

His whole body went cold. How the fuck could he get out of this? His mind went blank, and he panicked. Before he could think of a good enough reason to decline them without arousing suspicion, Lisa had taken his hand and begun to lead him upstairs, followed by Zoe and Jasmine.

"Keep the noise down." Tony chuckled and turned up the volume on the speakers.

Max followed in a daze of panic. Everyone would think it odd if he refused their advances, and he couldn't risk drawing attention to the state of his love life. All he could think about was that he was about to cheat on Rick—after worrying so much about being able to trust him, he was now going to betray Rick—and it made him queasy. But there wasn't a single thing he could do about it; there was no way out. It was too late.

WHEN THE lights were off and the girls asleep, Max lay awake until the dawn light shone through the blinds. He'd never felt guilt like this before. The sight of piles of clothing strewn across his bedroom floor made it even more unbearable.

Max floated downstairs as if in a waking nightmare, made coffee, and sat outside in the quiet of the early morning. Zoe and Lisa usually waited for him to contact them, so not finishing things with them had seemed like the perfect plan for now—so as to not raise suspicion about him and Rick—especially as they knew things were only casual. He dropped his head forward and lit a cigarette, pinching the bridge of his nose as he inhaled, and tried to calm the fuck down.

The back door rattled. "You okay?" Sian asked.

"What are you doing up? I thought you'd gone to bed."

Sian grimaced. "Work. I'm on the early shift at the bakery. Craig's sick." She snatched his cigarette and took a drag as she sat down on a yard chair, yawning. "What's going on?" She handed back the cigarette and narrowed her gaze. "And don't you dare tell me it's nothing. You've been acting weird for days."

Max clawed his fingers through his hair. He wanted to talk to someone about all of this, but how could he? The second they found out the truth, they'd look at him differently—judge him—and that would be the start of him losing everything. Why was this so fucking hard?

"I take it the girl you're hung up on isn't upstairs right now?"

Max froze for a second and then shook his head. If he pretended Rick was a girl, maybe he could talk about this after all.

"Talk to me, Max."

He took another drag of the cigarette and placed it in the ashtray. "I met someone who I think I could be serious with, but I'm not sure, it's early days, so I haven't told Zoe and Lisa yet, and then fucking Tony gets involved, as usual, and fucks the whole thing up for me."

"Why didn't you say anything last night?"

"How could I?" Max stared at Sian, his vision blurry from tears. "They were right there expecting me to carry on as normal."

"I'm sure they would have understood—"

"No, Sian. No. They wouldn't have fucking understood." He spat out the words and blinked furiously, willing his emotions to bury themselves back down again.

"Hey." Sian grabbed his hand and squeezed it as Max used the back of his other hand to wipe his eyes. "You listen to me. Look at me.

What're you so scared of? If you tell them the truth, they'll understand. If you don't go with what feels right, you'll regret it for the rest of your life. It's no fun living a lie."

"But what if... what if people react badly?"

"Then it's their problem. This is your life, babe, and you get one shot at it. You have to do what makes you happy, not what you think is going to make everyone else happy."

Max took a shaky breath. "I'm going to have to finish it with Zoe and Lisa, aren't I?"

Sian nodded and released his hand. "I can't believe you're dating someone properly. I can't wait to meet them."

"Oh my God, Sian, what if they find out about last night. What will I do then?"

"Claim cowardice and idiocy, they're not likely to question that, and then beg for forgiveness."

"I thought you were supposed to be my friend," Max grumbled, folding his arms and scowling at her.

"I am, and that's why I'm giving it to you straight." She stole his cigarette from the ashtray and took a final drag before stubbing it out and blowing smoke into the fresh, cool air. "I have to go to work. Message me and let me know how you get on, okay?"

Max leaned back in the chair, stretching his arms out behind him as he watched Sian leave. He could go back to bed, he was tired enough, but he couldn't bring himself to. It felt wrong to lie in bed with anyone other than Rick. He sighed and went indoors to fix another drink.

LATER THAT morning he was in the lounge watching a movie when Zoe and Lisa came downstairs. Everyone else was still in bed. He took a deep breath when he heard them coming. It was now or never, and then maybe he could relax. All this tension was running him ragged. How had his life gotten so complicated?

"Morning," they said in unison and sat on either side of him on the couch.

"Where's Jasmine?"

"She had to go."

"Oh. Good. I need to talk to you both about—"

"Look, Max." Lisa placed her hand on his knee. "Do you mind if we go first? There's something important we need to say to you."

Max scrunched his brow. He supposed he could wait a few moments longer. Besides, he was outnumbered. "Okay, sure. What is it?"

Zoe took his hand in hers. "Max, I know we've had a lot of fun over the past few years, the three of us, but Lisa and I have decided we want something a bit more serious now." Max's jaw dropped. This was the last thing he needed right now. "We wanted our last night with you to be memorable, which is why we invited Jasmine along, but Lisa and I are going to be exclusive from now on."

What the fuck just happened? Max tried to speak, but words failed him.

Zoe mistook his reaction for distress and rubbed his shoulders, apologizing profusely, trying to soothe the blow.

Last night didn't need to have happened. Max felt sick. He could've avoided cheating on Rick. His whole body was trembling, and he took a ragged breath.

"We're going to go now," Zoe said, and Max stared at her through glazed eyes. "I'm sorry; we never meant to hurt you. I hope we can still be friends." Zoe kissed him on the cheek, and they both left.

Max sat on the couch, staring into space, stunned. Sian was right. Fuck. Claiming idiocy was looking like the best plan right now. It was still very early days, so hopefully Rick would be able to forgive him. He didn't dare think about what he'd do if Rick couldn't. It wasn't like he had any choice but to tell him. He'd rather Rick heard it from him than from Pete or Tony.

Messaging Rick, Max told him he needed to see him as soon as possible. He fidgeted as he waited for a reply. He didn't have to wait long.

Is everything okay? I'm teaching all day but I have a break at three. Meet me then?

He took a deep breath, relieved this mess would be sorted out today, one way or another. Relaxing into the couch, he tried to ignore thoughts of how badly this could turn out, but the longer he sat there, the more he panicked. There were still a few hours before he was meeting Rick, and he was exhausted. With his bed now empty, he padded upstairs, stumbled into his room, and fell onto his mattress. Despite how edgy he was feeling, within moments he was fast asleep.

"MAX!" HE jolted awake to the sound of Sian knocking at his door, and he rubbed his eyes.

"What?" he said, grumpy at having been woken.

"I'm coming in." Sian opened his door, which he'd left unlocked. "Are you decent?" Her hand was covering her eyes, and she peeked through her fingers.

"Very funny." He rolled over to face her and pulled the comforter up to his chin. "What do you want?"

"I—"

Max caught sight of his watch on the bedside table. "Fuck!" He leaped out of bed, and Sian shook her head as he pulled some pants onto his naked body.

"What is it?" she asked, bemused.

"I'm meeting someone at three."

Sian snickered. "You've got five minutes."

Grabbing his jacket and motorcycle helmet, Max kissed Sian on the cheek and dashed past.

"Tell them I said hi."

He slid down the banister, sprinted to his motorcycle, and rode as fast as he could.

As he parked outside the dojo, ten minutes late, he saw Rick leaning against the building, waiting for him.

"Sorry," Max said as he removed his helmet.

"That's okay." Rick pushed off the building and sauntered over. "Nice bike."

"Thanks."

"Come on, let's go for a walk." Rick led Max toward the back of the building, and they joined a tree-lined path that ran alongside the stream, heading away from town. "What's so important?" Rick nudged Max's shoulder. "Not that it isn't great to see you."

Oh fuck. This was going to be a disaster. With all the rushing about, he'd not had a chance to plan how he was going to broach this. He waited until a couple of approaching cyclists had passed to give himself a chance to gather his thoughts before speaking.

"How're your classes going today?" he asked, trying to buy a little more time.

"Max." Rick stopped and touched his arm. "Don't tell me you've come all this way to make small talk." He took Max's hand—and Max hoped Rick wouldn't feel how nervous he was—and led him toward a bench, releasing him when another cyclist approached. "What's up?" he asked once the stranger had passed.

"I need to tell you something."

"Okay," Rick said.

"I don't want you to find out from someone else, or to find out later and have it cause problems for us... but I wanted to tell you anyway, didn't want to hide anything from you—"

"I don't see what could be so important as to cause a problem, but go on." Amusement danced in Rick's eyes. Fuck, he was not getting this.

"Right... well... um, anyway... last night. I wasn't expecting it and didn't plan—"

"Max, spit it out. I haven't got long until my next class."

Max cringed and felt queasy as the words left his mouth. "I kind of slept with Zoe, Lisa, and Jasmine last night." He couldn't bear to look at Rick, terrified of his reaction. When Max eventually risked a look, his mouth dropped. "What are you laughing for? It's not funny."

"You can sleep with whoever you want. It's not like we ever said anything about being exclusive."

"Wh-wh-what?" A wave of horror engulfed him, and despite the warm sun beating down, he was cold.

"You know I want you. That's all that matters. Three at once, huh?" He raised his eyebrows.

"You're not mad at me?" He couldn't believe what he was hearing. This was not what he thought he'd signed up for.

"I know your reputation. And I knew you had two girlfriends. Don't worry. Besides, I'm not looking for a serious relationship at the moment. I need to focus on my career. I'm going into this with my eyes wide-open, trust me."

"I wish I was," Max mumbled.

"What's that?"

"Nothing." Max tried to act cool as he organized his thoughts.

"Look. I really like you, you know that, and I want to spend a lot more time with you. But let's take this one step at a time, huh? My career is so up in the air at the moment...." Rick looked at the time on his cell phone. "Come on. We need to start heading back."

Max stood, his head in a daze as they retraced their steps.

"So are we still going to have our date?"

"Um, yeah, sure."

Rick touched his arm, and Max looked at him. "You okay?"

"Yeah, fine."

"After my fight we could come back here, maybe?" He winked at Max. "I've got an idea about how we can spend time together without worrying about being interrupted. The fight should be a good matchup. It's over at Elfinbrook Stadium, so if you meet me here, we can take my motorcycle?"

"Sure."

They stopped by Max's bike, and Rick stroked his cheek. "I wish I could kiss you right now."

Max flinched away and put his helmet on, wondering how many people Rick had kissed since they'd met, and it made him feel sick.

IT WAS Wednesday, and the intense heat of the afternoon sun burned Max's bare skin as he dangled his legs out of his bedroom window. He hummed along to his music and watched the world go by, as he so often did.

He was trying to avoid thinking of anything to do with Rick, but it was near impossible. The thought of Rick with someone else had haunted him for days. He'd never in his wildest dreams thought that Rick would be more promiscuous than him. Max had finally felt the urge to commit to someone, only to find out that it wasn't even an option. How was that for fucked-up?

Shunning Rick's persistent texts was proving more and more difficult as the week went on, but Max didn't know if he could do this Rick's way, and didn't want to see him until he had this figured out.

The bitch of it all was that the thought of sharing Rick was heart-wrenching, but the thought of not being with him was excruciating. It'd only been a few days since he'd seen Rick, and he was already missing him like crazy.

The gentle rumbling of a motorcycle slowing jolted him from his thoughts. He opened his eyes to see it pulling into the driveway and watched with vague interest as it parked. He didn't recognize it. It must be one of Tony's friends. He was about to close his eyes when the rider looked up at him and took a cell from their pocket, waving it as if to get his attention. Max jumped as his cell began to ring.

CHAPTER EIGHT

Rick

"Aren't you going to answer your cell?" Rick called up to Max's window and then removed his helmet. "I've been trying to reach you for days. If I didn't know better, I'd think you were avoiding me." He tilted his head and held Max's stare. "Fancy a bike ride?"

Max looked away and smoothed his fingers through his hair.

"I think we need to talk, don't you?"

Max swung his legs around and disappeared inside, and Rick was relieved when Max finally emerged from the front door, dressed in his leathers.

"Did you bring water?" Max asked as he pulled on his helmet, which was black with a grinning silver skull painted on the back.

"Yeah, I've got some here." Rick patted the saddlebag of his dad's customized Harley and wished Max was pleased to see him.

Max's black Yamaha had matching skulls on the fairing that gleamed in the sunlight as he fired up the engine. He revved it a few times, and Rick barely heard him above the noise. "Where are we going?"

"Someplace we can talk away from prying eyes. Marigold Lake."

Rick was nervous as he backed the Harley off the driveway. Max seemed distant... too distant. He took a deep breath and slowly pulled away, checking over his shoulder to make sure Max was actually following him. He was. And the sight of him didn't help Rick's nerves one bit. He'd always believed there was nothing sexier than a guy on a powerful motorcycle—but Max took it to a whole other level.

If he'd blown his chance with Max, it'd be a long time before he stopped kicking himself for being so stupid.

He'd surprised himself with his reaction to Max's confession—he'd been relieved, and then he'd panicked. He knew he should've told Max about Angelo there and then.

By the time his brain had caught up with his mouth, it'd been too late.

Rick's thoughts were in loops as they rode along the dusty desert roads. He always came out here when he needed to clear his head, the combination of riding a powerful bike and then the peacefulness of being out in nature worked every time. He hoped it had the same effect on Max so they could have an honest discussion about what was going on between them.

By the time the rocky desert landscape began to change, becoming greener as they drew closer to Marigold Lake, he still wasn't sure exactly what he was going to say to Max. He hoped he could avoid making things worse.

They pulled into the empty gravel parking lot and left their bikes in the shade of the trees, then walked along the overgrown grassy track that led to the lake. The scent of the towering pine trees perfumed the breeze and guided them along the steep path. Despite the cooler temperature up here compared to town, it was still hotter than he'd been used to back in Leatherton. Rick handed Max a bottle of water, taking a sip from his own, and they walked in silence.

The lake was a deep, dark blue today, with a hint of glistening yellow-green at the far edge where the lake was shallow and the sun strongest. As they reached the bank of the lake, Rick knew he was going to have to be the one to get things started. After walking to a secluded spot by some trees, he reached for Max's hand, sat on the grass, and pulled Max down to sit next to him.

Rick exhaled. "You want to tell me what's going on in that head of yours?"

Max shrugged and gazed across the lake, clutching his knees to his chest. "Not really."

"You're pissed at me. That's why you've been avoiding me?"

Max glanced at him. "Not pissed… just… I dunno."

"What?"

He didn't answer.

"If you don't talk to me, we can't sort this out. Do you *want* us to sort this out?" Rick held his breath as he waited for Max to answer. He knew he was taking a gamble, but surely Max wouldn't have come all the way out here if there wasn't some hope.

"I guess I needed time. It's been pretty intense." Max finally looked him in the eyes, and Rick's stomach flip-flopped as Max's expression softened a little.

"Yeah. It has."

"Urgh, I dunno what I'm thinking right now." Max huffed and rested his head in his hands. "It's all so messed up."

"Messed up?"

"It was never this hard when I slept with girls. And we're not even sleeping together yet."

"Yet?" Rick couldn't help but smile.

"Tell me, Rick, would it really affect your career so much? Being with me? How demanding do you think I am? Seriously? 'Cause I'll tell you now, I know it's still very early days for us here, but I don't want us to be able to sleep with other people."

"But you sleep around all the time. It's all over the internet. Are you telling me that you suddenly don't want that?"

Max pulled a handful of grass and opened his hand, letting the strands catch in the breeze. "You shouldn't believe everything you think you've seen."

"What are you talking about?"

Max sighed. "Let's just say I've become pretty good at this over the years."

"At what exactly?"

"Making people believe what I want them to about me." He picked up a rock, examined it, and threw it toward the lake. "You don't have to have sex with someone if you've passed out drunk. Luckily for me, most people aren't as honest as they claim. I've lost count of the number of pictures girls have put on social media where I'm in their bed and naked, but nothing happened."

Rick's jaw dropped. "Are you serious?" Had he really read Max that wrong? His palms were damp, and he wiped them on the grass.

"I had to make it look like I was sleeping around to keep Tony off my back. I guess he thinks that's how normal people live their lives, because that's what he likes to do."

Rick tried to ignore the heavy feeling in the pit of his stomach. After his talk with Tony, he knew Tony was doing his best to look out for Max and take care of him. If only Tony realized how much damage he was doing to Max in the process. "That's why you drink so much?"

Max squeezed his eyes shut and nodded. "It makes it easier."

He needed to convince Tony and Max to talk to each other. Properly. "Max—"

"I told you. I don't want an open relationship. I never have." He stared at Rick. "I even broke up with Lisa and Zoe. There's no one else now. Do you agree with Tony? Is that what's going on? Or is it that you're doing this because you feel sorry for me and are planning to finish things as soon as I'm not a shiny new challenge anymore?" His eyes were pleading. "Be honest with me, please. I'd rather know the truth. I'm fed up with all this pretending."

Rick sucked in a breath. There was no way he could keep the truth from Max after what he'd said. It was confession time. "Like I said, I wanted an open relationship… partly because it makes it easier to focus on my career, as I'm not sure what my next step will be, but also because I messed up too."

Max's jaw dropped. "What?"

"You hadn't called me. I thought you were blowing me off. I didn't realize—"

"Angelo." Max jumped to his feet, breathing heavily as he paced back and forth toward the muddy banks of the lake.

"How did you—"

"I'm not blind, Rick." Max spat out the words, but then his shoulders sagged. "How could I be so fucking stupid?"

Rick's mouth was suddenly as dry as the desert road. "I didn't want you risking everything for me if you weren't completely sure. How was I supposed to know you were going to change your mind?" Rick closed the distance between them and tucked a strand of hair behind Max's ear like he'd done before, his fingers lingering. "You're the one I want, not him. Look, we've not been on a proper date yet, so perhaps we could start fresh from here? Forget how we both messed up."

"Can you promise me it'll be just us from now on? Nobody else?"

"Yeah, just us." Rick kissed Max tentatively on the lips. If this was what he had to do to have a chance with Max, he'd do it. Thoughts of London and Neil's gym flashed into his mind, and he shoved them back down. He'd figure out a way to deal with that later—besides, Neil might not even offer him a position. And then there was the matter of Max being firmly in the closet. He couldn't help feeling that his life was about to get all kinds of complicated, but the thought of giving up this chance with Max was unbearable. "You do realize what that means, though?"

"That we're gonna have loads of hot sex?" Max grinned at him, and Rick laughed, pulling him closer.

"That too, I hope."

"Then what?"

"You're gonna have to tell Tony and your friends about us." Max went rigid in his arms. "You can't hide who you are forever… remember? Especially if we're gonna be exclusive."

He took Max's hand and laced their fingers together, relieved when Max eventually squeezed his hand and said, "Let's see how things go for a while, see how hot that sex is first."

Rick ignored Max's attempt to distract him. "Your friends will guess."

"No, they won't. If they guess, I'm denying everything, I told you that already. If they find out, it'll be by me telling them in my own time. When I'm ready."

"I hope you realize how hard that's gonna be… hiding it from them." He wished he could tell Max that Tony already knew, but it wasn't his place to say. Tony needed to tell him himself… and soon.

RICK HUMMED along to a country song playing on the radio as he packed up the MMA equipment they'd need for the competition. He wasn't sure what he was more nervous about: finally going on a date with Max or fighting a guy fifty pounds heavier than his current weight. That was the problem with fighting in the heavyweight division, there was a high upper weight limit, and usually the bigger the other guy was, the more it hurt when you got caught with a punch. Rick was only just classed as a heavyweight at two hundred and ten pounds, and his opponent tonight was two hundred and sixty pounds.

He kneeled and scanned the duffel bags in front of him on the dojo floor. There were four of them fighting tonight, and that meant taking a hell of a lot of kit with them. Art had offered to take the equipment in his car and drop the bags back afterward so Rick could take his motorcycle. He had such a great surprise for Max after the fight and was looking forward to making their date as special as possible.

"Art, can you grab another set of focus pads?"

"Another set? Are we leaving anything behind?" Art grabbed them from the cabinet and hurled them in Rick's general direction.

Deftly catching them, he said, "Makes sense for us all to warm up at the same time. There's not much gap between our fights."

"Oh yeah, I forgot."

It was Art's first proper competition, and he didn't seem nervous at all. Rick wasn't sure if that was a good or a bad thing. He hoped Art was taking it seriously. You never knew who was watching at these fights.

"What?" Art said and frowned.

Rick shook his head, realizing he'd been staring. "Nothing. Just making sure we've got everything. Did you pack the nail glue?"

Art laughed. "What in God's name do we need nail glue for?"

"You'd better hope you don't need to find out." Rick stood and stretched. "I'll go get some. Can you check we've got enough water?"

"Sure."

Rick made his way into the office and rummaged in one of the filing cabinet drawers. He really ought to get around to sorting all this out. His mouthguard was tucked into one of the filing slings; that was close—he wouldn't have been able to fight if he'd forgotten it. Rick fished it out, leaned back to throw it onto his desk, and nearly had a coronary. Max was standing on the other side of the desk, watching him.

"Jesus! You scared me half to death. How did you get there so quietly?"

"You know, that's the first time I've heard you nearly swear," Max said and grinned. "So do I pass ninja level one?"

"What?" Rick's heart was still pounding, and he turned to properly face Max.

"Ninja level one. You know, like stealth? Isn't that a ninja thing? Do you know nothing about ninja-shit grading levels?" Max looked thoughtful. "Are you gonna be okay fighting tonight? Should I be worried? Do you want me to fight for you instead? I've been practicing real hard after my lesson the other day."

The thought of Max stepping into the ring and fighting was ludicrous. His opponent tonight was probably double Max's weight. "Stealth's not gonna help you much when you're in the octagon. What kind of weird grading system is that, anyway?" Max opened his mouth, but Rick cut in before he could speak. "I'll be fine. Get in the dojo and help us pack up the kit, will you?"

"You're not taking those smelly gloves, are you?" Max wrinkled his nose and headed for the dojo door. "I'm not touching those again."

"No, we're not. And quit calling it 'ninja shit' while we're around the others."

"You're no fun."

Rick leaned forward and whispered in Max's ear as they reached the door. "I guess I'd better change what I had planned for later, then."

Max shivered and then glanced over his shoulder. "Fine by me."

"You don't even know what I planned."

"Did it involve you fucking me?" Max whispered, and Rick's breath caught.

"Are you serious?"

Laughing, Max opened the door and said, "See? No fun."

Rick watched in disbelief as Max walked over to Art. Was he messing with him? He had to be… didn't he? Rick sighed and shook his head. It was going to be near impossible to concentrate on his fight now.

"Rick," Max shouted across the hall, "what the hell is this for?" He held up a metal block and waved it in the air.

"It's called an enswell. It's an eye iron. You use it to help delay bruising during a fight," he said and made his way toward them.

"This ninja shit is weird. I was right."

Rick glared at him, but Max laughed as he threw the enswell back into the bag.

"Ninja shit," Art said. "I like it. Are you going to help in the corner tonight?"

"No, he's not," Rick said.

"Na." Max sat down next to the bag, picking up random items and throwing them back in. "I'm here for cheerleading or something."

"Don't you dare."

Max winked at him. "Maybe not. I'm sure I'll find *something fun* to keep me amused tonight."

Rick's cheeks heated, but luckily Art wasn't looking in his direction. "We should finish packing up. We don't want to be late."

THEY ARRIVED at Elfinbrook Stadium at six o'clock, two hours before the first scheduled fight. That would give them enough time to get checked in, weighed, and warmed up. Rafael, one of Rick's black belts, would be fighting first, and Rick was a little worried for him, as his opponent was a seasoned fighter with a ton of experience. As featherweights, they were lightning quick, and Rick had been working with Rafael on increasing his speed—he just hoped all their preparations would be enough for a victory.

Rick waited for Max to climb off the back of his motorcycle before dismounting. It had been nice to have Max riding with him, holding on tight around his waist, and he was excited about spending time alone with him later. Max had told his friends he was meeting up with some girl so they wouldn't start asking awkward questions. Rick wasn't sure how he felt about that, but it did mean they got the whole night to themselves, so he wasn't about to make a fuss. Right now he had a job to do and needed to focus. Art pulled up next to them in the parking lot. William and Rafael were meeting them there and were waiting by the doors to the stadium.

"Hey!" William shouted as they approached. He looked relaxed and was holding a large bottle of water that was half-empty; that was a good sign. It meant he'd been keeping hydrated and wasn't burning out on nervous tension before he even got in the octagon.

"How are you feeling?" Rick asked.

"Really good. Rafael and me went for a run. Thought we'd start warming up."

"Great stuff."

Art opened the trunk and began unloading the bags, and Rick picked up the two heaviest. "Let's take these inside. Get signed in."

He led the way into the building. They would be fighting in the hall. It was a pretty decent venue compared to some of the dives he'd fought in over the years. Being in a sports club meant that the fighters had access to the gym and changing rooms, unlike some places where you were shoved into a room, all the fighters together—including your opponent—and had to get on with it and make the best of the situation.

"Welcome, guys," the man on the sign-in desk said. "Can I take the name of your club?"

"Bernstein's School of Martial Arts," Rick said and dropped the bags to the ground.

The guy looked down his list and made some marks on the paper. "There's four of you fighting. That right?"

"Yeah, that's right."

"Rick Bernstein, Art Garcia, William Johnson, and Rafael Miller." Rick nodded. "Okay. Great. Rick, can you step on the scales, please?" He indicated to the left of the desk, and Rick did as asked. "That's great. You can get off now." The man wrote down his weight. "Art, you next, please."

Art was one hundred and eighty-seven pounds. Two pounds over the maximum for the middleweight division. Rick was going to have to talk to him about how to make weight, give him some more specific instructions. Two pounds should be okay; once he'd removed his sneakers and pants he'd make weight. Art looked horrified when the sign-in desk guy asked him to strip and get back on the scales.

Trying not to laugh, Rick said, "Leave your underwear on." For now, that was. If he still didn't make weight, they would make Art get on the scales totally naked. Art undressed in front of them decidedly uncomfortably.

"Okay, you're good to go," the guy said, and the tension left Art's face immediately.

"Shit, that was close," Art said and laughed.

While the others were getting weighed, Rick took him to one side. "That's actually good you were in danger of being over. The closer you can be to the maximum weight, the better. It's definitely not good to be over, though. Your opponent can refuse to fight you, or the other option is that you forfeit some of your fighter's purse."

Max whistled. "Jeez, that's pretty serious."

"That's nothing," Rick said. "If you come in overweight for a title shot, then even if you win, your opponent keeps the belt."

"I'll be more careful next time," Art said. "Sorry, Sensei."

"Don't worry about it. It happens a lot. I've got some tricks I can show you for next time that won't weaken your body for the fight." Rick patted him on the shoulder.

"I need you to sign this form, and then you are good to go," the check-in guy said to Rick. "They've opened up the football field to use for warmups if you like. Your fight times are on this card." He handed it to Rick. "Somebody will come find you when it's time."

"Thanks," Rick said.

"The changing rooms are through that door there." He pointed straight ahead. "You guys have a good night."

"This is exciting," Max said, bouncing along next to them. "It's kinda like being backstage at a gig, only with way more rules."

Rick laughed. "Is that so?"

"Yeah. Lee used to deal with all the serious stuff, like money and things. I guess Tony will be doing that now. How long until your first fight?"

Rafael said, "Am I still up first?"

Rick glanced at the card as he held the door open for them. "Yeah, you are. Ten past eight."

"Will all three of you be in my corner?"

"It'll be me and William." Rick frowned at the card. The fight order had been moved around without anyone telling him. "Hold on. Art's fighting right after you."

"What about my warmup?" Art said. "Does that mean I'll be on my own before my fight? That doesn't sound right."

Art was right. That wouldn't give them much time. And it certainly wasn't ideal leaving him on his own before his first fight. But there was nothing he could do about it. Rick needed a second person with him ringside. Tending to any wounds Rafael might get, keeping him cool and hydrated, and giving him instructions for the next round of the fight would be too much for one person in the short amount of time they were given. It wouldn't be fair on Rafael if Rick tried to do all that on his own.

"I can stay with Art. It'll be okay," Max said, and Rick gaped at him.

"But you've never even been to a fight before. You won't—"

"Maybe not, but I know what it's like to have to get out there and perform for hundreds of people, and what it takes to prepare for that."

Rick had never considered that what Max did for a living had any overlap with fighting, but when he thought about it, Max definitely had a point. Maybe he could do this—

"Just give me instructions on what you need me to do." Max grabbed his arm and stared at him. He was serious, and somehow Rick had every faith that Max would have his back with this. That he would have Art's back too.

"You sure about this?"

Max nodded and Rick smiled.

"Thanks. I owe you one."

"You don't owe me anything." Max winked at him. "Consider it payback for helping me out with the bass situation."

They found a spot in the changing rooms, which were already pretty full. The organizers of this event had sensibly separated opponents between the two changing rooms so there was less chance of fights kicking off before the event. Mostly Rick found that fighters respected one another and stayed out of the way of their opponents before their fights, but occasionally he'd seen fighters playing mind games and trying to unsettle their opponent to gain the advantage later.

"Are we going to run around the football field?" Art asked. He looked a little too excited by the prospect, but then he was a massive football fan.

"Yeah, let's do it. Max, do you want to come with us?"

Max narrowed his gaze. "How fast will you be going?"

"It's just a jog. Don't worry, it won't be a warmup like in class," Rick said. "To start with, anyway."

"I'll come and watch."

On their way to the field, Rick said hi to the other trainers and fighters he knew. It was usually the same clubs attending these events, but they changed up the fighters they brought pretty regularly. There were a few fighters Rick knew well, and who he knew were trying to make it big and took it very seriously. It was tempting to try to lure them to his club and have them as part of his stable, but he was struggling to compete with even these smaller clubs in terms of equipment and funding.

After the warmup, Rick took his fighters through some stretches and made sure they drank plenty of water. Max was starting to look bored. He was kicking at the grass at the edge of the field.

"Hey, Max." Rick beckoned him closer.

"What's up?"

"I reserved you a seat ringside for when we're fighting. Shall we go take a look so you can see where you'll be? It'll be pretty packed in there when you go out after Rafael's fight."

"Sure."

Rick left William in charge and told them they'd meet back in the changing room in a minute. As they headed inside, Rick said, "What do you think so far?"

"Honestly? It's just like a gig, only with loads of hot guys running around half-naked." Max grinned at him, and Rick gave him a gentle shove.

"Mm, I guess I should've thought harder about my choice of first date. Taken you somewhere with less competition."

A fighter ran by. Sure enough, he was bare-chested and wearing the standard tight fighting shorts, and Max made a point of staring as he passed them. He was still smirking, though.

"You're gonna tease me about this all night, aren't you."

"You have nothing to worry about, Rick. You know that." Max glanced up at him.

God, he looked sexy. "I wish it was time to leave already."

Suddenly, Max was serious. "No. You need to focus. This is important to you, right?" Rick nodded. "Then pretend I'm not here as your date. There's plenty of time for us to be on our own later, okay?"

"Now I'm thinking about later. I wish I could kiss you right now."

Max raised an eyebrow and looked pointedly at a group of fighters a few yards away.

There was no way they would have heard him. Rick sighed and wished Max wasn't so far back in the closet.

"Tell me what I need to do with Art while you're not there," Max said.

RAFAEL WAS fighting well. He'd improved a lot since his last professional fight, and that had all been down to Rick's instruction. Rick watched him from the sidelines as Rafael darted closer to his opponent with a flurry of punches and then quickly got out of there again. When Rafael had first come to him from another club, Rick found he had picked up the bad habit of moving within reach of his opponent before starting his attack. The problem with that was that it meant he was also in range of his opponent's fists. That bad habit had totally gone, and Rafael was now looking strong.

The horn sounded, and Rick grabbed the small stool. He and William dashed into the octagon and began their work. William handed Rafael some water, got the enswell on a potential bruise at the corner of his left eye, and did his best to try to cool him down. Rafael had a split above his right eyebrow, to which Rick applied Adrenalin Chloride 1:1000—to constrict the blood vessels—before packing the cut with Vaseline to help any incoming punches slide off it so they didn't split the wound open farther. While Rick was working, he shouted instructions for the next round.

"Your footwork is looking good. Keep on with the short, solid attacks, and then take him to the ground. He's starting to look tired, so look for the submission as soon as you get the opportunity. Try for the rear naked choke we've been practicing."

The horn sounded and Rafael leaped to his feet, shoving his mouthguard back in, and Rick and William hurried out of the octagon.

"He's doing well," William said. "I think he might have him in this round."

"Yeah. Let's hope so. It's a nasty split above his eye. The sooner he gets to the ground the better. All the time they're exchanging punches, he's gonna keep aiming for that split." Rick grimaced.

After some heart-stopping moments in which he nearly got himself knocked out, Rafael finally got his opponent to the ground and the odds turned in his favor. His opponent's ground game wasn't strong, and Rafael got the choke and a tapout just before the horn.

"Yes!" Rick punched the air and hugged William.

"Think you can get a tapout quicker than Rafael?"

"Is that a challenge?"

"Sure is."

"Okay, you're on." They shook on it as they entered the octagon to clean Rafael up a bit and celebrate. "Loser has to do burpees throughout the entire warmup next class."

William grinned. "Game on."

IT WAS a swift changeover when they got out back. Art looked really focused, but fired up and ready at the same time. Max had done an astounding job with him. Rick threw an energy drink and protein bar at Rafael and grabbed his sweats for him to put on over his kit. It wasn't an ideal situation by far. They only had a couple of minutes before they were back out there again. Max helped Rafael get himself sorted while Rick slipped on the focus pads and did a super-quick warmup with Art. Next time he was gonna have to bring more students with him. There were a couple who were nearly ready to give it a try.

"Art Garcia, we're ready for you."

"Okay, let's go," Rick said to William and Rafael. "You ready?" They both nodded. "Thanks for your help, Max. Do you want to go watch out front now? I'll come find you after my fight," Rick shouted over his shoulder. Max gave him a thumbs-up.

FINALLY, IT was his turn to fight. Rick felt a mixture of nervous excitement and overwhelming confidence as William held the pads for him as he warmed up.

It was time to go. Rick made his way to the hall entrance. It looked dark after the bright light of the changing room, but his eyes soon adjusted, and he took several deep breaths as he waited for his walkout music to begin. At the first beats of the dance track, the flashing lights came to rest on Rick, and he jogged out onto the walkway between the barriers that held back the fight fans, waving, and slapping any outstretched hands. The fast beats of the dance track always energized him, and it was like a switch was flipped inside him whenever he heard it: it was time to fight. He was 100 percent focused.

He was checked at ringside by the officials, and then he made his way into the octagon. With the more impressive fight record, Rick had been given the option whether he wanted to be first or second to walk out to the octagon, and he had chosen to come out second. It gave him the advantage of making his opponent wait, and it also meant there was less time for Rick to overthink the fight and become nervous. The mind games were almost as important as the fight itself.

Their fight was announced, and then the referee brought them both into the middle and reminded them of the rules. Rick and Chad, his opponent, touched gloves and backed off, waiting for the horn to signal the start of their fight.

Rick had a game plan, and it went perfectly at the start. His biggest weapon was the fact that he could switch stance and fight just as strongly both orthodox and southpaw. If his opponent hadn't done his homework, then it was guaranteed to catch them out. Rick stuck to the orthodox stance for now, with his left foot forward, and traded Thai kicks to Chad's shins. It was then that Rick noticed Chad was copying his actions. Rick would kick and then Chad would do likewise. If Rick kicked a little higher, Chad's next kick was also higher. He loved it when he came across a fighter like this. He'd seen it all too frequently, and it made it so easy to set them up for a knockout.

Moving in closer, Rick went for a combination of jab, cross, hook to the head, and then quickly darted out of range, his fist by his jaw to protect himself. Sure enough, Chad retaliated with a jab, cross, and hook—all of which Rick easily blocked. What he didn't expect, however, was Chad's kick that followed: a spinning hook to his right temple that dragged across his eye. What the hell? Rule one of fighting: you never kick high on a fresh opponent. Rick fell to the canvas, his fists covering his face, but it was too late. The damage had been done. He scrambled to get to his feet before he got counted out, hanging onto the octagon netting while he waited for his vision to stabilize. The ref finished counting and peered at him. Rick knew he was checking if he was okay to continue, so he put on his best smile and hoped he didn't look as dazed as he felt.

"Okay?" the ref asked.

"Yeah." Rick nodded, and the ref signaled for them to continue fighting. Chad was holding out his hand, and Rick touched gloves with him before they circled each other again, each of them looking for the perfect opening. There was no way Rick was going to let him get the upper hand again. He couldn't believe he had been so complacent. He was always telling his students to never underestimate their opponent, and he had gone and done just that.

Settling back into the fight, Rick set up a series of punches, which Chad again copied, but this time Rick then switched to southpaw stance, using his speed and the element of surprise to go in for the kill.

CHAPTER NINE

Max

WATCHING RICK in the octagon was the single most terrifying thing Max had ever had the misfortune to witness. Each time Rick's opponent caught him with a heavy punch, it made Max wince and wonder how Rick didn't seem to even register the pain.

It was the kick that caught Rick across the face and knocked him to the canvas that had Max leaping onto his seat, trying to get a closer look to make sure Rick was okay. He watched through his fingers after that… with his eyes closed. Somehow, Rick had managed to get up and went on to win the fight, and Max had never been so relieved.

Max realized that one, MMA was brutal and he was glad he hadn't agreed to take it up properly; two, Rick was as tough as they came and very well-known in the ninja scene—he was totally in his element here; and three, watching someone he knew putting themselves in a position where they could get seriously hurt was something he never ever wanted to experience again. He'd even found it hard watching Art and William fight, who he barely knew. Oh, and four, he apparently cared about Rick more than he'd realized. It was absolute torture watching some guy kick the shit out of him. Fuck, he needed a drink after that.

"What did you think?" Rick asked as he slid into the seat next to him. He'd showered and smelled so good, and Max tried not to let it distract him from how upset he was. "Pretty awesome, huh?"

"Awesome? You're going to have some dude's footprint on your fucking cheek tomorrow."

Rick laughed. The guy was batshit crazy. Max had thought he was worried for Rick before the fight. He hadn't even been able to stomach any dinner, but that was nothing compared to how worried he was going to be in the future when he knew Rick had a fight.

"He caught me across my eye, not my cheek, and it was my own fault. I should've seen that spinning hook coming."

Max shook his head. "You're crazy. You're officially crazier than I am. That's gotta fucking hurt."

"Yeah, not until tomorrow, though. Adrenaline's still working. You ready to get out of here?"

Thank fuck for that. "Yeah, let's get the hell out of this place." The arena was filled with tough fighter types, and Max was very aware of how out of place he looked and the funny stares he was getting. It wasn't much fun being out there on his own, and he'd already witnessed a couple of fights starting out in the crowd. Thankfully security dealt with them fast before they got even more out of hand.

Max climbed on the back of Rick's lime-green-and-black Kawasaki and held on tight, grateful Rick had come away from the fight mostly unscathed. A few minutes later, Rick pulled up in the dojo parking lot. "Art will be here any minute with the gear," Rick said as they climbed off his bike. "Listen. How would you feel about staying here tonight?"

Max removed his helmet and took out a packet of cigarettes from his pocket. "Here? Like at the dojo?"

"Yeah. I got a mattress and some other bits so we'd be comfortable. We wouldn't have to worry about anyone disturbing us. My parents have the only other key, but I can bolt the door from the inside."

"You're serious?" Max shook his head with a smile and lit a cigarette. "We can stay here?"

Rick pulled Max into the shadows and rested his hands on Max's waist. Turning his head, Max blew smoke to the side so it didn't go into Rick's face. "Well, we're not supposed to," Rick said. "But yeah, we can stay here. If anyone sees you leaving, just say that I was giving you a private MMA lesson."

"What if someone sees my motorcycle here overnight? Pete lives opposite, he's bound to notice."

"Mm, good point. I've got a tarp you can borrow for tonight."

"That works for me," Max said and took a step away as Art pulled up in his car.

"Hey," Art said. He had a shocking purple bruise on his cheek, and his nose was held in place with tape. That was definitely going to hurt tomorrow. Despite the state of him, he had won his fight.

"We're sorting out your guard next class," Rick said.

"I think I've learned my lesson, Sensei," Art said and jumped out of the car.

"Seriously, though, you did really well tonight. You can be proud of yourself. Do you two want to bring the bags into the office and I'll sort them out?"

"Sure," Max said and gave Art a hand.

After they waved Art goodbye, Max slid inside and shut the door.

"Here," Rick said and handed him the tarp for his bike.

"Thanks. Saves us dropping my bike at mine tonight and coming back here after."

When Max came inside after covering his bike, he locked and bolted the door. Rick had stowed the equipment away and was waiting for him by the door to the hall.

Max's nerves ratcheted up as their eyes locked. They were finally alone.

Rick must have reached for him at the exact same moment, and their lips met in a desperate kiss. Max pressed his body as close to Rick as he could, digging his fingers into Rick's hips and pulling him even closer, but still it wasn't enough to relieve the pressure in his aching cock. Something sharp dug into Max's back, and he realized Rick had him over his desk. Were they really going to do it right here? His first time with a guy was going to be on a desk. Nervous laughter bubbled inside him, and he forced it down.

"Comfortable?" Rick's lips were right by his ear, his teeth grazing the delicate nerves and sending shivers down Max's neck.

"Fuck." Max reached for his balls and pulled down hard, breathing heavily. He couldn't remember ever being this turned on. Squeezing his eyes shut for a second, he tried to focus on something other than the overwhelming desire that threatened to end this far too soon.

Rick ground against him, a slight smile on his lips. He knew exactly what he was doing. What effect he was having on him. "Shall we move this into the hall?" He kissed Max's neck beneath his earlobe and worked his way to the crook between Max's neck and shoulder, where he bit down.

Max groaned and leaned into him. "Jesus, Rick." Max thrust against him. Hard. And the friction against his solid cock both eased the tension and made him want Rick even more. "I'm not gonna make it into the hall if you keep on like this."

Grabbing Max's hand, which was damp from nerves, Rick pulled him up off the desk and dragged him into the hall. By the far wall was a mattress, complete with comforter and pillows, and there was even a lamp to the left of it, casting a gentle glow around the room. It was perfect.

Rick let go of Max's hand and lifted his T-shirt over his head, then threw it to the floor, and Max followed suit and removed his. His heart was pounding. What if he got this wrong? What if he was no good at this and didn't satisfy Rick? His hands were trembling as he wiped them on his pants.

Rick reached for Max's hand again and pulled him down on top of him on the mattress. "Relax. It's okay," he whispered. His tongue traced the shell of Max's ear and sent all coherent thought away in an instant as Max leaned into his touch. "Tell me what you want."

"I'll take whatever you want to give me." Max wrapped his arms around Rick. He never wanted this to end. Wanted to experience everything. For Rick to show him what he'd been missing out on all this time.

Rolling them so he was on top, Rick ground his hips, grazing Max's cock with each revolution. It was sweet torture. Rick was as hard as he was. It had to be agonizing for him too. Rick kissed him, deep and slow. "If you want me to stop at any point, just say the word. Okay?"

"Uh-huh." Max let his head fall back against the pillow and closed his eyes to take in the sensation of Rick's lips on his collarbone, his chest, his nipples. Max gasped as Rick sucked on one and then the other, his tongue flicking them before moving down to his abdomen, his hips…. *Oh fuck.*

Rick's fingers were on the button of his pants, and Max bucked, trying to get him to hurry the fuck up. Soon he would be inside Rick's mouth. The thought of it alone nearly made him come. Luckily, Rick seemed to be in as much of a hurry as he was. Max opened his eyes and tilted his head to watch Rick undo his zipper. Then Max lifted his hips so Rick could pull his pants down. He removed them completely and threw them to the side.

Kneeling up, Rick was watching him with hooded eyes as he undid his own zip and pulled out the thickest cock Max had ever seen. His breathing quickened and his cock jolted at the sight.

"This okay?" Rick said. "Do you want me to stop?"

"Hell no. But if you were gonna fuck me, I might need a minute to prepare."

Rick laughed. "Actually I was going to suck you. If that's okay?"

That was more than okay. He couldn't wait for Rick's warm, wet mouth to bring him off. The thought of it had him trembling. To calm himself, Max pressed their bodies together, aligned their cocks, and took them both in his hand as Rick kissed him and rocked into his grip.

"Or we could just do this?" Rick said, thrusting harder and kissing him deeper.

It felt better than he'd ever imagined it could. A total sensory overload. It was tempting to let go and come together like this, but more than anything he wanted Rick's talented mouth around his cock. Rick placed his hand over Max's, and the pressure on them both increased.

"Fuck." He wasn't going to have any choice if Rick kept doing that.

Rick released his grip slightly and moaned. His cock jerked in Max's hand. "That feels so good, but we need some lube. Don't move." Rick let go and reached to the side of the mattress.

The loss of pressure on his cock was unbearable, so Max pumped himself a couple of times, taking in the sight of Rick's muscular torso and imagining what he would look like as he came. Sexy as fuck. Max jerked himself faster.

"You look so hot like that," Rick said, watching him for a moment, then pumping lube into his hand and warming it slightly before applying it to his cock with long, slow movements. He shoved down his jeans and kicked them off the mattress. He started to lean down.

"Wait," Max said. "Let me watch you."

Now naked, Rick rested back on his heels. "What, like this?" he asked.

"Don't you want to touch yourself?"

"Like this?" Rick gripped his cock, sliding his hand back and forth slowly.

Max jerked himself faster, his breathing ragged. That was the hottest thing he'd ever seen. It turned him on all the more, knowing that all of that was just for him.

"God, that lube feels good," Rick said and groaned, his fingers flying over his cock.

"Get over here," Max growled, then whimpered as Rick took them both in his strong hand.

The glide of the lube made it more intense. Rick's rigid cock sliding against his as he rode the brink of orgasm was too much, and he thrust into his hand one final time, grabbing Rick's shoulders and crying out as he came hard over Rick's hand and cock. His body was trembling from his release when Rick suddenly gripped him tighter and yelled, his muscles tensing and eyes clenching shut as he coated Max's chest with thick white ribbons.

Rick kissed him and then rolled next to him. Both of them were breathing heavily.

Max had never felt so content and satiated… so lucky. To have found Rick and been able to experience this. He rested his hand on his forehead and smiled as he replayed the image of Rick coming. That was something burned to memory for life.

Rick was the first to catch his breath, and he leaned up on his elbow and stared down at Max, grinning.

"Sorry I didn't get to blow you, but you're just too damn hot."

"Hey, don't blame me." Max grinned back. "You'd better follow through next time, though."

"Mm. And when is that likely to be, do you reckon?" Rick kissed him. Gently this time.

"Whenever you like." Max reached across for Rick's hand and placed it on his softening cock.

"Maybe we should get cleaned up first," Rick said, wiping his hand across Max's chest.

"Hey!"

"You're covered in it. A bit more isn't going to make much difference." Rick smirked. "Come on." He pulled Max to his feet.

"Where are we going?" Max let himself be led across the cool hall floor.

"To the showers."

"Are you going to blow me in there?"

"If you're lucky."

Max laughed.

THE NEXT morning Max opened his eyes, and it took him a second to remember where he was. He smiled at the memory of the night before and rolled over to look at Rick. He was still sleeping.

Snuggling deeper under the comforter, Max took a moment to study Rick. The bruise over his eye had turned a nasty shade of purple, his typically immaculate hair was scruffy against the pale blue pillow, and blond stubble a shade darker than his hair was beginning to show through. Max reached out to stroke Rick's jaw, and he stirred at the touch.

"Morning," Max said.

"Morning." Rick smiled at him.

"How are you feeling?"

"Like I've been hit by a truck."

"What?"

Rick laughed. "Don't worry. That's normal the day after a fight. I got up earlier and took some painkillers, so it's not too bad at the moment. It's the second day that's usually the worst."

"You've been awake already?"

"Yeah. I don't normally sleep this late, but we didn't go to sleep until after two, was it?"

"Yeah." It had been an early night for him. And it was kind of a novelty to be waking up without a hangover. His greatest fear had been that he wouldn't be good enough at this to satisfy Rick, but he'd made Rick come three times last night, and each time he'd gained a little confidence—in some things at least. He'd feel more relaxed once he'd tried everything. He wasn't used to being out of his depth when it came to sex, and it was unsettling.

"Any regrets?" Rick asked.

"About?"

"Last night."

Max grinned. "No. You?"

"Definitely not."

"Good."

"How are you feeling?"

Max grabbed Rick's hand under the comforter and placed it on his morning wood.

"Mm, I was hoping you were going to say that." Rick shuffled closer until their bodies were touching. Max kissed him, chaste at first, but then deepening it as they thrust together, his need growing.

"Actually," Max said. "I do have one regret about last night."

"What's that?" Rick pulled back, looking alarmed.

It was reassuring to know Max wasn't the only one who wanted to make sure this went well. "That I didn't get to taste you."

"I'm sure we can fix that right now." Rick kissed him and waggled his eyebrows. "How do you want me?"

Max sat up, his back slumped against the wall, and pulled Rick up onto his knees so he was straddling him.

"How does this work for you?"

Rick reached for the wall behind them, placing one hand on it and the other on his straining cock as he guided it toward Max's mouth. "I've got no complaints."

Oh hell yeah, this was what Max had been waiting for. He wetted his lips, and his nerves kicked in all over again. He knew how good this could feel. But what if he wasn't able to recreate that for Rick? He tried to recall all the things that had felt incredible on him… the things Rick had done to him last night that had blown his mind.

The soft head of Rick's cock pressed at Max's lips; his mouth watered and he opened wide, allowing Rick's rigid length to slide along his tongue. The weight of it felt so right as it filled his mouth. He groaned and moved his head forward to take more, then eased back and coiled his tongue around the head. God, he tasted good. A salty drop of precome exploded on his tongue, and Max bobbed back and forth, concentrating on keeping his teeth out of the way as Rick thrust into him. Rick stiffened even more, quickly pulling out with a gasp after Max took him to the very back of his throat. It had almost choked him, but he didn't care.

"Too much?" Max asked with a smirk, his confidence building. He was doing something right. Rick's eyes were black and his breaths heavy.

"You sure you haven't done this before?"

Max kissed him and reached down to ease the tension in his own cock. "I got a few pointers last night." Rick laughed. "Do you want to come in my mouth?"

"Seriously?"

Max's voice was husky as he replied, "Yeah." Fuck. He longed to watch Rick come undone as he fucked his mouth.

He opened wide as Rick guided his cock back into his mouth, and took everything he gave him as Rick rocked his hips. Blowing him was turning him on almost as much as receiving it had last night. He jerked himself as Rick's movements became more ragged.

"I'm gonna—"

Rick's cock stiffened and Max's eyes widened as Rick's release filled his mouth faster than he could swallow it—and it kept on coming. His eyes watered, and he began to choke. Rick quickly withdrew, and come dribbled from Max's mouth.

"Fuck," Max said as his choking fit subsided, and wiped his chin. Rick was rubbing his back.

"You okay?" Rick asked and kissed his cheek.

"Shit. There was tons of it."

Rick laughed. "Yup. It gets easier. Promise."

Max froze. Had Rick enjoyed it? He'd been so caught up trying not to choke to death that he'd forgotten all about trying to make it good for Rick. "Was it good enough? For you, just now, I mean."

"Hey, look at me. You made me come, didn't you?" Rick put his hand on Max's jaw and made him look him in the eyes. "I'm glad I got to be your first." He pressed a kiss to Max's ear and whispered, "It was perfect."

"Yeah?"

"Yeah. How are you doing? Do you want me to finish you off?"

The moment had kind of been lost, and Max's erection was flagging. He was about to say no when Rick closed his lips around him. It took seconds for Max's arousal to return. He groaned and thrust up into Rick's mouth, and soon he was coming. Damn, Rick was good at that. Max stared at him through hazy eyes. Rick hadn't spilled a drop. He had to learn how to do that. And he was sure Rick wouldn't mind him practicing.

"How about some coffee?" Rick asked. "I wasn't sure what you'd want for breakfast. I've got some cereal, but that's about it."

"That sounds great. As long as you're not cooking again."

"Mm, funny." Rick gently swatted his head, but Max was too blissed out to care.

"What have you got planned for today?" Rick asked him as they sat on the mattress, eating their cereal.

"Trying out some new basting recipes."

"Some what?"

"Basting recipes. For the whole-hog competition at the jamboree in a couple of weeks. I'm entering with Sian."

"Oh wow. You're entering that?"

"Yeah."

"I got that you're good at cooking, but I didn't realize you took it that seriously."

"It's just a bit of fun." Max laughed. "Okay, maybe I do want to win as well."

"I think it's great that you're doing something like that. My dad used to do barbecues all the time. Never a whole hog, though."

"How about you? What are you doing today?" Max asked.

"Putting ice on my eye and trying not to hobble about too much when I teach later."

"You're teaching later? Straight after a fight?"

"Yeah. I'll get them sparring, though, so I can rest my body. One of my black belts can take the warmup. It'll be good practice for them."

"Speaking of your fight last night." Max took a sip of coffee. "We need to have serious words about your walkout music."

"You don't like it?"

Max pulled a face. "Are you kidding? It's such an obvious choice that it's cheesy as hell."

Rick leaned across and nudged him. "You think you can come up with something better for me?"

"Definitely. Let me think on it."

A WEEK later, Max parked outside Rick's dojo in the ambulance. He was unloading the small amplifier, guitar, and duffel bag when Rick came out to meet him.

"Morning," Rick said.

"Hey," Max said and yawned. He still hadn't got used to being up this early, but it was the only way he could get to see Rick without anyone knowing. Rick didn't tend to have classes in the mornings, and all Max's friends were sleeping, so it was the perfect time to slip out unnoticed. The problem was that all this lack of sleep was catching up with him. "I finished your walkout music, if you wanna hear it? I've recorded it, but I brought the guitar so we can play around with some riffs if you want anything changed."

"That'd be awesome. Thanks." Rick took the bag and the guitar from him, and Max locked the ambulance. "We should do your MMA lesson first, though."

Max scowled. Rick had been insistent that Max have a lesson each time they spent time together. "Can't we skip it today? You've already taught me, like, a hundred ways to kill someone with my bare hands."

They walked to the dojo, and Rick held the door open for him. "I've taught you *three* ways to defend yourself so you can get away if you were ever attacked. Don't you feel better armed with this knowledge?"

"I guess."

"Well, it makes me feel better knowing you could protect yourself."

"Fine, we'll do the ninja lesson first." Max sighed and dumped the amplifier on the floor near the mattress that Rick hid in the changing room whenever Max wasn't there. "What time are you teaching today? How long do we have?"

"Art has a lesson at one. We're going to work on his guard now that his bruises have gone down. So that gives us three hours."

"Great. I brought some food for later too." Max threw himself down on the mattress and closed his eyes.

Rick grabbed his hand and tried to pull him up, but Max groaned. "You've worn me out."

Chuckling, Rick climbed on top of him and kissed him. That was more like it. Max kissed him back, trying to deepen the kiss, but Rick took advantage of him being distracted and hauled him to his feet. Max stood there, glaring at Rick. "Can't believe you'd rather do ninja shit than me."

Rick ducked his head and kissed Max again, then slid his arms around Max's waist. "We've got plenty of time for that later. Come on. This is important." He dragged Max toward the blue mats laid out near the heavy bags. "I thought we'd do a silat move today."

"A sil-what?"

"Pencak silat. It's a particularly nasty form of fighting. Great for self-defense."

"What do you need me to do?" Max asked.

"Stand behind me and grab me around the waist."

Suddenly the ninja lesson wasn't looking so terrible. Max did as he was told and then thrust against him.

"Hey, stop it!" Rick said, but he was laughing. "Stop trying to distract me. This is a serious lesson."

"Is it working?" Max asked, sliding his hands down to Rick's semihard cock. "Yup, definitely working."

Rick grabbed Max's hands and placed them firmly around his middle. "The quicker we get done with this, the more time we'll have later for that."

That was true. "You have my undivided attention, *Sensei*."

"Shut up," Rick grumbled. "Okay, so if someone grabs you around the middle and you need to escape, this is what you need to do. First, scrape your boot down the front of their leg from below their knee, and then stomp on their foot. They'll flinch from the surprise 'cause it hurts. A lot. When they flinch, make a fist with your right hand and hit them as hard as you can on the back of their hand below their first two fingers. If you need to, do this twice. Their hand will open, and with your right hand you grab the first two fingers of their left hand, and then you step around to your left and push against the back of their left arm, just above their elbow. They'll end up on the ground. Once they're on the ground, that's when you run away. Got it?"

"Show me?" As always, that was a lot to take in until he tried it for himself.

Rick demonstrated, slowly at first, and then he did it faster. That was when it fucking hurt once he was on the floor. It felt as though his arm was going to snap. Max tapped the ground as quickly as he could, and Rick released him.

"Ready to give it a try?"

"Sure. That's a good one." Max rubbed his arm as he got up.

When Rick grabbed Max around his middle, Max couldn't resist pushing his ass backward into him. "Concentrate," Rick whispered into his ear, sending shivers down Max's neck.

"That's not helping."

"First slide your boot down my shin...." Max followed Rick's instructions, and soon he'd gotten the hang of it and was able to do it quite fast. Rick seemed pleased with him. After he'd learned that one, they practiced the others he'd been taught.

"Four ninja moves," Max said, grinning as he flopped on the mattress. "How many do I have to do until I get a badge?"

Rick lay on the mattress next to him and turned his head to stare at Max. "You want to do the gradings? I thought you weren't interested in all that."

"Hell no! I was kidding. Seriously, though, how many more ninja moves are you gonna be teaching me?"

"As many as you want. There're thousands of them." And then he whispered, "We could keep on going forever."

Max rolled on his side to face him, and they stared at each other for a long moment. His nerves were tingling with anticipation. What was Rick saying exactly? Were they still talking about the martial arts?

They lay there in silence, the possibilities in Rick's words sending light shivers of happiness through Max's body.

Rick stared at him and tucked a strand of hair behind Max's ear, his fingers lingering. "Do you feel ready for me to fuck you?"

"Oh, hell yeah." Max's tone was light and teasing to mask the emotions still rushing through him. "I thought you'd never ask." He needed time to process Rick's words. What if he hadn't meant them the way Max desperately wanted to take them?

Max climbed on top of him and kissed him deep and hard while he rid Rick of his T-shirt and then removed his own. He ran his hands over the taut muscles of Rick's chest as he sat up, looking down at Rick as he asked, "How do you want me?"

"On your front? Or you can ride me if you want? That might be easier for your first time. You'll get to control it that way."

"I'll go on my front." Getting to control it sounded good in theory, but he wanted to totally lose himself in the sensations, and that meant trusting Rick to take care of him. And he did. Completely. Max unzipped his boots and shoved down his pants, watching as Rick did the same. Rick was hard, and Max swallowed as he watched him jack himself a couple of times, making himself even bigger—if that was possible. Was this a good idea? Would he be able to take all that? He guessed there was no turning back now. He'd heard and seen how good it could feel, and right now he hoped the guys in the porn he'd watched hadn't been faking. But what if they had been? Oh God.

"Relax." Rick moved behind Max on the bed and trailed kisses down his spine. "I've got you."

When he reached the base, he kept on going, and Max groaned at the warm, wet caress of his tongue between his asscheeks as Rick gently probed his hole. That felt incredible. Nobody had ever done that to him before. How could something so simple feel so fucking amazing? When Rick reached his balls, Max arched up to meet him, and Rick took one of them into his mouth, and then the other. Max slowly stroked himself, wanting to make this last.

He couldn't wait until he knew what he was doing with all this. It was kind of terrifying, and he hoped Rick didn't expect too much from him this first time. Max blew out a breath to steady his nerves. Maybe if he did something he was getting better at he'd feel more relaxed. "Want me to suck you for a bit?"

"Sure." Rick grinned at him. "Definitely won't say no to that."

Rick lay back, and Max shuffled down the mattress and took him into his mouth, enjoying the now-familiar feel of Rick sliding to the back of his throat. He moaned as salty precome coated his tongue, savoring the taste, and forced Rick even farther into his mouth. Fuck, that felt good.

"Hey." Rick's voice was husky, and Max glanced up at him. "I thought you wanted me to fuck you? That's not gonna happen if you carry on like that… especially if you do that thing you did last time."

Max smiled. He was doing something right, then. That was good to know. He cupped his lips around Rick's tip and sucked harder, holding the base and jacking him in time with the motions of his mouth.

Rick suddenly groaned and shoved Max's hand until he popped out of his mouth.

"Hey!" Max said. "I was enjoying that."

Rick narrowed his eyes at him with a smirk and rapped him on the nose with his cock. "So was I. Too much. Don't give me that innocent look. You knew exactly what you were doing." He leaned up and kissed Max before pushing him over onto his back and looking down at him. "We don't have to do this today if you don't want to."

"No." Max took a shaky breath and nodded. "I want to get it over with."

"How romantic." Rick laughed and kissed him thoroughly until Max almost forgot all his fears. "Ready now?" Rick whispered.

"Ready." Max hoped his voice was convincing. Turning onto his front on his hands and knees, he tried to relax as best he could. He knew this was gonna fucking hurt, and he hoped it was worth all the pain.

He heard the click of the lube bottle and then felt the warm slide of Rick's fingers at the entrance to his hole. "Let me know if you want me to stop. I'm gonna go slow, though, okay?"

Max grunted, trying to ignore his trembling legs, and arched up even more as Rick's fingers slid inside him. He was used to the sensation, having done this to himself many times before, especially since seeing how big Rick was. There was no way he was going to chance being too tight to take him. He hoped he'd prepared himself enough.

"You feel so good," Rick said as he kissed the back of Max's neck, his cock pressing against Max's thigh and leaking precome.

"Do you think you're ready?" Rick asked after Max had managed to take three of his fingers. Rick had big hands, and even three of his fingers stretched him more than he was used to, but the gentle burn felt good so far.

"Do it," Max gasped, letting go of his straining cock so he didn't risk coming the second Rick pressed against his hole. He heard the rip of a condom foil and turned to watch as Rick rolled it on and then added more lube. As Rick straddled him and lined up, Max rested his forehead against the pillow and closed his eyes. This was it. No turning back. Rick rested his solid cock between Max's asscheeks, and Max took a deep breath as Rick slowly pushed inside, creating even more of a burn, stretching him even wider.

He stopped and gave Max a chance to get used to the feeling, and somehow read Max's body perfectly. Each time Max relaxed enough and felt like he could take more, Rick edged inside without him having to say anything. It still hurt like hell. But he had Rick inside him. Max squeezed his eyes shut and smiled. Being so close to him was gut-wrenchingly special—not like he'd ever experienced before—and he wished it didn't have to end, that they could stay like this forever. Rick gripped his hips and edged inside a little more, and finally he was all the way inside. Max took hold of his flagging cock and jerked himself, and the pain gave way to the most incredible sensation. He groaned and fell forward, willing Rick to take total control so he could savor every second. Rick's strong grip held him in place, and he stayed with him as he fell, the weight of his body on top of him just enough and not crushing him at all.

"You feel amazing," Rick said and kissed the side of Max's neck, and Max pressed back against him with a groan. "You okay for me to move?"

"Uh-huh."

When Rick began to pull out and then thrust back inside, Max was in heaven. "Go as hard as you like," he breathed.

"You sure?"

"Yeah."

"I won't last if I do that." Rick's voice was husky.

"Don't care," Max managed, and suddenly he didn't. He pushed back against Rick and gripped himself hard as he jerked himself faster. He was so close to coming now, it was all he could focus on. The delicious friction inside his ass as Rick thrust harder added with the sensations from his hand and tipped him over the edge. He came hard, clenching and releasing around Rick's cock deep inside him as come spurted from his cock. Rick's hold on his hips tightened and his movements became sharper, and then he was shouting out as he came.

Rick collapsed against him, breathing hard. He seemed to realize he was crushing Max—not that Max minded much right now, if he died like this he'd die happy—and then he pulled out. It was the weirdest sensation, kind of tickly, and Max almost laughed.

"You okay?" Rick asked as he lay on his back and dealt with the condom.

"Fuck, yes." Max draped his arm across Rick's chest and closed his eyes as he caught his breath. "God, that's gonna ache later."

"Yeah. But it's totally worth it," Rick said. "I think so, anyway. I love getting fucked."

"I'm sure you're right. That felt so good." He opened one eye and caught Rick staring at him.

"Yeah?" Rick asked and held him tight.

"Yeah," Max said and sighed, cuddling up as close as he possibly could.

MAX MUST have nodded off. When he opened his eyes again, Rick was sitting on the mattress holding the guitar and quietly pressing his fingers against the strings. He didn't notice Max watching at first and jumped when Max spoke.

"I can give you some lessons if you like?"

"Maybe next time," Rick said and laid the guitar carefully on the floor. "I didn't realize you were awake."

"Yeah, sorry. I only got a couple of hours sleep before I stopped by. We didn't finish band practice until about four." Max shoved back the comforter, sat up, and stretched. He could still feel where Rick had been inside him earlier, and he smiled at the memory.

"Are you hungry or can I get you a drink?" Rick asked.

"I'm starving, actually. How much longer have we got?"

"About an hour."

"Is that all?" Their stolen moments together never felt long enough. Max had dared to stay the night a couple of times, and he had posted on his social media so it looked like he was out drinking and had stayed at some girl's house again to keep Tony off his back and from asking awkward questions about where he'd been. It had worked, but Max didn't dare do that too frequently in case he got caught out.

"Did you say you brought some food?"

"Yeah, I did." Max jumped to his feet and rummaged in his bag until he found the tub.

"What have we got?"

"Burritos. I found this great new recipe that uses a ton of beans and different spices. There's no meat in them but they taste so good, even when they're cold." He handed one to Rick and took one for himself.

"No meat?" Rick frowned and cautiously sniffed at it.

Max laughed. "Don't you trust my cooking by now?"

Rick took a tiny bite and then groaned. "That is so good. You'd better not turn me vegetarian."

"Hardly." Max tucked into his own burrito and then asked, "How are things at home? Didn't you say your dad's friend was staying this week?"

"What, Dietmar? Yeah, he arrived yesterday afternoon. He's actually staying for ten days, not a week, so he'll be here for the jamboree. He's helping my dad show the Harley."

"Will you be there?" Max glanced at Rick. He'd been hoping Rick would be going, but hadn't asked him because he knew Rick was usually really busy on Saturdays.

"Yeah. I've cancelled the classes that weekend, so I'll be there the whole time. There was no point in holding them. I think the entire town will be at the jamboree."

"True." There was always a good turnout. Max couldn't wait to perform there. After that, he'd be busy with the whole-hog competition with Sian. "You'll have to come and say hi. It'll be difficult for me to get away."

"I'll come find you." Rick finished the last of his burrito and then leaned across and kissed him. "So what was this you said about changing my walkout music? I'm dying to hear it, and we don't have much time left."

Max was so excited about this. He'd spent most of the week trying out different riffs to find something that would sound awesome as well as suiting Rick's personality and taste. It had to be powerful too. Something to get him fired up and ready to fight. Combining those elements had been seriously tough. But he thought he'd hit on something. The one thing he still didn't have were the lyrics, but he could figure those out later.

"I have it recorded on my cell phone. I also put together a decent playlist for you to use for your warmup."

"Yeah?"

"I'll send it to you. It's a mix of heavy electronica. Kind of like what they use at Black Ivy."

"Oh, I liked what they were playing in there."

"And there I was thinking it would be a challenge to convert your music taste." Max grinned and scrolled through his cell to find the latest version of Rick's walkout music. "Here it is. Ready?" Rick nodded. "Close your eyes and pretend you're about to walk out for your fight. See if it feels right. We can change it however you like. Or start again if you hate it."

Rick obediently closed his eyes and Max hit Play, holding his breath and watching Rick to see his reaction.

The track intro had a light, fast guitar sequence. It had a cheeky feel to it, Max thought, and sure enough Rick smiled at those first bars. The slow, deep drumbeat came in next, and then Max had mixed it up. A short verse that had a funky rhythm followed, and then he'd used heavy chords that led into the faster chorus. He'd included some of the slap-bass riffs he'd been playing at Hugh's the day they'd gotten his guitar, and also used an interesting, but slightly unusual, drumbeat to give the chorus a unique feel. The track finished after the verse had played for the second time. Max was planning to add the rest in later if Rick liked it.

"What do you think?"

Rick opened his eyes. His grin couldn't have been any wider. He leaned over and kissed Max. "I love it—"

"I was thinking of adding some vocals maybe… what do you reckon? I've been struggling to come up with anything good at the moment, though."

"Would it be you singing them?"

Max nodded. "If you wanted, that is."

"I'd love that."

"Is there anything else you want changed? Please be honest. There are a couple of—"

Rick pressed his finger to Max's lips. "Don't change a thing. Honestly. I can't believe you did this for me. Thank you." He removed his finger and kissed Max again, deeper this time, and as they fell back onto the mattress, Max wished they had longer together. He hadn't realized Rick was going to be this grateful. If he had, he would've played it for him as soon as he'd arrived.

CHAPTER TEN

Rick

"HAND ME the wrench, will you?"

Rick rummaged through the toolkit and shielded his eyes from the glinting metal before handing it to his dad. It was the perfect day for the Elfinbrook jamboree. It was late July, and there was a rare cooling breeze that cut through the early morning heat. He hoped it stayed for the rest of the day, or he was going to get burned.

"How many others are showing their bikes, Jakob?" Dietmar asked.

"About another fifty, I think."

"I'm surprised by the turnout. I didn't realize Elfinbrook was so big."

Rick picked up a rag and polished the fairing of his dad's Harley. "People travel here from all over. It's quite a big deal."

"What time is your friend's band playing?"

"Not until lunchtime." It had been such a great week, and he'd seen Max almost every day, although it was usually only for an hour here and there as Max had been busy preparing for today. They'd even been doing Max's "ninja" lessons—Rick smiled as he remembered how Max hadn't been kidding about his total lack of coordination. He was doing really well with the self-defense stuff, though.

He had such a great surprise for Max. Dietmar ran a chain of music venues over in England, and after Rick had played him Purple Method's first two albums, Dietmar was seriously considering offering to fly them over to perform at his alternative music clubs in London.

The smell of grilling bacon and onions wafted in the air, and Rick looked across the field to the food court. His dad had insisted on them leaving at five in the morning to get there before the crowds, as he hated being rushed, but it had been a bit early for Rick, so he'd rolled out of bed and into the car without so much as getting coffee. It had just passed eight now, and he was starving.

"Looks like the food trucks have fired up. Shall I get us some breakfast?"

"Would you like a hand?" Dietmar asked, and Rick shook his head as his dad handed him a fifty-dollar bill.

"No, I can manage. Back in a bit."

Running to the first food truck, he joined the short line and was deliberating between a breakfast burrito and a bacon panini when somebody head butted his back. What the hell? He spun around, about to confront them, but then he realized it was Max, who looked barely in the land of the living. "Hey. You're up early."

"One hour's sleep." He peered up at Rick, his eyes bloodshot. "I had one fucking hour's sleep."

"Want me to hold you up until you get coffee?"

Max nodded and leaned against Rick's arm.

He had been kidding, thinking Max wouldn't want this kind of contact with him in public, but he seemed too out of it to care. He'd closed his eyes, and Rick wouldn't have been surprised if he'd fallen back asleep even though he was still standing. "You gonna be okay to sing later?"

"Yeah," Max said, his voice muffled against Rick's T-shirt.

"You're cute when you're sleepy."

"Fuck off."

Rick snickered and maneuvered Max forward as the line moved, nudging him as they reached the front of the line. "What are you having?"

"Biggest coffee they have, black, sugar."

"Any food?"

"Na."

"Sure? My dad's paying."

He waved the fifty-dollar bill in Max's face, and Max briefly opened one eye. "Bacon panini, all the fixings."

Rick made their order and was handed four coffees, one extra-large, Max's panini, and three breakfast burritos. "Can you give me a hand taking these back over there?" He nodded toward the bike show as he scooped up the drinks carrier. Max held out his hands, and Rick loaded him up with the burritos. Somehow, Max also managed to eat his panini as they walked.

"How come you're here so early, anyway?" Rick asked.

"We've got to get set up for both the gig and the hog competition."

"I thought the hog competition wasn't until tomorrow?"

Max's eyes opened wide, and he looked at him as if he were stupid.

"What? What did I say?"

"You really don't cook at all, do you." Max shook his head and sighed. "We gotta start it today. There's the meat inspection at nine, and it takes a long time to prep and cook a whole hog. And then there're all the fixings to get perfect. The competition's tough even at a small event like this one."

"I thought you came sixth last year?"

"Yeah, and this year we're gonna win."

"If you can wake up in time, that is."

Max elbowed him in his ribs, right on the spot where he was still bruised from a fight he'd had a couple of days back. It was a deep one, and although his ribs had ached, his skin hadn't colored until today. "That's not funny." Max looked up at him through his hair that had fallen forward. "We take this very seriously. We even got a new smoker for this year. Sian's setting it up now."

"Sian? Was she expecting you to get her a drink?"

"Yeah." Max sighed. "I'll get it on the way back."

Dietmar waved as they got closer, and Rick wondered if this was the best idea. It was too late to turn back now, though. Max was about to meet the man who could give Purple Method an amazing opportunity, and Max was barely with it and looked as though he had just fallen out of bed. Not that Rick was complaining about that last part. It had better not put Dietmar off; he'd kick himself if he thought he'd jeopardized this.

"Hope you're hungry," Rick said and put the drinks down on the toolbox. He took the burritos from Max and handed them out.

"Max, this is Dietmar, and my dad, Jakob."

"Hey," Max said with a mouthful of bacon and gave them a little wave as he reached for his coffee.

Dietmar was frowning, and Rick groaned when he saw Dietmar's outstretched hand that Max had ignored. He was willing to bet he hadn't even noticed.

"Max," Rick said and nodded at Dietmar.

"Sorry." Max clenched his panini between his teeth and shook Dietmar's hand. "Had a bit too much to drink this morning."

What? It was all Rick could do to stop himself from dropping his head into his hands and groaning. "Don't you mean last night?" He glared at Max, hoping he would somehow get the hint.

Max took a long slurp from his bucket of coffee. "Nah, it was definitely this morning. Tony and Kyle are wrecked too. We were all up till six. We wouldn't have made it at all if it wasn't for Sian waking us up. This gig today's gonna be interesting."

"Yes, I'd say it probably is," Dietmar said.

"You'll have to come see us. We're a bit heavy, though, so it's probably not your thing."

"Max," Rick said, "why don't I come with you to find the others, and you can show me where you've set up for the hog competition." The quicker he got him out of there, the better, although he couldn't see how it could get any worse.

"Sure. Hey, could you help them with the smoker? That thing's fucking heavy. We need to get everything unloaded quick so they can get back home to pick up our equipment for the gig. Luckily it's not far—"

"Them?" Dietmar asked. "Aren't you going to help too?"

"My talents lie elsewhere—"

Rick grabbed Max's shoulders and spun him around. "We should go. Dad, I'll be back later."

"Okay."

"What the hell was that?" Rick hissed once they were far enough away.

"What?" Max peered up at him and swallowed the last of his panini.

"That was my dad." Rick stared at Max's blank face and sighed. He really wasn't getting it. "Did you think telling him how hungover or drunk you were was going to make a good first impression?"

Max frowned. "You think I should've lied? How would that have made a good impression?"

"No… not lied, just… I dunno, maybe held back a little on the truth."

"Oh."

They walked in silence past the stunt-bike area toward the hog competition areas that were visible in the hazy distance. Every time Rick looked across at him, Max took a long drink of coffee and made a point of looking at anything other than Rick. Great. That was all he needed. He'd been looking forward to this weekend, looking forward to being able to spend some quality time with Max, getting to know his friends better, and to seeing a side of Max that still mystified him.

"You gonna ignore me for the whole rest of the weekend?" Rick asked.

"I dunno. You stopped being embarrassed by me yet?"

"You don't embarrass me."

Max gave him a sidelong glare. "I might not be as smart or as worldly as you, but don't you dare take me for a fool."

"That's not…." Max sped up and Rick jogged to catch him, grabbing his arm to stop him. "That's not it."

Max shrugged from his grasp and went on walking.

"For fuck's sake, Max, will you at least listen to me before you make up your mind that I'm some kind of asshole?"

Stopping and turning, Max stared at him with one eyebrow raised and a slight smile. "You're swearing now? I must've pissed you off."

"Have you never met parents before?" he asked, exasperated.

"Uh, no, not really."

He was about to groan, but there was a sadness to Max's answer that made him bite his tongue, reminding himself that Max's background was very different from his own.

"My parents don't drink a lot. They don't understand the whole partying thing, okay?"

"Oh, okay." Max kicked at the dirt. "What do they do, then?"

Rick held back a laugh at the confusion in Max's voice. "Their lives revolve around dance, mostly."

"What do they do to chill out if they don't drink?"

"My dad fixes up classic bikes, and Mom likes watching sitcoms on television."

Max frowned. "That's it?"

"Yeah, pretty much. Not everyone likes to party."

Max huffed a laugh. "Well, that explains why you can't hold your drink."

"Me?" Rick gently poked his chest. "You're the one who was so drunk you couldn't even climb the stairs that night we met."

Max's cheeks colored. "If it weren't for you, I wouldn't have had so much to drink."

"It's my fault? Should I feel flattered or guilty?"

He shrugged. "Up to you, but if you're feeling guilty, you could give us a hand lifting the smoker out of the ambulance, and we can forget it."

"Max," Rick sighed, "listen to me. You need to make a good impression with Dietmar, okay?"

"Why? He's not your dad."

"No, but trust me, okay?" He didn't want to tell Max why, especially after their meeting just now, didn't want to get his hopes up if nothing came of it.

"Okay." Max dragged out the word and squinted at Rick. "Why are you being so mysterious?"

"It's part of my charm." He threw his arm across Max's shoulders, but Max shrugged him off. "Too much?"

"You know it is. Don't make me regret this. You're not that charming. And you'd better tell me what this is all about."

"I will, but not yet."

After getting Sian her drink, they walked under the gigantic fluorescent banner advertising the Barbecue Cooking Contest, and wove their way through groups of people meandering past the entrants, who were at various stages of setting up. Some booths were still empty, and others were hives of activity with people cooking breakfast on their fancy contraptions and decorating their plots. It all looked very serious, and Rick was glad he was a spectator.

"That's us." Max pointed to a plot on the left-hand side. The ambulance's back doors were open, the huge steel smoker still inside, and Tony and Kyle were sitting in yard chairs, watching Sian paint a sign for their booth in massive stylized letters in purple glitter on a black background. It had the same feel as their band logo.

"The Porkaholic Method?" Rick raised one eyebrow. He couldn't quite decide whether it was a ridiculous or an ingenious name.

"What are you talking about? It's an awesome name—better than any of theirs, anyway." Max gestured toward their competitors in the surrounding booths, and took another gulp of coffee.

Rick snickered. Max was right; their name fit right in. The Piggy Protection Agency was on one side, and opposite was Pearls Before Swine. Pearls Before Swine, consisting of five rather straightlaced looking ladies, didn't look impressed by their booth location, and honestly, Rick could understand it—Tony and Kyle looked as tired and hungover as Max had before his caffeine hit.

Stepping over the rope marking their area, Max headed over to Sian, and Rick followed.

"Ready to move the smoker?" Max asked and handed over her drink.

Sian straightened up and admired her work. "Sure. What do you think?"

"It looks great. That glitter paint is awesome."

"Are you helping us?" Sian smiled at Rick.

"Yeah."

"No," Max said. "Not with the cooking at least. Just with the smoker."

"That's a bit mean, don't you think?"

Max pointed at Rick. "He can't cook at all. He even burns bread, like, all the time. He's not touching Lorette."

Sian looked between the two of them, frowning, and then grinned.

"Who's Lorette?" Rick asked. The whole thing was becoming very confusing.

"Our pig." Max sighed in exasperation.

Rick snorted a laugh. "You named your pig? Are you serious?"

"Yes," Max said. "Are you gonna quit asking stupid questions and give us a hand?"

"How much does that thing weigh, anyway?"

The smoker looked like it barely fit in the ambulance, and it was bound to be heavy. He was glad he'd been in training.

"Getting on four hundred pounds, I think. Don't worry. Pete said he'd give us a hand too."

"Four hundred pounds between four of us?"

"Six. You, Kyle, Tony, Sian, Pete, and me. I was kidding when I said I wasn't going to help. Don't look so panicked."

Rick tried to smile and hoped Pete was more awake than the others.

"Max, we've got fifteen minutes before the judges will be around," Sian said. "We need to get Lorette."

"Rick, can you help me?" Max asked and walked toward the front of the ambulance while shouting over his shoulder, "Sian, get the folding table set up?"

"I'm on it."

Max opened the passenger door, and Rick gasped. Lorette was strapped into the seat, her body wrapped in a silver emergency blanket.

He shook his head and watched Max lean across to unstrap her. "What have you guys done to that poor pig?"

"She wouldn't fit in the back with the smoker, so I wrapped her in ice packs; the blanket helps to stop them from melting—keeps her cool for longer. Can't have the meat turning bad in this heat before we even start."

"You're crazy, you know that."

Max grinned. "Thinking outside the box isn't crazy, it's awesome."

"Whatever. Come on, let's get poor Lorette out of here. Is she gonna fit in that smoker?"

"Yeah, just. I checked yesterday."

Lorette was ready for inspection as the judges reached them, and Rick unfolded a yard chair and sat next to Kyle, who was snoring. Max and Sian dealt with the judges, and Pete had wandered off.

"You got a problem with your hearing?" Tony asked.

"Only after your gigs."

Tony pursed his lips. "'Cause it's looking awfully like you hadn't heard me when I told you to stay away from my brother. Didn't you get how serious this is?"

"Yeah. I did. That's why I've been giving him self-defense lessons."

"You've been what?"

"He didn't tell you? He's actually picking it up really quickly."

"Rick, don't encourage him. Please. I'm begging you. You must have seen how he looks at you."

"You need to tell him that you know. It's doing more damage to him by not knowing the truth. How do you think he's going to feel when he finds out? It's only a matter of time before he's tired of hiding—"

"It's none of your business. You'd better not—"

"If I was going to tell him that you know, I would have by now. You can't protect him by lying to him. You need to talk to him. Soon. He needs to know. I'm not your enemy, Tony," he said, working hard to keep his voice steady and quiet enough that nobody overheard them.

Rick held Tony's stare until, out of the corner of his eye, he saw Pete approaching.

"Everything okay?" Pete eyed them suspiciously, and with Tony showing no intention of looking away, Rick turned to Pete.

"Yeah, fine."

"Good," Pete said.

"Lorette passed inspection." Max ran over to them and bounced on the spot. "It's smoker time. I hope you're feeling strong. Hey, Pete, how're things?" He gave Kyle's ankle a kick, and Kyle groaned. "Tony, wake him up, will you?"

"*Kyle, move your ass.*"

Kyle opened his bloodshot eyes and frowned. "I'm awake. There's no need to shout."

"Max is right, we need to get that monstrosity out of the ambulance so we can get our gear for the gig. They want us set up and ready to go by one."

"Can't believe we got such an awful slot," Kyle said, yawning and stretching as he stood.

"You were lucky to get a slot at all," Pete said. "I heard that was the last one."

"Well, we told everyone about it"—Max shrugged—"so hopefully we'll have a good crowd. Come on. Me and Sian need to baste Lorette before the gig."

The smoker was as heavy as Rick had feared, but somehow they managed to get it into position in the booth. Tony and Kyle then went back for the gear. Helping set up for the gig was easier. Rick was in charge of hauling the stuff from the ambulance to the stage while Tony and Kyle set it all up and Max and Pete did a quick sound check.

"I'm gonna head back to the booth and give Sian a hand with Lorette," Max said to Rick as he jumped off the stage. "We prepared the mixture a couple of days ago, but it still takes a while to inject it."

Rick gaped at him. "You inject that poor animal?"

"Yeah." Max laughed. "Come on, I'll show you. We'll take the ambulance around to the booth."

They jumped in, and Max drove them back along the dusty paths, through the crowds, and parked up behind their booth. But he showed no sign of getting out.

"What's up?"

"I don't really have to give Sian a hand with the basting. She's got that."

"What? Why are we back here without the others, then?"

"I needed an excuse to get away." Max stared down at his hands. "You know what it's like, right? You can't just get up and go straight in the octagon."

"Yeah." Rick drew out the word, totally confused. Then he shook his head. "No. No, what are you talking about?"

Max looked up at him. "Promise not to laugh." Rick nodded. "Singing's the same. I need to warm up first. It's kinda like I've got a six-pack on my vocal cords. I can't sing as well cold."

"You sounded great at sound check."

"That's not the same. We only tested the midrange notes."

"So warm up. What's the big deal?"

Max huffed a laugh. "You can't tell Tony and Kyle."

"Why not?"

"They don't know I do this."

"Ah." Tony may have been doing his best for his brother, but he was doing more damage than good, in so many ways—he was sure of that. It was so frustrating. "Pete helps you?"

"Yeah." Max grimaced. "You can't tell anyone that either."

"Your secret's safe with me… all of them."

"Thanks. They'd better be."

"You're camping here tonight, right?" Rick put his hand on Max's knee and squeezed.

"You're not staying in my tent, if that's what you're asking," Max said and moved Rick's hand away.

"That's a shame." Rick put his hand back on Max's leg, sliding up the inside of his thigh and leaning in as if to kiss him.

"Out! Now!" Max leaned across and opened the passenger door. "You start doing that and I'll never get my warmup done." Rick climbed out of the ambulance, laughing. "And don't touch Lorette." Max slammed the door closed and climbed into the back, out of sight.

Rick gazed around. The smells coming from the other booths made his mouth water. Pearls Before Swine seemed to have a military operation going on. Everyone had a particular job, their booth was spotless, and it was decorated to perfection. He didn't know much about barbecue competitions, but they had to have a shot of first place with that kind of precision. He wandered over to Sian, who was holding a syringe that looked like it belonged in the hospital.

"How're you getting on?" He watched as she sucked up a load of green mixture from a large tub into the syringe. It looked disgusting but smelled delicious.

"Okay. I'd be better if slacker over there was helping." She nodded toward the ambulance. "Can you give me a hand?"

"Um, Max told me not to touch Lorette."

"You really gonna pay attention to him?" She raised an eyebrow and wiped strands of hair from her forehead with her arm. "You'd be helping him out more if you give me a hand. Honestly, it'd be impossible to do any damage to Lorette at this stage. He's being ridiculous."

Rick smiled and scanned Sian's work area. "What do you need?"

"Help me lift her so I can inject underneath?"

"Sure."

To the faint sound of Max working through his scales, Rick washed his hands, lifted the pig, and wondered when his life had become so bizarre.

"ARE YOU sure your friend is going to be okay performing?" Dietmar asked as he and Rick made their way through the stifling midday heat toward the stage.

"Absolutely. I'm not sure what came over him earlier. He takes his music very seriously… you'll see. They've been working really hard on their new album. That's why they were up so late last night."

"Oh, I see. They don't make a habit of it, then?"

"They've been figuring out a new sound since their bassist left. They reckon it's unique."

"I'm looking forward to hearing it after everything you've told me. It could be a good fit for the Scarab Lounge."

Rick hoped Purple Method didn't make this their one dud performance, and wondered whether he should have told them what was on offer so they were better prepared. It was too late now.

The bleachers were full of metalhead types, some Rick recognized from the Torrens Club. Angelo was sitting on the grass with Joe, and they were drinking beer already. Rick caught his eye and gave him a wave. Things hadn't been at all weird between them since the night they'd spent together, thankfully, because it was impossible to avoid each other. He'd had a chat with Angelo at the Villains gig and had made it very clear that for him it had been a one-time hookup. Luckily Angelo had felt the same.

Clusters of fans clutched the rails at the front. It was good to see that Purple Method had such a lot of support.

Pete came rushing over to him carrying two buckets. "Hey, Rick, would you mind helping us out and holding one of these by the exit over there when they're done with their set? Tony thought it would be good to raise money for the air ambulance."

"Tony suggested that?"

"Yeah. Don't ask."

Rick took the bucket. "Sure, I can help out. That's fine."

"Thanks, bud."

Pete rushed off, heading for the backstage area.

Craning his neck, Rick could see Max waiting in the wings. He was wiping his mouth and shouting at Tony. Max hooked the strap of his six-string fretless bass guitar over his shoulders and caressed the strings.

"Here we go." Dietmar pointed to Tony, who was taking his place onstage. Kyle followed, and finally Max took his place at the microphone stand at the front.

Rick cheered along with the rest of Purple Method's fans.

"There's only three of them?" Dietmar asked.

"Yeah."

Dietmar snorted. "You need another guitarist to make a decent sound. Especially in a heavy metal band."

Rick prayed Dietmar wasn't right.

"For those of you who don't know us, we're Purple Method, and we want to thank you folks for joining us and coming to see what we can do," Max drawled into the microphone. "For those of you who do know us"—he winked at Rick, and the groupies at the front cheered, thinking it was meant for them—"we've got something a little different for you. We hope you enjoy our new sound. Here's some melodic metalcore to wake you up this fine afternoon. This one's called 'Busted, Bolted, and Burned.'"

Max signaled to Tony, whose eyes glinted wildly as he raised his arms high and struck down hard against the drums, the first beats driving the power and energy of their new sound. Rick felt the excitement rise a notch as Kyle began their smooth, yet heavy, guitar riffs, and Max waited for them to finish the intro, a touch of a smile on his lips. He took a breath, and his powerful vocals above the complicated arrangement of indulgent yet meticulously precise notes of the swinging, punchy, slap-bass rhythm were mesmerizing. Rick had never heard anything like it, and judging by the volume of screams from the crowd—neither had they.

"You know." Rick jumped at the sound of Pete shouting close to his ear. "They may not be the most organized or dedicated, but they sure can pull it together when it matters."

"I heard Max warming up earlier," he shouted back. "You've been coaching him, haven't you?"

Pete held up his hands and grinned. "Guilty as charged. I'm surprised he told you. I don't think anyone else knows. It would be a crime to let a talent like that waste away. I wish he wouldn't hide how hard he works."

"Yeah, but I kinda get why he does. Tony's not the easiest to get along with." Dietmar's arm brushed against his. "Oh, sorry. Pete, this is Dietmar. Dietmar runs a chain of clubs over in England." Dietmar shook Pete's hand. "Pete's a vocal coach."

"Oh, nice to meet you." Dietmar moved so he was standing closer to Pete. "Are you responsible for Max?"

"I'm not sure 'responsible' is the right word for it, but yeah, I help him out sometimes."

"I can see that might be something of a challenge."

"He's a good kid."

"Incredible voice."

"One of a kind." Pete chuckled. "Don't tell him I said that, though."

"Tell me something, do you think they're ready for the next step?" Dietmar nodded toward the stage.

"Honestly… I think it's exactly what they need."

Rick smiled and his heart lurched a little as Max slid across the stage on his knees, his T-shirt riding up and exposing his abs. God, he was sexy. Perhaps Max hadn't blown it after all. Purple Method would finally get the break they were after, and so would he, with any luck.

The crowd was growing as the band delivered rapid-fire drumming, monstrous guitar riffs, and melodic, throat-grating screams and howls interspersed with tender and emotional choruses. The small music area looked to be filled to capacity, and the mosh pit was in full force when Purple Method's half-hour slot was up. Everyone was cheering, and Rick suddenly remembered the bucket he was in charge of.

"Pete, had we better get to the exits?" he shouted.

"Oh yeah, I nearly forgot." Pete grabbed his bucket and pointed it toward their left. "You take that one, and I'll take the other side."

Dietmar followed him as Max bounced to the front of the stage. The cheering was deafening.

"Thank you so much," Max yelled over the microphone. "You've been amazing to play for. We hope you'll come see us again real soon. We're collecting for Elfinbrook's air ambulance charity, so if you liked what you heard, then please show your support. Oh, and we're selling a load of T-shirts over at our hog booth if you want to come say hi."

Rick caught Max's eye, and he grinned at him. Max waved one last time, threw a handful of Kyle's plectrums into the crowd, which Kyle didn't look too impressed about, and they all left the stage.

The bucket was heavy by the time the crowd had cleared, and Rick rested it against his hip.

"Should we catch them now while they are packing up? I'd like to meet them," Dietmar said.

"Yeah. I'm not sure what needs to happen to all this, so I should get it to Tony." He shook the bucket.

Purple Method was in a huddle behind the stage, and Tony looked a bit emotional as he said, "This is the start of something very special."

Dietmar coughed.

"Hey, how much did we raise?" Tony asked Rick.

"I dunno. You'll have to count it." He thrust the bucket at him.

"Oh wow, there's loads," Max said, peering at it. "Guess we must've done all right, then. We'd better get back to the booth and give Sian a hand selling the merch."

"You may as well go while we pack up," Tony said. "Not like you ever help us anyway."

Max scowled. "Yeah, I do."

"Guys, this is Dietmar," Rick said before their bickering could get out of hand. "He wants to talk to you."

"Oh yeah," Max said. "The guy from the bike show. I guess we weren't too heavy for you after all?"

"Max, will you shut up a minute." Rick glared at him, and Max looked shocked. He'd make it up to him later, but this was too important.

"Actually, I know a thing or two about heavy metal," Dietmar said. "I own a chain of clubs over in England, and several of those are alternative venues."

"Fuck," Max said and smiled sheepishly at Rick. "Sorry. I didn't realize. You didn't say anything—"

"You have bands play at your venues?" Tony asked.

"Yes. It's mostly live music, and then we have a few club nights too. I really liked what you did out there. You have a very interesting sound." Dietmar shook each of their hands. "I'd better get back to Jakob. He'll be needing a hand with his bike. It was nice to meet you all."

Dietmar walked away, and Rick hurried after him. "What was that?"

"You were right. They're excellent, but their sound is so unique I'm not sure who I could get them to open for, sorry," Dietmar said and patted Rick on the shoulder. "I should get back to Jakob."

"Dietmar, please."

Dietmar shrugged his apology and disappeared into the crowd. Rick's shoulders slumped, and he wandered back over to Max and the others.

"That was weird," Tony said as he hauled one of his drums off the stage.

"Yeah," Rick said and rubbed his hand across his face. He'd been convinced Dietmar was going to make them an offer. "Look, I'm going to get something to eat. I'll meet you back at the booth." He needed some time to figure out a way to convince Dietmar that not inviting Purple Method over to London would be the biggest mistake he'd ever made.

SIAN HAD sold all the merchandise and was carefully weighing some dried spices into a large tub when Rick got back to the booth. The others had returned after having dropped off the band equipment back at the house.

"How's it going?" Max asked her as Rick joined them by Lorette.

"The marinade is all injected. You've just got the rub to put on her."

"Aren't you helping?" Rick asked Sian.

Sian removed the tub from the scales and handed it to Max. "I've done all the work so far. It's Max's turn. Besides, it's nearly three now. I need to go pick up the blind boxes."

"What's a blind box?" Rick asked, taking the beer Pete handed him.

"It's what we have to present our meat in once we're done," Max said. "It's so they can't tell whose is whose. Makes the judging fairer."

"Oh. I had no idea it was all taken so seriously."

Sian snorted a laugh. "This is nothing. The bigger competitions are governed by societies that have very strict rules, and they even have professional teams competing."

"One day." Max tasted the rub.

"What's in it?"

"It's our secret recipe," Sian said. "Only Max and I know exactly what's in it."

"Oh, come on. Tell me?" Rick said. Kyle and Pete were sitting in yard chairs by the ambulance while Tony fiddled about with their sound system. There was no one close by. "I won't tell anyone."

"Uh-uh." Max shook his head. "We don't crack that easy. What if you're working for the opposition?" He nodded toward Pearls Before Swine.

Rick grabbed a wood chip from the bag lying next to the smoker and flicked it toward Max, hitting him gently on the forehead. "Hey!" Max vigorously shook his head. "Quit messin' around. This is serious."

Sian laughed. "I'm gonna get those blind boxes and take a break. Don't forget to cool Lorette once you're done with the rub."

Max waited until she was out of sight and then produced a bottle of bright green liquid. He emptied it into the marinade that was left over.

"What was that?"

"You didn't see anything."

"What's it worth?" Rick folded his arms. "Sian doesn't know the secret recipe either, does she?"

"This whole competition was my idea. She would never have gone with this, and I wanna win this year."

"What is it?"

Max sighed. "It's something to make the sauce pack more punch. The judges only take a couple of mouthfuls. If the marinade isn't strong enough, then we won't stand a chance against everyone else."

"Surely Sian would understand that."

"I already talked to her about it. She wouldn't do it. She preferred the recipe she thinks we're using. Trust me, it's for the best."

Rick held up his hands. "I'm not saying a word. This is all on you. So how come if you have these blind boxes, you're cooking Lorette whole? Wouldn't it be easier to smoke each bit separately?"

"That's the point." Max tipped the dry mixture onto Lorette and began to massage the rub into her skin. "Everything has to be ready at the same time. It's difficult to get right because all the cuts are different thicknesses. All the hams, shoulders, and loins need to be cooked perfectly for us to have a chance at being placed." He patted the smoker with his elbow, as his hands were covered in the rub. "This baby will make it easier. It's a reverse-flow offset smoker with auto gas and auto water. If we can't win with this, we may as well give up now and go home."

Tony inspected Lorette from a distance. "How much longer are you gonna be doing that pig?"

"A while, why?"

"We're heading back to the stage, see what other bands they have playing. You coming?"

"Na. Got too much to do here. I've got the decoration for the boxes to do yet, and besides, someone's got to guard Lorette."

"Rick, coming? Can't imagine this is much fun for you, hanging about here."

"Thanks, but no. I've got to head back over to see how my dad's getting on with his Harley." Tony seemed satisfied with his answer, thank God. Max's brother really was a pain in his ass, and not the good kind.

"Tell Sian where we are when she comes back?" Kyle said and Max nodded, and finally they were on their own.

"What time do you have to go see your dad?"

"I don't."

Max stopped massaging the pig. "But you said—"

"Did you want your brother to think we were hanging out again, on our own?"

"I guess not." Max frowned and continued massaging more slowly. "Why, has he said something?"

"You know how he is. Don't want him to cause problems when I've finally got you to myself." Rick winked at him, and he could have sworn Max's cheeks colored.

"You know nothing's gonna happen here, right?"

"I know." Rick smiled and reached across to squeeze Max's forearm. He was trying to be understanding but was finding it almost impossible to not touch him. "When do you start cooking her, anyway?"

"We'll fire up the smoker at about eleven, and then she'll go in from about one."

Rick frowned. "One… tomorrow afternoon?"

"Tonight." Max laughed. "Judging is at twelve thirty tomorrow, and it's gonna take about ten hours to smoke her. Then we've gotta get her looking her best."

"In the blind boxes?"

"Exactly."

"That's hours away, though, so why did you say to Tony that you needed to get them ready now?"

Max concentrated hard on Lorette. "Helps intensify the flavor the earlier we get the marinade on. Besides, you're not the only one who's finding my brother a giant pain in the ass lately." He glanced up at Rick and back to the pig. "No way was he gonna hang out here all afternoon. Can you give me a hand with her?" Max gave Lorette one last check. "I need to get her in the cooler."

"You have a cooler?" Rick looked around their empty booth. "Where?"

"Ice packs. In the ambulance. Like before."

After Rick had helped Max to wrap Lorette up, they placed her in the paddling pool in the back of the ambulance to keep her nice and cool until the middle of the night, and then they lay on the grass, sipping beers in the late afternoon sun. Sian had delivered their blind boxes and had gone to find the others in the music section.

"That was weird with your buddy Dietmar," Max said, taking a drag from his cigarette.

"I guess." Rick stretched out on his back and adjusted his sunglasses. This was the last conversation he wanted to be having with Max right now. He still hadn't thought of a way to convince Dietmar to change his mind.

"Why didn't you tell me what he did? Is that why you were so worried about how I behaved around him?"

"He's just an old friend of my dad's."

Max punched Rick's arm, and Rick turned his head to look at him. He was sitting cross-legged and looked very thoughtful. "Yeah, but he might've wanted us to play at his clubs. That would've been awesome, you and me in London, Purple Method showing England how great we are. Then again, maybe they're not ready for our kinda sound. I guess I was right about us being too heavy for your friend."

"Wait... what did you say?" Rick pushed himself up onto his elbows.

"What? That it would be awesome to play in England? I've never been there. Have you?"

"Yeah, a few times," Rick said slowly. "When we lived in Germany."

"You lived in Germany? When was that?"

"Until I was five," Rick said distractedly.

"You never said." Max looked a little hurt.

"You never asked." Rick smiled at him and leaped to his feet. "I'll be back in a minute, okay?"

"Where are you going?"

"I won't be long," Rick called back over his shoulder to a very confused-looking Max.

Breaking into a run as soon as he was through the worst of the crowds, Rick headed straight for his dad, hoping to find Dietmar there too. He was in luck. Slowing to catch his breath, Rick waved at them as he approached.

"How's it going?" he asked his dad.

"Great. Loads of people have taken her picture." Jakob patted the gleaming Harley and smiled.

"That's good. Dietmar, have you got a minute?"

"Sure, I'm not going anywhere." Dietmar leaned back in his chair. "This about your friends?"

"Um, yeah. I had a thought."

"What's that? By the way, I spoke to Neil about your MMA, and he's very interested in seeing what you can do."

"He is?" Rick's stomach somersaulted. "What did he say?"

"To send him a recording of one of your classes, and he'll think about it."

"That's brilliant, Rick," his dad said.

Rick almost bounced with excitement. "I've got a better idea."

Dietmar sighed. "Why do I get the feeling I'm not going to like this?"

"How about I visit with Neil in London instead?"

"Okay," Dietmar said slowly.

"When Purple Method plays at your clubs." Dietmar opened his mouth, and Rick hurried to continue. "It's only a matter of time before Purple Method makes it big. Surely you can see that? Their music is as authentic as it gets. And they're unique. You said it yourself. Aren't they worth the risk? Once they've opened for a couple of generic metal bands, you could have them headlining, and when they make it big, you'll be the one that discovered them. It would be great publicity for your clubs."

Dietmar laughed, but it looked long-suffering. "You make a convincing argument, I have to say." He studied Rick for a moment with a knowing smile. "Fine. They're booked in four weeks on Friday, August 31, at the Scarab Lounge, and I'll see where else I can fit them in. I'll talk to Neil for you and get him to set something up at his gym."

Rick leaned down and hugged Dietmar. "Thank you. You won't regret it. I promise."

Dietmar growled. "I'd better not."

WHEN RICK got back to the Porkaholic Method booth, Max was busy frying bacon on a portable stove.

"Mm, that smells good," Rick said, giving him a quick squeeze and leaning down to sniff the bacon.

Max frowned. "Where did you get to? What happened to us spending some time together?"

Rick tried to snatch a piece of bacon from the pan, but it burned his fingers and he let it go.

"Serves you right," Max said.

"I've got good news. Want me to tell you now or wait until Tony and Kyle get back?"

"What have you gone and done?" Max lifted the bacon from the pan with the tongs and placed them on a plate before looking up at Rick.

"You don't want to wait?"

Max narrowed his eyes. "Tell me."

"We're going to London in four weeks, and you're playing at Dietmar's club, the Scarab Lounge."

Max stared at him in disbelief. "Are you serious?" Rick nodded. "And you're coming too?"

"What do you think? Shall we go tell the others?"

"No." Max grinned. "Why should Tony always get to be in charge of the band? I know the perfect time to tell them. Will you help me book the airplane tickets? I guess we should do that right away." He bounced on his toes. "Oh my God, we're playing in London. I can't believe it." Max stared at Rick. "And you arranged all this for us? Thank you, Rick. It means a lot."

"You can thank me later." Rick winked at him and stole a piece of bacon from the plate. "Do you think anyone would notice if we disappeared into the back of the ambulance for a while?"

Max snorted a laugh. "We can if you want, but Lorette's still chilling in there. I don't know about you, but right now I could do without an audience."

CHAPTER ELEVEN

Max

SECOND PLACE. Second place! Max still couldn't believe it. The judges had said it had been a close call, but losing to Pearls Before Swine was soul destroying. He was still seething three days later. Scrambling out of bed, Max grabbed the silver trophy from his desk and shoved it in the back of his closet, hiding it away in the dark. At least now he wouldn't be reminded of his failure every time he woke. Maybe that would help him forget about it… until next year.

His door opened and Tony walked in dressed in his Elfinbrook hockey team shirt. "Hey, you're up."

"Everything okay?"

"Yeah, great. We're just heading off now."

Tony, Kyle, and Sian had tickets to watch Elfinbrook take on the Leatherton hockey team. It was their local derby, and there was a huge rivalry between the two teams.

"Have a great time. I guess I'll see you later." Max crouched down by his stacks of vinyl to pick out something to listen to.

"Yeah. About that. Sian surprised us and booked a motel room."

"You won't be back tonight?" Max tried to hide his excitement. Would he really have the place to himself? He couldn't remember the last time that had happened—if ever. As soon as they left, he'd be calling Rick to come over. "Well, that's great. Saves someone having to drive."

"Yeah. Be good to have a few beers after the match." Tony sat down on Max's bed. "You going to be okay on your own? Want me to ask Pete to come over and keep you company?"

"Na. I'll be okay."

"Will you go to the Torrens Bar, do you think?"

"Probably."

"You know, I'm sure I could still get you a ticket if you want. Or I could stay. Some of the guys—"

"Tony, I'll be fine here. Go. Have a good time. You know hockey's not my thing."

Tony went to stand, then sat back down again and opened his mouth, but Max beat him to it. "Seriously. I'll be okay. It's not like I'll burn the house down or anything."

Why was Tony so hesitant to leave him? It didn't make any sense.

"Tony! We're going," Kyle called upstairs.

Tony glanced at the door and then at Max and slowly got up.

"Good luck," Max said.

"Yeah. We'll kick their asses, don't worry. Don't have too much fun without us."

"Can't guarantee that." Max grinned.

"And call me if you need anything."

"Tony!"

Tony patted the doorjamb. "See ya, then."

The front door slammed, and Max waited until the ambulance had left the driveway, then dialed Rick. They'd have the whole night and most of tomorrow together. He couldn't wait. Rick had classes until nine in the evening, and Max counted down the minutes until they got to be together again. It was kind of scary how strong his feelings were for Rick. To the point that he'd caught himself wondering what it would be like if his friends did know about them. He'd see Sian and Kyle together, or Tony with his latest conquest, out in the open and not having to hide. Not being able to share with his friends and Tony that he might be falling in love for the very first time was constantly getting harder, but the thought of how they might react still terrified him. They'd never look at him in the same way again.

"IT'S WEIRD being here with it so quiet," Rick said after he had kissed Max hello.

"Oh yeah. I forgot you haven't been here since the party. God. That was nearly six weeks ago. I can't believe it's been so long. Come on down to the kitchen. Are you hungry?"

"Starving. I didn't get a chance to eat dinner before the last class like I normally do."

Max jogged downstairs and into the kitchen. "What do you want? I could make more bean burritos like the ones we had the other day. Or I could do"—he rummaged in the refrigerator—"chicken taco salad. Or cheeseburgers and homemade fries?"

"I don't have a fight for a couple of weeks, so maybe the burger?"

"Good choice." Max removed the ingredients and stacked them on the counter. "Do you want a beer or a soda?"

"What are you having?"

"Mm, soda probably."

"Okay, I'll have one too."

Max handed him a can and opened one for himself.

"Art was asking whether you'd be coming back to class."

"Really? What did you tell him?"

Max diced an onion and then opened the packet of ground beef and tipped it into a bowl with an egg, the onion, and some seasoning while Rick watched.

"I told him you'd decided to take private lessons for a while to get you started."

"What the hell? He'll be expecting me to come back to the class."

"I also said you were more interested in learning the silat and kali systems. I don't teach much of that in class, so he was quite impressed with your decision, actually."

Max snorted a laugh. "You make it sound as though I know what I'm talking about. I almost feel obliged to return the favor and teach you how to cook."

"Almost?" Rick came up behind him and slid his arms around Max's waist, kissing him on the neck.

"You start doing that and you won't get any food or a cooking lesson."

Rick laughed and rested his head on Max's shoulder, as Max squished the ingredients in the bowl to make patties, which he laid on a baking sheet.

"I didn't realize burgers were that easy to make."

"Yeah, they don't take long." Max reached across to the sink and washed his hands before slicing the potatoes into thick fries, which he then threw into a bowl of cold water. "Can you pass me the oil?"

"Sure." Rick let go of him and went to grab it from the opposite counter, and Max took out the pan he used for deep frying. "Are we still going to book the flights to London today?"

"Yeah. Is that okay?"

"Of course. It's not hard. Shouldn't take long. I brought my passport, so we should have everything we need."

"Why do you need your passport?"

"You have to put the number in when you make the booking."

"The number? Well, how the hell am I supposed to get those for the others? It's a good thing we all had to get passports for the gigs in Toronto."

Max added the oil to the pan. It wouldn't take long to heat up, so he fished the fries out of the water and dried them with a cloth.

"You're going to need to tell them," Rick said and sat at the table. "How long were you planning to leave it before saying anything, anyway?"

Sighing, Max said, "I've never had any involvement in the running of the band. It was always Lee and now Tony. I guess I just want to prove to Tony and Kyle, and myself, that I could do all this other stuff if I had to… and maybe I want to someday."

Rick smiled and took a gulp of his soda. "Then we'll find a way to do it. Do you know where they keep their passports?"

"I know where Sian keeps hers and Kyle's. She's super organized. I called Craig to book her time off work so she can come. He promised to not say anything to her, so that's good. I haven't got a clue with Tony, though." Max carefully lowered the fries into the oil. He was going to triple cook them so they were extra crispy. "I think we're gonna have to search his room."

AFTER THEY'D eaten, Max took Rick upstairs. Luckily Tony had left his door open, as Max could never remember his code.

"I feel like I'm intruding," Rick said.

"He's not exactly a private person. Don't worry about it."

Tony's room was a mess. Cosmetics and drumsticks littered the surfaces. Clothes and magazines were strewn across the unmade bed, and Max narrowly avoided tripping over Tony's hockey skates, which were in the middle of the floor without the blade guards on them. That could've hurt. "Watch your feet," Max said and picked his way over to the dresser. "If you were Tony, where would you keep important stuff?"

Rick frowned. "I dunno… in the bedside cabinet maybe?"

"You check there. I'll look through the dresser."

As Max was rummaging through one of the drawers, Rick suddenly gasped.

"What is it? Did you find it?" Max spun around, and Rick looked stunned.

"I'm officially scarred for life."

"What? What is it?"

After making his way across the room, Max slid an arm around Rick and crouched down to look inside the cabinet. Inside was a clear Fleshlight next to a massive bottle of lube and the superhero porn DVD Tony had bought the other week.

"I guess that'll teach us for looking through his stuff," Max said and shuddered. "We found what we were looking for, though." Tony's passport was tucked between the lube bottle and the side of the cabinet. Max gingerly reached in and grabbed it, then wiped it on his pants.

Getting Sian's and Kyle's passports was far less traumatic. After collecting what they needed, they sat on Max's bed with his laptop. Rick had his back to the wall, and Max sat between his legs with Rick watching over his shoulder. "My credit card is gonna take a hammering," Max said as they were entering the details for the flights, with Rick showing him what he needed to do. "Okay, so that's everyone done. We need to book a hotel, and I guess we should sort out shipping for our gear as well. I hope they can do it at such short notice."

"Do you know what company to use?"

"Yeah. Pete gave me what I needed. He's done this before when he toured with his band years ago. They went all over the world. Luckily, the company they used is still going strong. I wouldn't have a clue who to use otherwise. I also arranged with Pete for us to record our album in a couple of weeks. Gives us some time to get the tracks perfect. Hopefully we'll get some sales off the back of these gigs in London."

When they were done organizing everything, Max placed his laptop to one side and relaxed back against Rick, closing his eyes when Rick kissed his head. It was nice being able to relax like this, in his own room, on his own bed, without any risk of interruptions.

"Can I use your laptop a minute?" Rick asked.

"Sure." Rick's torso flexed beneath him as he reached for it.

"I thought I recognized that website logo."

"What's that?" Max asked, half opening his eyes. *Oh no!* A naked man was on his laptop screen, jacking himself. "Give me that." He tried to grab the laptop, but Rick held it out of reach.

"It's okay. I look at this site sometimes too."

"You do?" Max turned around on his knees to try to reach for it to turn it off. How mortifying. The next thing he knew, Rick had used some ninja move on him and Max was lying on his back with Rick straddling him. Rick moved Max's hand onto his groin. He was semihard. Max raised an eyebrow. The shock of Rick discovering his secret was suddenly full of possibilities.

"We could watch it together? That could be fun. What do you think?" Rick leaned down and whispered, "I bet I can last longer than you can."

Max caressed him through his jeans. Fuck. He liked that idea. "You're on."

"Mind if I take a look at your playlist?"

"That'd be cheating. I think we should pick one together." Max knew he would probably lose. He was getting hard just thinking about it. He'd definitely lose if Rick picked any of his favorite videos.

"How about this one?" Rick stopped scrolling. He'd stopped on one of a really hot muscular guy with blond hair who was going to be jacking off.

"No way. To make it fair we should pick one where they don't look like either of us."

"Mm, somebody wants to win." Rick kissed him long and hard, and Max almost forgot all about their game. "I know which one we should choose," Rick murmured as he pulled away. It turned out to be a video that started with three fully clothed dark-haired guys lying on a bed.

"Yeah, looks good to me." Max shuffled across so he was sitting up next to Rick with his back against the wall, and Rick moved the screen so they could both easily see it. "Have you watched this one before?"

"Yeah, a few times. You?"

"No."

Rick pressed Play, and Max watched as the three guys began to undress one another as they exchanged brief kisses. "What ones do you usually like?" Rick asked.

"You first."

Rick shrugged. "A mixture, I guess. Depends on what mood I'm in. I like the ones where you can tell the guys have a good chemistry."

"Yeah, that's true. Watching them getting blown is pretty cool. I like those."

"You're so gonna lose," Rick said and laughed as one of the guys dropped to his knees and the other two took turns feeding him their cocks.

Max groaned and rested his head back against the wall, staring at the ceiling fan. He was aching to touch himself, and after one of the guys started moaning, he couldn't help looking back at the screen. After unzipping his pants, he reached inside and squeezed himself. He glanced across at Rick. His jeans were still fastened, but he was rubbing himself through the material. He looked to be fully hard, though, so it couldn't have been comfortable.

The two guys getting blown started making out, and the guy kneeling held their cocks together, running his tongue along their lengths and then sucking the tips into his mouth. Max's cock twitched, and he shoved down his pants so they were out of the way while he stroked himself as slowly as he could.

Rick's breathing was getting louder, and finally he gave in and removed his jeans and his T-shirt. Fuck, he looked hot. Max watched him as Rick jacked himself by alternating a couple of fast strokes followed by several slower ones. A bead of precome was at his tip, and Max wondered if it would be considered cheating if he licked it away with his tongue.

"How far through do you normally get before you come?" Max asked after a while.

"I try to wait and come at the same time as them." Rick was watching Max's hand, so Max sped up his strokes.

"Do you always manage?"

"Sometimes I fast forward." Rick's breathing was becoming slightly ragged now, and the slap of his hand as his fist slid up and down his solid length was making Max even harder. Max loosened his grip as he tugged on his balls with his other hand.

"Ugh. That's a good idea," Rick said and removed his hand to copy Max, and his cock slapped back against his tight abs. Rick gave him a small smile as he steadied his breathing.

"What does the winner get?" Max asked. He was seriously considering jumping Rick right now.

Rick reached across and kissed him, hot and wet. "I'll get to watch you come undone as you pleasure yourself. It'll be so hot that you'll drive me over the edge, but I'll hold myself back until you've spilled every last drop, and then I'll come wherever you want." He trailed his tongue around Max's ear and then whispered, "Where do you want me to come?"

"Fuck." Max pushed Rick away and reached for himself again, pumping at a steady pace so he didn't tip himself over the edge. "That sounds so good. But maybe I want to watch you make yourself come hard first."

The guys on the screen were fucking now. One guy was standing facing the wall, bracing himself against it while the other two took turns inside him. The guy currently fucking him was slamming into him with every thrust.

"How long until they—?" Max nodded at the screen.

"Not for ages. You want me to fast forward it?"

"Fuck. How do they last so damn long?"

Rick's leg was touching Max's as they sat side by side, and every motion of Rick's hand as he jerked himself rippled through Max, turning him on even more. He risked a look down as he loosened his grip a little. The head of Rick's cock was red as he strained to stave off his release. It was then that Max realized Rick was watching him more than the screen. He desperately wanted to touch Rick, to feel how turned on he was for him, but even more than that, he wanted to watch Rick lose control all on his own. There would be plenty of time for them to touch later.

With Rick watching him, Max thrust up into his hand, slowly, deliberately. "God, that feels fucking good." He shifted his grip so he was holding himself from underneath, to allow Rick an uninterrupted view of his length.

"That's cheating," Rick gasped and let go of his cock. He stared back at the screen, breathing hard.

"How much do you want to win?" Max asked. "Are you sure winning is worth all this?"

"You want me to rewind to when those guys were getting blown?"

"That'd definitely be cheating." Max secretly hoped he would, but that could very well mean the end for him. Watching that had turned him on so fucking much. "Don't you want to watch these three guys make each other come?" Rick gripped himself as he watched the screen, and Max glanced up to see what had captured his attention. Instead of watching the two of them fucking, the third guy was lining up behind, ready to take them both.

Max and Rick watched in silence for a while, and other than the video, the only sounds were an irregular rhythmic slap as they jerked themselves and their breathing getting deeper and jagged.

Finally, one of the guys on the screen said, "I'm getting close." In the next shot, the three guys were on the bed. One of them was lying on his back, and the other two were kneeling on either side of his head with their cocks aimed at the guy's mouth.

They were getting ready to come, the camera going in for a close-up. Was Rick about to go too? He was watching the screen intently, his eyes hooded and his hand now flying over his cock. He was, Max was sure of it, and he couldn't take his eyes off him. Each time Rick breathed out it became more erratic than the breath before.

"Fuck, I'm coming," Max heard on the screen, but he didn't look at it. He desperately tried to hold himself on the edge as he heard the guys on the screen climaxing, and then Rick squeezed his eyes together and yelled out. His hand was moving impossibly fast as thick spurts of come coated his chest right up to his neck. His body was still shuddering as Max's orgasm took hold, and Max was aware of Rick watching him as he kneeled up on shaky legs. He steadied himself by holding Rick's thigh, and pointed his cock at Rick as his orgasm thundered through him and he coated Rick's chest with his release.

Max flopped down next to Rick. Once he had caught his breath, he said with a grin, "Looks like I win."

"I want a rematch."

"Fine by me."

"I'm sure you cheated."

"Hey, you chose the video."

"Maybe we should see who can come first next time."

Max laughed and rolled onto his side so he could kiss him. "I'd still beat you."

They spent the night sharing their favorite clips until Rick had to admit defeat and gave in to sleep. That had been at about three in the morning, and Max lay awake watching him for hours as he slept.

He had had the best time tonight. It was effortless being around Rick, and Max felt as though he could truly be himself when it was just the two of them. He'd never been able to do that around anyone before. It scared him a little—the strength of his feelings, that is. Plus, the sex was incredible. That was definitely a bonus. Max sighed and lay back, hoping that Rick wouldn't sleep too long. He was ready for another round, and they had the whole morning to themselves.

SEVERAL WEEKS later, Max was wondering whether it had been the best idea to keep the London trip from the others. He was nervous about telling them, but he couldn't leave it any longer. Today they would be recording their new album, *Languid Lunatics*, and Tony and Kyle would want to know what the hurry was.

After using Tony's special body wash and spending enough time in the hot shower that he couldn't see through the thick steam, Max bounced downstairs.

It was still morning, so none of the others would be up yet. As he reached the kitchen, he wished that wasn't the case. He was too excited, and not just about recording the album. It had been difficult to keep it secret for so long, but immensely satisfying knowing that he'd coped with arranging everything.

Max whistled a random tune and fired up his skillet, ready to cook maple bacon, pancakes, and over-easy eggs. Things had been going so well with Rick. It'd been two months since they'd first kissed, and they had been the happiest two months of his life. He let his mind travel back to the night they'd spent here in his bed. It had been incredible. He'd never experienced anything like it. And getting so much uninterrupted time together had felt so right. It was a shame they would rarely get to do that. If ever again. A sadness washed over Max, but he pushed it away. Part of him ached to be with Rick and it was getting harder to resist by the day.

He took his breakfast into the garden and sat in the shade of the garage to eat. Max waved away a bug that flew in his face and took a sip of his coffee. It was hot out there already today, and the sun wasn't even at its peak. It was peaceful, though, with the sounds of lawnmowers humming and someone splashing in their pool. He could've stayed out there all day. But they had an important job to do. He hoped the others wouldn't take too long to get up, but three hours later he had warmed up his voice and was still waiting for them.

Two o'clock. Two fucking o'clock. This was ridiculous. Max paced his room. The loud music he was playing hadn't made the slightest bit of difference. Perhaps it hadn't been his greatest idea to keep this from them until today.

Pete was expecting them at three to record their new album so they could upload their music before they went, and also so they could take some CDs with them to sell. He'd rearranged a load of work so they could do this. If they didn't show up, Pete would be pissed. He had no other option left; he was gonna have to wake them all. Tony first.

Banging on Tony's door didn't get him a response. Cringing, Max eased the door open. Thankfully, Tony had left it unlocked. He shielded his eyes with his hand and approached the bed, catching his foot on something and swearing as he fought to stop himself from face-planting onto Tony's bed.

"What the fuck, Max." Tony rolled over and stared at him with bleary eyes. "This'd better be a fucking emergency."

"It is." Max picked up a T-shirt from the floor and threw it at him. "Get dressed. We're recording *Languid Lunatics* in an hour. I booked studio time with Pete."

"We're what?" Sitting bolt upright, Tony leaned back on his elbows and narrowed his gaze. "What's the—"

"We've got a gig in London in a week, and so we need our new album online by then. Surprise!"

"London?" Tony scrubbed at his eyes and shook his head. "What the fuck have you gone and done?"

Max grinned. "Think this is the chance we've been waiting for? Purple Method's big break?"

"What I think is why the fuck you didn't mention this earlier," Tony shouted and leaped out of bed, pulling on some jeans. "How did you—"

"Dietmar, Rick's friend—"

"But that was three and a half fucking weeks ago that he saw us. Have you known all that time? I might have guessed he'd be involved."

Max froze, his pulse suddenly pounding. "What's that supposed to mean? What's wrong with Rick helping us out? He's a friend—"

"Is he?" Tony paused before pulling the T-shirt over his head. "Is that what he is? A *friend*?"

"I don't know what you mean."

"Wake the fuck up. Rick is gay. You think friendship is all he wants from you? How can you be so fucking naïve? You're acting like a sixteen-year-old virgin. Grow up, Max. Un-fucking-believable. You think he's giving you self-defense lessons out of the kindness of his heart?"

Max was stunned. "How do you—"

"And he'd better not be coming to London with us."

"But… it's his friend."

"Fucking perfect." Tony shoved past him. "Do you want everyone to think you're sleeping with him?"

Max watched as Tony brushed his hair and finished getting ready, and then he took a deep breath and looked Tony right in the eyes. Not being able to be with Rick out in the open when he was with his friends had become unbearable. And hearing Tony speak about Rick in that way was just awful. Rick had become too important to him to keep this up any longer.

He felt amazingly calm as he said, "But I am sleeping with him, Tony. I'm gay."

Nervous relief washed through him. He was tired of pretending; it was exhausting. It felt amazing to finally say those words. To finally own who he was and stand up to his brother. Rick had given him the confidence to do this, and he knew Rick would take care of him if this went badly. There was no way he could've stood by and not defended Rick, not defended himself.

Max stared at Tony, defiantly watching as a multitude of emotions crossed Tony's face.

Tony's eyes widened. "No!"

"Yes." Heat flushed through his body, and he screamed, "I always have been, and I'm not going to hide it anymore. You need to accept this is a part of who I am."

"No! You can't. You can't be." Tony broke down with uncontrollable tears, which chilled Max to the core. He'd never seen his brother cry before, not since they'd been adults. "I can't lose you, Max." Tony's voice was shaky, and he dropped to his knees, his body trembling. "Please don't do this. I'm begging you. Please…."

Max's heartbeat was racing. Tony looked defeated, and it was terrifying. Tears soaked Max's cheeks as he got down on the ground next to Tony and hugged him close. "You're not going to lose me. Why would you think that?"

"Todd from Vanquished Villains, Kris from Norshell Arachne, Damon from Coco Mashita…."

Suddenly Max got it, and a lump formed in his throat. "I'm not going to kill myself, Tony. Hey, look at me." He lifted Tony's chin. His eyes were red and puffy, his face wet. Max lifted the bottom of his T-shirt and dried Tony's face. "Is that why you've been making this so hard for me?" Tony wouldn't look him in the eyes, and Max huffed a laugh. "You're a fucking idiot. You've been making my life hell." He lay back on the floor and placed his hand on his forehead, trying to process what had just happened and what that meant for the future. "So… let me get this right. Are you even bothered that I like guys? Other than it might make me want to kill myself."

Tony sniffed and punched his arm, hard, and lay on the floor next to him. "I don't give a fuck who you're sleeping with." He sighed. "It's everyone else's reaction that worries me. You saw what happened in the media with Todd. They didn't leave him alone. And they were really cruel and intrusive."

"Yeah. I know." Max scrubbed at his face. "I guess it's a good thing we haven't hit the big time yet."

"But we will, though. What then? What if you're right and this London gig takes us to the next level?"

"I guess we have to take it one step at a time." Max turned to stare at Tony. "Is it okay if we just tell our close friends at the moment?"

"Yeah. Sure." Tony reached for his hand and squeezed. "So, Rick, huh?"

"Yeah." Max couldn't help grinning.

"He's a good guy."

"Yeah, he is."

"Think it's serious?"

Max took a deep breath and chewed on his bottom lip. "Yeah. Yeah, it is."

Tony banged their hands against the floor. "We should go wake up Sian and Kyle. You want to tell them when we get to Pete's? You can tell everyone at once then."

"Yeah.... How do you think they'll react? Do you think Pete will be okay with it?"

"Pete's gonna be fine, and so will Sian and Kyle."

"I thought he'd guessed at one point."

"Na, he doesn't know. I don't think he'll be surprised, though."

Sian poked her head around the door and sniggered. "You guys okay down there?"

"Yeah," Tony said. "Is Kyle up? We're all heading over to Pete's."

"ONLY AN hour late. I'm impressed," Pete said as the four of them shuffled through his front door.

"Sorry," Max said. "There was an incident."

Pete sighed and showed them through to the studio. "There usually is. Don't worry about it. Everything's set up. Did you bring the equipment you needed?"

"Yeah," Max said. "Actually, I've got something I need to tell you guys first, if that's okay?" Max sat on the stool by what would be his microphone.

"Sure. What is it?" Pete said.

Kyle frowned. "You'd better not be leaving the band."

"No, it's nothing like that."

Max's hands were clammy, and suddenly he felt nervous. Everything was about to change with a few small words. He clenched his fists. "I've been dating someone, and it's getting pretty serious."

Sian shrieked. "Oh my God, that's so exciting!"

"That's great," Pete said. "Who is it?"

Max took a deep breath. "It's Rick."

Pete's and Kyle's eyes widened.

"I knew it!" Sian said and hugged him.

"You did? How?" Max said.

"Rick?" Pete said. "What, my friend Rick?"

"Yeah." Max rubbed the back of his neck. "I'm gay."

Pete gaped at him.

"I know it's a lot to take in—"

"Na. I'm happy for you, bud," Kyle said and shook his hand. Then he turned to Sian. "How come you knew and didn't say anything?"

"She didn't know," Max said. "I told Tony this afternoon. He's the first person I've said anything to."

"Apart from when we talked in the garden that morning," Sian said. "Don't you remember? I had a feeling you were hiding something. You don't usually hold back on telling me the details, but you wouldn't even tell me who it was."

Max scowled at her, and she laughed.

Pete still looked shocked, and Max's nerves returned. "Pete?"

"Sorry. Um. Yeah. It's a bit of a shock. That's all. It's a lot to take in, you know?"

"But you're okay with him being gay?" Tony asked. His brow was furrowed.

"Oh. Yeah. Totally." Pete shook his head. "I just want to make sure you're not rushing into anything. You said it's serious between you and Rick?"

"Yeah. It is." He was so relieved that Pete was okay with him being gay. He guessed it must be a bit weird for Pete that he was dating his friend. "Rick's a good guy. He's taking care of me. Don't worry."

"Yeah. I know. It's just… promise me you won't rush it, okay?"

"Yes, Dad," Max said and rolled his eyes.

"Well," Pete said. "I guess we should get started on recording your album, then. How did you want to do it?"

"We've got twelve songs to get through," Max said. "It should only take a couple of hours I think. I thought we could record it like a 'live in the studio' album and maybe video each track at the same time? That way it wouldn't matter if it's not perfect. I know we're cutting it fine with this."

Tony laughed. "If it wasn't for you hiding this from us, we'd have had plenty of time to record it. Anyway, what is this 'not perfect' bullshit? You think you can't keep up?"

"Of course I can keep up."

"Awesome. Let's get started, then." Tony smashed the cymbal in quick succession. "Pete, you got any beer?"

"You can have some after."

"What?"

"If you're doing this drunk, tonight's going to be a living hell."

Kyle snorted a laugh. "Yeah, don't want you falling off your stool if we're recording this—"

"Let's get started before you all kill each other," Pete said. "I'll grab the video recording equipment."

CHAPTER TWELVE

Rick
Two hours earlier

RICK ACCEPTED the beer Pete handed him and took a long drink. His thoughts drifted to the upcoming trip to London, which was only one week away, and his nerves multiplied tenfold. It was going to be difficult for him and Max to keep their relationship secret while in such close proximity to the others. But that wasn't what was stressing him out the most.

"You've been hanging out with us too much," Pete said as he dropped into the kitchen chair opposite him.

"What?"

"You." Pete waved his beer bottle toward Rick's. "Drinking. You barely touched the stuff a couple of months back."

"I shouldn't be drinking at all." Rick sighed. He'd been training all morning, so it wasn't like he was slacking off, but Pete was right. What had happened to him? He used to be so disciplined with martial arts training his sole focus.

Max.

Max had happened to him and had turned his world upside down.

"I was only messing with you. One beer ain't gonna hurt you."

"That's just it. It might."

Pete frowned. "What you talking about?"

"Can you keep a secret?"

"Sure."

"I've got an interview in London for a job training world-class fighters."

"That's awesome." Pete held out his hand, and Rick halfheartedly high-fived him. "Isn't it? I thought that's what you'd been working toward."

"It is. Was. I dunno." He took another pull from his beer and then slammed it down onto the table. "It's not that simple anymore."

"Thought so."

"What?"

"You've been acting all distracted these past weeks. It's been pretty obvious that you've been seeing someone. What's their name?"

He shook his head. "You've got the right idea staying single."

"That bad already?" Pete whistled. "You sure they're worth it?"

"They are...."

"But?"

"But what if I have to move to London? Their life is here in Elfinbrook."

"Ask them to come with you."

"That's not even an option." He sighed and pushed the beer bottle away with his fingertips. "How can that be a possibility when he won't even tell his friends about me, let alone anyone else? How can I choose him over my career when I don't even know if we have a future together?"

"Thought about doing it long-distance, then, maybe?"

Rick raised an eyebrow. "How many couples do you know who've made that work?"

"Dunno. One, maybe?"

"They happy?"

Pete grinned. "Occasionally, I think."

"It's difficult enough when we're living in the same town, let alone different continents." Rick groaned. "I never should have agreed to being exclusive. There was always a high chance I'd have to move away for my career, and that it would cause problems for us if the relationship wasn't casual."

"He insisted on it?"

Rick nodded. "If I wanted to be with him, it had to be this way. It just feels like I'm the one making compromises all the time. And the closer we get, the harder it becomes. Especially now with this interview. I haven't even told him about it yet. Don't feel that I can. I'd forgotten how hard it is to date someone who isn't out."

"What are you gonna do?"

"I don't want to lose him. Things are going great, and I really care about him." Rick grimaced. "But is a relationship I have to keep a secret, maybe for forever, worth throwing away my career over? Ugh. I don't see a way to have both. I don't want to give up on either. It feels like an impossible choice."

Pete huffed a laugh, but there was a sadness to it. "Well… I made the wrong decision four years back now. Letting the love of my life go was the biggest mistake I ever made. Gets kinda lonely after a while."

Rick stared at him. "I only get one shot at this, don't I?"

"You talking about your relationship or your career?"

He let his head drop into his hands. "Both," he mumbled.

"You'll figure it out." Pete gathered up their empty beer bottles. "My advice? Don't make any rash decisions. And don't keep no secrets. Living with regret for the rest of your life ain't no fun. Beer?"

"You got any soda?"

"Sure." Pete gave his shoulder a squeeze as he walked past. He grabbed a can out of the refrigerator and handed it to Rick. "You want to stick around for a bit?"

"I would, but I have a ton of paperwork to get through."

"Shame. I know just the thing that would've cheered you up. Ever witnessed a crazy-ass band trying to record an album when half the band don't even know about the recording session?"

Rick snorted a laugh and tried to ignore the little flip his stomach did. He knew what Max had arranged, but he couldn't tell Pete that. Rick hadn't been able to see Max today because of this recording session. He sighed as he was reminded once again of all the secrets he was being forced to keep because of Max's situation. He'd known it wouldn't be easy dating Max. But he hadn't realized it would be this hard. "Thanks, but I should get going. Thanks for the chat, Pete."

"Anytime."

Rick made his way along the hall toward the front door. He paused with his hand on the doorknob and squeezed his eyes shut. The last thing he wanted was to hurt Max, but what if Neil did offer him that job? He was running out of time to figure out what he was going to do, and right now he couldn't see a solution.

LATER THAT evening, Rick was in the lounge, jotting down ideas for tomorrow's classes, when he let out a loud yawn. He glanced at the clock on the mantelpiece. No wonder he was tired. It was nearly ten and he'd had an early start that morning.

"You going to head up?" his dad asked, checking the time and switching off the television.

"Yeah." Rick stretched his arms above his head.

The doorbell rang and his dad frowned. "Who could that be?" He shook his head. "It's very late. I hope that didn't wake Lily."

"You want me to get it?"

"No, it's okay. You go on up. See you in the morning."

"Okay. Night."

Rick began to climb the stairs as his dad opened the door, but listened in to make sure everything was okay.

"Hi. Is Rick there?"

He froze. He recognized that voice intimately. But it couldn't be.

"Um, yeah," his dad said. "Rick, it's for you." Rick turned to look at the door, staying on the stairs, his mouth gaping as his dad walked past him and patted him on the shoulder.

Max poked his head around the door. He was smirking. "Uh. Is it okay if I come in?"

Rick shook himself. "Yeah. Of course it is." He edged down the stairs. "What are you doing here? My parents are—"

"Yeah. I saw."

Rick craned his neck to make sure his dad wasn't watching and then placed his hands on Max's arms. "Wha-what are you doing here?"

"Surprise," Max whispered and kissed him.

He was so stunned, he barely kissed him back.

"Is it okay that I came over?" Max asked, resting his arms around Rick's waist. "I can leave if you want…." Max pressed their cheeks together and nuzzled Rick's ear, making him groan and drop his head to Max's shoulder. God, he smelled good. The mix of leather, smoke, and the light musk of Max's aftershave was fast becoming his favorite scent. "Or I could stay?"

"This is either the worst tease ever or the best—"

"It's not a tease." Max's grip around his waist tightened. "It's okay if your parents and Isla know about us. You can tell them if you want."

Rick snapped out of the spell Max had cast on him, and leaned back so he could look at him properly. He had so many questions but didn't even know where to begin.

Max grinned sheepishly. "So is it okay if I stay over?"

Rick narrowed his eyes as he took in what Max had told him, and he said slowly, "Yeah. It's totally okay if you stay over. Let me go tell my parents you're staying." He started up the stairs and then turned to look at Max. "You're absolutely sure this is—"

"For fuck's sake, Rick, it's fine. Tell them whatever you want. I came out to Tony, and the guys. They all know about us. All the important people know."

Rick hadn't dared hope that was what had happened. Hearing Max speak those words sent a rumble of joy flashing through him. He bit his lower lip as he reached for Max's hand, and prayed he didn't wake tomorrow to find out this had all been a cruel dream.

RICK RANG the doorbell of the Diaz house. He still couldn't believe it. Max had actually told his friends about them. When Max had turned up at his house after the recording session to tell him, he had been speechless. It was such a massive step forward for Max... for them as a couple. Rick didn't dare let himself hope that Max would be ready to tell everyone else soon. He longed for the day where he could hold Max's hand in public—where Max would let him put his arm around him when there were people watching. It felt so unnatural not being able to express his affection for Max.

Tonight would be the first time he had seen them all since Max's big announcement three days ago. Max had invited him and Pete over for dinner. They were going to have a barbecue.

"Hey!" Max said, his face lighting up when he saw Rick on the doorstep. "Come on in."

Once the door was closed, Max kissed him. "I'm so proud of you," Rick said again, pulling him into a hug.

"Everyone's been great about it. Well... Pete's been a bit weird. But he is your friend and all, so I get it."

"Really?" Rick frowned, and then his heart sank when he recalled the conversation he'd had with Pete where he'd told him *everything*. Had he said anything to Max about his job interview? Max seemed happy to see him, so it didn't look like it. He was going to have to get Pete on his own later. "Um, I brought this." He held up the bag, which was filled with bottles of beer.

"Thanks!" Max took it from him. "I'll go get them chilled. Everyone's in the backyard. I'll meet you out there in a minute."

Rick watched as Max jumped down the stairs to the kitchen, then braced himself as he opened the back door.

The barbecue smoker was set up differently than how he'd seen it at the jamboree, and Sian was flipping burgers. A table by the garage was filled with burger fixings and sauces. It all looked and smelled delicious.

"Hi, Rick," Kyle said, and everyone turned around and smiled.

"Hi, everyone." He felt really awkward, but then Tony came over to him and draped his arm across Rick's shoulders.

"How do you like your burgers?" Tony asked.

"I don't care so long as they're not burned," Rick said and laughed.

"Rick," Sian said and beckoned him over. "Come over here and tell us all the details. When did you two get together? Max has been so cagey over the details."

"That's 'cause you're too nosey and want to know everything," Max said. He was laughing and handed Rick one of the beers he was carrying. "And I mean everything. She asks the most inappropriate questions."

"I'm your best friend. You're supposed to tell me all the inappropriate details. The burgers are about done if anyone wants one."

Rick copied the others and loaded his plate with as much as he could. He knew Max's cooking was fantastic, and this meal was no exception. He joined them as they all sat around the table and tucked in. Pete still hadn't spoken to him, and he was dreading that conversation.

"So, when did you actually get together?" Tony asked. "I reckoned about a week after the party. Am I right?"

"No," Sian said. "It was much later than that. Kyle, what do you think?"

"I have absolutely no idea."

"Don't you just love being discussed?" Max said and shook his head.

"So, come on, then, when was it?" Tony said.

Max looked at Rick and shrugged. "I guess it was two weeks after the party? The day Lee left the band?"

"Our first date wasn't until a week after that, though."

"Where did you go?" Sian asked eagerly and frowned at Max. "You didn't tell me anything."

"I took him to one of my fights over at Elfinbrook Stadium."

"Yeah," Max said. "And I never want to do that ever again. You should see how hard they hit one another. Rick got kicked right in the eye, and I thought it had knocked him out."

"Thanks for that!" Rick laughed. "I didn't get knocked out. I won the fight."

"How're your martial arts lessons going?" Tony asked.

"Good, maybe I'll show you some later," Max said. "How did you know about those?"

Rick stared at Tony. He wasn't going to be the one to tell Max.

Tony nodded at Rick. "He told me at the jamboree." Rick's stomach lurched at the reminder. "The day I told him to stay away from you for the third time."

"You did what?" Max gasped. "I can't believe you, Tony."

"What? I was looking out for you."

"Sorry about my brother," Max said and reached for Rick's hand. Rick could feel everyone's eyes on them. The sooner everyone got used to this the better. Rick squeezed his hand and gave Max a kiss on the cheek.

"That's okay. I think we understand each other. Right?"

Tony cocked his head. "All the time you protect my brother we don't have a problem."

Rick held Tony's gaze. "I would never do anything to hurt him." Rick caught Pete staring at him. "On purpose," he added, and Pete shook his head. "I'll be back in a minute. Just gonna go to the bathroom."

He got up and hoped Pete would follow him. They really needed to clear the air. Thankfully, Pete got the message. "Anyone want more beer?" Pete asked, and Rick went inside, down to the kitchen where he knew Pete would be headed.

"Pete—"

"Don't even start with me," Pete said. "I… what the hell are you thinking? Max was who you were pouring your heart out about to me the other day? What? You didn't think that one day I would find out and put the pieces together?"

"Pete, I—"

"Max is like a son to me. You know that. How could you tell me all that stuff about him and the way you're feeling? I can't believe you still haven't told him about the job yet. I should go and tell him right now. Do you know what a difficult position you've put me in?"

"I would never—"

"But you have, Rick. This is gonna break his heart when he finds out. I've never seen him behave this way about anyone before. Do you understand how hard it was for him to come out? And he did that for you. How do you think he's going to react when he finds out that I knew what you have planned?"

"You're going to tell him?"

"I should," Pete spat out and pointed his finger in Rick's chest. "But I'm not. I'm giving you a chance to make this right. Don't you dare fuck this up and hurt him."

Pete grabbed the beer, and Rick followed him back upstairs. Pete barely spoke to him again all evening, and he couldn't blame him. Rick hoped he could fix this, that he hadn't ruined his friendship with Pete. They'd gotten close over the past months. He'd find the right time and tell Max. He had to.

"Do you want to stay over tonight?" Max asked Rick hours later as everyone moved from the garden into the garage.

"Yeah, I'd like that."

Max pulled him around the corner. "This is where you kissed me. Remember?"

"Yeah, I remember." Rick put his arms around Max and kissed him again. "How could I forget." He rested his forehead against Max's. "And I told you I didn't believe you when you said you'd never kiss me again."

"I'm glad I was wrong," Max said and kissed him so sweetly that it made Rick's heart ache.

There was no way he could give up Max. Or risk losing him. He'd go along to the interview—it was too late to cancel now—and then if Neil offered him the position, he would turn him down. Maybe he could try to get some funding so he could expand his gym. Make it more attractive to top fighters. If that failed, maybe he could get a bank loan. Rick held Max tight and prayed that he could figure this out.

FLYING OVER England was something Rick had always enjoyed as a kid. It was the vast expanse of lush green fields, spires of old churches, and pockets of tiny villages that he loved the most. It had been years since he and his parents had visited with Neil and Dietmar, and he realized now how much he'd missed it. It was certainly a welcome change from the desert of northwest Nevada, especially during these hot summer months.

Rick was beginning to wish they hadn't booked the night flight, even though the countryside looked beautiful in the morning sunlight. He hadn't gotten a wink of sleep, worrying about what the next few days would bring. Rick had looked into getting funding and bank loans, but all those options had been nonstarters—in part due to the monumental amount of debt he had in student loans.

He now knew he was going to have to take the job if Neil offered it to him, but still Rick hadn't been able to bring himself to tell Max about the interview. Things had been so perfect between them over the past couple of days that he hadn't wanted to break the spell. He knew it was selfish, but he'd wanted to make the most of that time together before it would all likely come crumbling down once Max found out what Rick was keeping from him.

They arrived at their hotel in Camden late morning. Sian and Kyle were sharing a room, as were Max and Rick, and Tony had the room next to them on his own. As soon as the door to their room had closed, Rick dropped his suitcase to the floor and fell onto the bed, puffing up the already-plump pillow and closing his eyes. Thank goodness the hotel had let them check in early.

Tony knocked on their door, and Max came out of the bathroom, where he'd had a quick shower, to let him in.

"Don't we have to meet with Dietmar soon?" Max asked.

Opening one eye, Rick stared at Max, who was perched on the edge of the bed, watching him. Rick took his cell out of his pocket and groaned.

"Yeah, we should've been in the hotel bar ten minutes ago."

"The bar?" Tony said, his head appearing around the bathroom door. "Why didn't you say so before? What the hell are we still doing in here?"

"Sleeping," Rick said, shutting his eyes as pure exhaustion took hold. Dietmar would understand if he didn't go. He wasn't in the band, after all.

"Up," Max said and grabbed Rick's hands, pulling him to his feet. "You'll feel better with a beer inside you."

Rick wasn't convinced. And the last thing he needed was to drink alcohol before his interview tomorrow.

"Besides, I want to go explore." Max was bouncing on his toes. He had way too much energy for Rick's liking right now. But then he had managed to sleep on the airplane. "Can't you show us around?"

"Fine. But we're gonna be stopping for coffee, a lot."

"Awesome."

Tony was holding the door open for them, and Rick followed Max outside into the corridor, which had burgundy walls and a matching mottled carpet, old paintings of the aristocracy lining the walls, and floorboards that creaked as they made their way toward the elevator. It felt like they'd stepped back a hundred years in English history. They collected Kyle and Sian on their way.

It was actually a pretty decent hotel—right in the middle of Camden and a few blocks from the Scarab Lounge, where Purple Method would be opening for Death Charm the following night. The hotel was a quaint building tucked away down one of the side streets off the main street. Away from the hustle and bustle, but close enough that they'd be right in the thick of it after walking a few yards.

"You're late," Dietmar said, standing as they approached the large table he sat at in the hotel bar.

"Sorry, Dietmar," Rick said. "It took forever to get through customs."

"It's nearly lunchtime. It must have." Dietmar shook their hands and gestured for them all to sit. "I've ordered some coffee for us, so please, help yourselves."

"The traffic's so busy in the city. It's worse than I remember it," Rick said and laid out the cups, ready to pour coffee for everyone. Tony looked disgusted at the fact that they weren't getting beer, but thankfully had the sense to keep quiet and accept the drink Rick handed him.

Dietmar laughed. "I guess I don't really notice it anymore. I've lived here so long now. It's certainly nothing like Elfinbrook."

"Yeah. We're looking forward to exploring," Max said with a grin. "Rick's gonna show us around this afternoon."

"Mm," Dietmar said. "You should have enough time to see a small amount of London today. Probably best to keep it local, Rick. We've got a pretty packed schedule." He handed Tony a sheet of paper. "This is your itinerary while you're here. I expect you to be on time for everything."

"Did all our equipment arrive okay?" Max asked.

"Yes, I believe so. We received some of your boxes last night. This afternoon I will need you to check that you have everything you need for tomorrow night. In fact, we can go straight from here, and that way I can show you the venue."

"Hold on," Tony said, frowning. "What's this on Sunday night?"

"You'll be playing ten gigs while you're here… assuming tomorrow's goes well, that is. You are here for several weeks, after all."

"Awesome," Tony said.

"Two will be at the Scarab Lounge, and the others will be at some of my other clubs. The addresses are all on that sheet."

Rick snatched the paper from Tony and photographed it before he had a chance to lose it. It wasn't worth taking any chances.

"Is there anything else we need to know?" Max asked.

"No, I don't think so," Dietmar said. "As soon as you've finished your drinks, we can go to the club."

"Is it far?" Kyle asked.

"A five-minute walk. You will need to be back there at five tomorrow to sound check, so that gives you a few hours to sightsee. Any idea what you want to do while you're here?"

"Abbey Road Studios," Sian suggested.

"How about that big wheel by the Thames?" Kyle said.

Rick laughed and drained his coffee. "The London Eye?"

"Yeah, that's the one."

"You get a great view of London from there. However, I suggest you find something a bit more local to see today. The queues can be pretty long, and I'm sure you must be jetlagged," Dietmar said. "Ready to go?"

"Sure, let's do it," Tony said.

Camden was just as Rick remembered it. As they reached the end of the road and joined the main street, delicious aromas of cooking street food wafted in the air. The tang of exotic spices combined with the comforting earthy aromas of bread warming and potatoes baking.

"This place is amazing," Max said, his gaze darting from food outlet to food outlet. "Never mind visiting the landmarks, I could easily spend all my time hanging out here and trying all these foods." He pointed at a sign at one of the takeout storefronts. "What the hell is kimchi?"

"Fermented vegetables," Dietmar said. "It's good. You should try it." Max didn't look convinced. "It's a Korean dish. Very popular."

"Korean?"

"There's food from all over the world here," Rick said as they walked over the bridge that crossed the river, and he looked across to where long trails of willow dipped into the water and a group of ducks was arguing. "And you'll love the market, 'the stables' section of it, that is. There are a lot of alternative clothing stores in there."

"There's nothing alternative about the way I dress," Max said and laughed when Dietmar gave him an odd look. "Not my fault if everyone else wants to dress strangely."

"Here we are," Dietmar said as they reached some double doors in between a tattooist and a body piercing place. The Scarab Lounge was written above the black doors in stylized old-fashioned writing.

"It doesn't look like much," Kyle said and frowned.

"Wait until you see inside," Dietmar said. "It's a much bigger venue than it looks."

He was right. A long, dark corridor led to a balcony that looked down over the stage. As Rick looked behind him, he saw there was a bar and booth-style seating that had a gothic-Egyptian feel to it. The lighting was eerie, the electric candles throwing shadows against the dark blue walls. It was going to be perfect for Purple Method.

"This place is awesome," Tony said.

"Follow me and I'll take you to your kit," Dietmar said and gestured for them all to follow him through a door at the side of the bar and to a steep staircase that led to the basement and then around the edge of the main area to backstage. "There's another door that leads to the street that you can use tomorrow night once the venue is open. Your set will be thirty minutes."

It was quite pokey backstage, but Rick stayed with Purple Method as they checked through the boxes they had shipped and then helped them stack them out of the way, ready for tomorrow.

"I think we've got everything," Tony said. "It all looks good to me."

Max grimaced. "I don't have any spare bass strings. I'll need to get some more before the gig in case I snap one."

"There is a music shop not far from here that sells them. It's a short tube ride." Dietmar scribbled down the address on a scrap of paper.

"Thanks," Max said and shoved the paper into one of his pockets. "I'll head down there tomorrow."

"I think that's everything. Unless you have any questions?" They all shook their heads. "Great. I'll see you tomorrow. Don't be late."

As they headed outside into the bright sunlight of the busy street, Kyle said, "So, what now?"

"I could use a drink," Tony said. "Looks like there's plenty of bars around here. Which one shall we try first?"

Kyle suddenly gasped, and Rick spun around to look at him. He was pointing excitedly at a poster in the tattoo store window. It was advertising an ice hockey match that evening. "We have to go to this, Tony."

Tony's grin said it all. "We'll all go."

"Absolutely no way," Max said. "You should go, though. We'll hang out here and check out some of these food places and those clothing stores."

"Yeah. I'd rather stay around here," Rick said and let out the yawn he'd been holding in. "I need to get some sleep."

Tony said, "We'll only be gone a few hours, and then we can all have a drink afterward."

Max shrugged. "Sounds good."

"Tony, we should head over there now to get tickets. Maybe we can see about skating while we're there too, if they've got a session before the match?" Kyle asked.

"Sure. It'll be weird not having our own skates. If they're really shit, I'm sure they'll have a bar we can go to instead."

"Great," Sian said. "What's the best way to get there?"

"Tube," Rick said and pointed toward the station. "Definitely the best way to get around London."

"We'll see you later, then," Kyle said to Rick and Max.

"Are you thinking what I'm thinking?" Max said as they watched the others walk away.

Rick smirked. "Hotel?"

"Yeah," Max said. "But we're stopping for some takeout first."

Rick reached out to put his arm around Max, but Max shrugged him off.

"What do you reckon... Greek chicken skewers with triple-cooked fries or filled Indian puris?"

"Whatever you want. You choose."

By the time they reached their hotel room, they'd finished their skewers. Rick could have done with a sleep. But he wanted to make the most of his time with Max before tomorrow. Before he found out what his future held.

"Are you tired?" Rick asked as their hotel room door slammed closed.

"A bit," Max said and slid his arms around Rick's waist, kissing him and then resting his head on Rick's shoulder.

"Nervous about tomorrow?"

"No, not particularly." Max went over to the bed, puffed up one of the pillows, and slumped against it.

"Not even a little jittery?"

"No, not at all. Why?"

Rick came over to the bed, climbed on top of him, and sat straddling him. "That's a shame. I guess the bubble bath in my case will have to wait until another time, then."

"You know, now you mention it, I do feel a little tense," Max said and cracked his neck for effect.

"Yeah. Thought you might be." He smiled and leaned over to kiss Max.

Pulling him closer, Rick deepened the kiss, savoring Max's taste.

"I'll go get the bath started," Rick breathed and reluctantly pulled his lips away.

Once the water was running, Rick poured in the bubble bath and inhaled the steamy aroma of rosemary and thyme. This was a great idea. He could do with a decent soak after that long airplane trip and then the rushing about from the second they'd arrived. As he stripped off his clothes, he glanced in the mirror and decided to shave his two days' worth of stubble—he'd feel better after.

The mirror was already steamed up, and Rick wiped it clear with his hand as he took out his shaving kit. He jumped as Max slid his hands around his waist and pressed his hard shaft to Rick's bare skin.

"You're such a tease," Max said and thrust his hips toward him so his leaking cock rested between Rick's buttocks. Rick groaned as lust shot through him and spread throughout his body.

"You need to learn to have some patience." Rick caught Max's eye in the reflection and winked at him.

Sliding his hand around the curve of Rick's hips, Max cupped his balls in one hand and caressed them, allowing his fingers to brush against the underside of his shaft. He pressed his thumb over Rick's tip and smeared the silky precome over the head. Rick couldn't help groaning, it felt so good.

"Really? You're the one who keeps on losing our races," Max murmured, reaching up to grab Rick's jaw, turning it toward him, glancing his lips across Rick's, and trailing kisses down the side of his neck.

Max gasped as Rick grabbed his hips and swung him around so quickly that Max reached out to the basin to steady himself. Leaning forward, Rick pressed his mouth against the nape of Max's neck. "I have no self-control when it comes to you." Rick took a firm hold of Max's cock and used what he hoped were agonizingly slow strokes. "Turn around," Rick said and nipped at his neck, reaching across to turn off the running bath.

As soon as Max obeyed, Rick grabbed some lube from his dopp kit, dribbled it between Max's asscheeks and teased him by gliding his thick cock between them, deliberately not penetrating. Instead he gyrated against him, making damn sure Max could feel how wet he was for him.

Max's body trembled as Rick let go of his waist and ran his fingers around his rim, sliding them inside, Max's breathing quickening as he pressed back into his touch. Dropping to his knees, Rick withdrew his fingers and took hold of Max's cock with one hand as he ran his tongue around Max's entrance, darting inside. Max bucked against him, but Rick was ready for him and didn't allow his tongue to penetrate farther. Pumping Max harder, Rick held his other hand across Max's lower back to hold him in place as he darted his tongue deeper this time. His hand stayed clenched around Max's cock, and Max flexed against his grip as Rick's tongue traced the ring of muscle at his opening.

"Just fuck me, will you?" Max gasped.

Slowly standing, Rick said, "What was that? You want me to fuck you?" He held his body rigid, resisting Max's attempts to force their bodies together. Pressing his lips to Max's neck, he waited for an answer.

"Yes," Max choked. "I want you to ram your cock into me so hard that I have to beg you to stop."

Rick caressed Max's neck while he grabbed a condom from his dopp kit and put it on. His sheathed cock teased Max as it rested against him. "You got it."

Max cried out as Rick penetrated him, pushing in just far enough that he could feel resistance, waiting for the ring of muscle to relax before thrusting deeper. Max was ready for him and pushed against him, forcing him deeper as he slowly thrust back and forth. He whimpered as Rick changed angle to glide over his prostate.

"Ready?" Rick whispered, and Max moaned in response.

He thrust harder, and once again Max cried out. Rick clasped his hand over his mouth to remind him to stay quiet. Max wouldn't want the entire hotel hearing what they were up to. It felt so good being inside him like this. It was these moments, when they were able to be together like this, that everything felt perfect, like they were meant to be together.

Rick was getting close, and he rested his head against Max's back as Max writhed beneath him. He reached around and batted Max's hand away, gripping his rigid length as he pumped him, his balls slapping against Max's bare skin, and pistoning his hips as he thrust into the delicious heat of his body. Max yelled as he tensed, clenching around Rick's cock and spilling into his hand, tipping Rick over the edge. Rick jerked into him, breathing heavily as he emptied his load, white-hot sparks shooting through him and blinding him for a moment, and then he slumped against Max as he fought to catch his breath, kissing Max's neck before pulling out and taking a few moments to enjoy the afterglow. "It was supposed to be the other way around."

Max was still gripping the basin. "I can do you in a minute if you want?"

Rick huffed a laugh. "I meant I'd thought we could take the bath first. But I like your thinking." He dealt with the condom and lowered himself into the bath. "You going to join me?"

"How much of the bubble bath did you use?" Max laughed and flicked water into Rick's face. "You sure there's room in there for me?"

He sighed and relaxed back, reaching for Max's hand and pulling him down on top of him with a splash, closing his eyes, and smiling at the weight of Max's body pressing down on him. This was pretty damn near perfect. He wished this moment could last forever.

"I CAN'T believe how much equipment you have in here," Rick said in amazement as he looked around Neil's MMA gym the next morning.

He'd managed to slip out before Max had woken, and had left him a note to say he'd gone to the gym.

Over to the right of the entrance was a large area of black mats where some fighters were stretching and others were practicing takedowns. There were floor-to-ceiling mirrors covering the walls at the far end, reflecting the octagon to his left and rows of heavy bags. A cornered-off section directly to Rick's left contained high-tech gym equipment and free weights.

Neil gripped his shoulder and smiled. "Why don't I show you to the changing area and we can run through some training drills while we talk?"

"Sounds good. I can't believe it's been seven years since I last saw you. You haven't changed a bit."

Neil laughed. "Thanks. I'm a bit grayer these days." He scrubbed his hand over his shaved head. "I have to say, I was excited when Jakob told me you might be interested in joining us here. Do you remember when you visited when you were twelve and I gave you your first kickboxing lesson?"

"Yeah." Rick grinned. "I don't think Mom's forgiven you for that, even now. As soon as we got back to the States, I gave up dancing so I could do kickboxing instead."

Some of the fighters in the changing rooms eyed Rick as he walked in with Neil, sizing him up. He recognized a couple of them from televised fights, but he didn't flinch. He was used to other fighters trying to psych him out and make him doubt himself, and knew he could handle himself against any of them in the ring.

Concentrating on getting changed, Rick stripped to his fighting shorts, and then Neil surprised him by saying, "Grab your MMA gloves and mouthguard. There's an advanced class about to start. How do you feel about joining in?"

"Sure." That sounded like fun. He was getting twitchy from not training for a few days. Hopefully the caffeine he'd taken that morning would keep him going through the jetlag that was threatening to knock him out.

"Great. It'll give me a chance to see where you're at and for you to see how we work. They'll do a warmup, then some drills, and they'll finish up with some light sparring in the octagon."

There were nine other guys in the class, including the two he recognized from the changing rooms. Their toned, muscular bodies, gloves that were heavily abraded and falling apart, and relaxed, confident manner made it obvious they were all professional fighters. Rick studied each fighter as they started on the warmup, running along the track marked out around the outer edge of the gym. He noted the way each of them moved—his chiropractor training making it easy to spot what injuries, if any, the fighters had—as well as their levels of competitiveness and aggression. Some of them raced, and others were happy to be at the back. Rick kept pace with the middle of the pack, careful not to let any of his own weaknesses show, as he'd be stepping into the ring with them today.

"Rick, why don't you pair up with Shawn," Ian, the trainer, said once they had finished warming up.

"Sure," Rick said, smiling at the tall dark-haired man shuffling toward him. He felt they were evenly matched based on what he'd seen so far, certainly in terms of weight and build. Their reach was probably about the same. He'd have to make sure he dominated in the drills and then again if they fought. If he couldn't handle Shawn, there was no way Neil would offer him the position. He had to be able to cope with whatever was thrown at him, and at the highest possible level.

Ian was demonstrating a pretty standard drill of jab, cross, hook, spinning backfist, jumping snap kick, roundhouse, and a compass half-moon capoeira kick.

"You want to pad first?" Shawn asked as they grabbed some water.

"Sure." Rick picked up his focus pads from the floor and slid his hands through the straps. "How long have you been training here?"

"Since it opened a year ago."

"It looks like a good setup."

"Yeah." Shawn dropped his water bottle and put on his gloves. "Much better than my last place. Plus I'm able to compete in the big competitions. We did quite well over in Japan last month."

"That's great." Rick held up the pads, ready to start the drill.

"I hit pretty hard, so make sure you hold the pads steady, yeah?"

Rick suppressed a laugh, nodded, and indicated for him to begin. The guy was quick, but if he thought this was hitting hard, he had another thing coming. He was going to get a shock when Rick took his turn. "Swivel your left foot more when you turn into the spinning backfist.

It'll give you more momentum and will set you up better for the snap kick. You're a bit off-balance at the moment."

Shawn frowned. He clearly didn't like the "new guy" trying to give him tips, but then he relented and nodded. Rick held up the pads, and this time Shawn's form was much better. His backfist had more power and his roundhouse was much more controlled. From the sidelines, Rick was aware that Neil was watching him and that he'd smiled and turned away, nodding.

He was right about Shawn not being used to powerful punches and kicks. With his first punch, he saw that the pad had knocked back and had struck Shawn's mouth, but he didn't show any sign of pain. With the second punch, Shawn staggered backward, and by the backfist he had securely anchored himself ready for the kicks, almost. With his roundhouse, Rick sent Shawn flying backward.

"Sorry, bud," he said and offered his hand to help Shawn up. "You okay?"

"Yeah." Shawn was laughing. "Haven't had that happen to me for a while. Who did you say you were again?"

Ian came over to check on them and watched with amusement.

Smacking Shawn on the back, Ian said to him, "Learn what you can from him." He winked at Rick. "Looks like the rumors were true. You've got one hell of a punch. We'll get you in the octagon in a minute, see what you've got." He stood back, and Shawn held out the pads again. This time Shawn was ready for him.

After one successful three-minute round in the octagon against another of the fighters who was lighter than Rick but very quick, he was watching Shawn fight someone who was about thirty pounds heavier than him.

He was clearly struggling to gain an advantage, and Ian was yelling at him to get to his feet when the other fighter took them to the mat. Ian was right. If you were fighting someone heavier, they would usually have the advantage when you were grappling, unless you were very good on the ground. Shawn was struggling. They were face-to-face on their knees, and Shawn was trying to overpower the fighter and flip him. Rick groaned and willed Shawn to listen to Ian, who was screaming at him now. He saw it coming, and there was nothing he could do to stop it.

Rick winced as Shawn's right shoulder dislocated. They carried on fighting, Shawn not seeming to notice. That would be the adrenaline, but his shoulder would hurt like hell later. No one else seemed to notice that Shawn had injured himself, and out of respect, Rick didn't try to stop the fight. They only had another thirty seconds anyway and the damage was already done.

Shawn lost the fight, and as he walked out of the ring, he was rubbing his shoulder and cracking his neck.

"Neil, mind if I take a look at his shoulder?" Rick asked.

"Yeah, go for it. Thanks, Rick."

Rick took Shawn to one side. He was a bit pale.

"Your right shoulder hurting?"

"Yeah, I caught it funny. It'll be okay."

"I think you've dislocated it. Mind if I take a look?"

"Dislocated? Fuck. Yeah, sure."

He checked his arm movement, and thankfully Shawn only had a partial dislocation of his acromioclavicular joint. At least it wouldn't need surgery.

"Is he okay?" Ian asked, and Rick filled him in. "Just pop it back into place and he can take some painkillers. I need him fight-ready for next week."

"Are you serious?"

"Yeah. You can do it, can't you? I thought you were a chiropractor?"

"Yeah." Rick shook his head. "Yeah, I can do it."

It took seconds to sort out Shawn's shoulder, and then he took some painkillers and carried on as if nothing had happened. He'd be taking the painkillers for a while.

That was something Rick had struggled with since he'd been training as a chiropractor—the disconnect between the mentality of "fix them up as quickly as possible and carry on as normal" and the "assess and administer a proper course of treatment." He was getting there, although there was one thing he would have to change in this gym for sure if Neil offered him a job, and that was to make sure fighters were more evenly matched in terms of their weight classes to try to limit injuries. Fighting someone you were not closely matched with could often do more damage than good.

"That fight knackered me out," Shawn said. "Thanks for fixing me up. How come you know so much about all this, anyway?"

"Like Ian said, I'm a chiropractor, and I run an MMA club back home."

"Guess I'd better listen to you, then, huh?" Shawn's breath caught as he tried to roll his shoulder.

"Put some ice on it as soon as you can. Once the swelling goes down, you should have the full range of movement back."

"Rick, can I have a word?" Neil asked and gestured for him to follow him out to the changing area. "I've seen enough." He smiled. "When can you start?"

"Are you serious?" Rick's heart was suddenly racing with excitement. "You want me to work here with you?"

"Yeah. It's obvious you know what you're doing. The fact that you're a chiropractor is definitely a bonus. I can pay you extra to take care of any injuries and to be our cutman when we go to fights."

"That sounds perfect. Thank you." Rick hugged him.

"Why don't you go and take a shower and get dressed and we can talk details."

Rick was so excited. He'd known he had the skills to make this work, and finally someone was willing to take a chance on him. He already had so many ideas of things they could change and improve in terms of taking care of the fighters and training routines. He switched on the shower and stood under the hot stream of water.

This opportunity was the most exciting thing that had happened to him since… since Max.

CHAPTER THIRTEEN

Max

IT WAS a bit scary, navigating London on his own, but Max eventually found the music store Dietmar had recommended. Thankfully, it had only been two stops on the tube in the end. He probably could have walked it. Rick had disappeared, leaving a note saying he'd gone to the gym, Sian and Kyle had gone out on their own to find someplace for lunch, and Tony had flat-out refused to go with him, choosing instead to stay in the hotel and sleep off his jetlag.

The music store was tiny compared to Hugh's, but they had a good selection of bass strings, and he was able to get exactly what he needed. He exited the store into the unfamiliar street. There was a posh-looking MMA gym a few doors down across the street, and it looked out of place among the takeout stores and foreign currency exchange places. His thoughts flitted to Rick and how much he would've appreciated seeing it.

Sighing, he took out his cell and checked where he was. It really wasn't too far back to the hotel, and it was a nice day, so he decided to walk back. As he approached the gym, he stopped and took a picture of it, and then leaned against the glass exterior as he sent it to Rick and messaged him.

See what you've missed out on. You should've come with me!

Max pushed off the glass and glanced inside the building as he shoved his cell into his pocket. There were two men near the reception desk. They had their backs to him, but one of them looked remarkably like Rick. The tall blond guy turned slightly as he shook the bald guy's hand. It was Rick. Awesome. They could walk back together. Shoving his shoulder against the door, he walked inside and waved to Rick as both men turned to look at him. Rick's smile dropped, and his eyes widened.

"Can I help you?" the bald guy asked.

"It's okay, Neil," Rick said. "He's with me."

"Okay, well, I'll leave you to it. It was great to see you again, Rick. Oh, I just realized we didn't discuss dates. Can you start at the end of September, or is that too soon?"

Start? What the hell was going on?

"Um." Rick glanced at Max and shifted his weight. "Is it okay if I let you know in a couple of days?"

"Sure. Like I said. The job's yours. Let me know when works for you. I'd better get back. I'll talk to you soon."

Job? Max had always wondered what people meant when they talked about their blood running cold, and now he knew. Was Rick leaving him?

"Okay, thanks, Neil," Rick said.

Max shoved open the doors, his muscles rigid as rage careened through him. His throat was so tight he could barely get the words out. "Something you want to fucking tell me?" His entire body was trembling. An elderly couple crossed the street, giving them a wide berth. Right now Max was beyond caring who witnessed this. Rick's face was flushed with guilt. It told Max everything he needed to know. "What, were you going to disappear and hope I didn't notice, or were you going to wait until just before you left to break up with me, huh? Do I mean so little to you that you'd move halfway around the fucking world without giving me a second thought? Doesn't our relationship mean anything to you?"

"Max, come on, be reasonable. We can figure something out. I wasn't going to break up with you—"

"Fuck you. I've been nothing but honest with you, and you hide something like this from me?"

"I didn't even know Neil was going to offer this to me until a few minutes ago."

"You didn't even fucking tell me you were meeting him. Don't you trust me at all? No, you know what, I don't give a shit whether you trust me or not. I don't care what you think. How could you not tell me about this?" Tears were falling down his face, and Max wiped them away with his sleeve.

"Opportunities like this don't come along very often," Rick said. "Do you know how many local MMA gyms I've applied to and been turned down—?"

"No, Rick, I don't, because you never fucking told me." Had he been so blind? "How could you not tell me about this when it's obviously so important to you?"

"What did you expect?"

Max walked away from him, blood pounding in his ears, but Rick grabbed his arm.

"You expect me to talk to you about my career and what I want in the future? We didn't even have a future all the time you wouldn't tell your friends about us, all the time you wouldn't let me tell Isla or my parents about us, let alone anyone else. Did you expect me to give up on my dreams, on what I've worked so hard for, for a future we'll never have all the time you're hiding away? You've come out to your friends, but what about everyone else?"

He couldn't believe what he was hearing. "You didn't tell me that you were planning to move to London because I might threaten your future? What about this, Rick, if the press find out about us, about the fact that we're together, then I may not have a future, period. Do you even care how much I've risked for you? For us to be together? I came out. For you."

"A few days ago. I couldn't put my life on hold on the off chance that you might come out at some point in the next fifty years. And even now, you're still not out completely."

"You said you understood," Max said quietly. "You said you'd keep it secret."

"I do understand, and I have kept it secret." Rick closed the distance between them and stared at him. "I want us to be together, but it was becoming impossible to keep things the way they were. Don't you see that? I have this one chance to make something of myself. One chance. You're a talented musician, Max; you've proved that with what you've been able to do with the bass. You'll have plenty of opportunities, even if the press do find out. You're too good not to. Why are you still so scared?"

"Purple Method is my life. I could lose everything. Why can't you understand that?"

"There has to be some compromise if we have a future together."

"Like me being okay with you living in London?"

"Like you understanding that my career is as important to me as yours is to you."

"You didn't even respect me enough to discuss it with me, or even to tell me. I'm not a fucking mind reader."

Max couldn't believe what he was hearing. That Rick had hidden something so important from him. Everything had been so perfect last night; were they really on the brink of breaking up for the sake of their careers? He couldn't bear to look at him.

Max turned and ran.

"Max, wait!"

Ducking around a corner, Max hid in a sheltered doorway. He had no illusions about being able to outrun Rick. As he struggled to catch his breath, his heart hammered in his chest. Had he dreamed what just happened? Had they broken up? He buried his head in his hands. His face was wet from tears, and more were coming. Years of tension, guilt, and frustration pouring out. He was losing the one thing that was more important to him than his music, and why? Because he'd been scared. Because he and Rick had been at different places in their lives when it came to what they were looking for in a relationship. In a partner. He'd been so excited about what their future might hold that he'd been blind to where Rick's head was at. He felt so stupid for letting himself feel so deeply for Rick, for assuming they were on the same page.

HE WASN'T sure how long he'd been hiding in the doorway, but it had to have been hours. His legs felt weak, as if the life force had drained from them along with his tears. Max wandered the streets, in a daze as he followed the directions on his cell, and found himself outside the Scarab Lounge, but couldn't face going inside, even though it was almost time for their sound check. He turned away and saw there was a bar next door, so he went in there instead. He was desperate for a drink and a dark corner to hide in.

There were quite a few metalheads in there wearing Death Charm T-shirts. It was weird being in a bar before a gig and nobody recognizing him. Right now, he was grateful for it. The last thing he needed was an audience while he fell apart.

His cell started to ring incessantly, and Max switched it off without checking who had tried to call, and he didn't even care. Losing Rick was the only thing he cared about right now. Screw Purple Method. Screw being a million miles from home. He'd never felt so lost and alone.

Five pints of beer and several shots of tequila later, the pain of losing Rick still hadn't numbed. If anything, it had made it worse. How could Rick have done all of this without telling him? Was the reason Max was here in London because of Rick's interview? Fucking hell. Neil... he was the one who had gotten Rick started in martial arts, he remembered now. He lifted his hand to his face and his beer glass went flying. The glass ended up on its side and beer cascaded onto the floor. The bartender glared at him.

"Sorry," Max mumbled and tried to act as sober as he could. He didn't want to have to find another bar to sit in. Hiding here in plain sight had worked well so far. While the bartender cleared up his mess, Max stumbled out to the restrooms.

There were two guys in there who eyed him suspiciously, but Max ignored them and went straight into the cubicle. They were whispering, but Max could make out what they were saying. One of them was a drug dealer and the other was buying enough weed for him and his friends, by the sound of it. Max had never tried anything stronger than cannabis, but right now the thought of erasing the last day from memory was very appealing. What was that stuff Kyle took sometimes? He couldn't remember. He'd always looked fine afterward, though. Hearing one of the guys leave, Max came out of the cubicle and made a decision. He'd buy something to help him forget. His life was falling apart, and he didn't want to be conscious enough to witness it.

"You selling weed?" Max asked casually as he washed his hands.

"Who's asking?"

"Look, I'm only in London a couple of days, and my dealer is back in the States. Can you hook me up or not?" The guy seemed to decide Max looked trustworthy enough, and he was able to buy some. "You got anything stronger? Something to help me forget about the shitstorm of today?"

"I've got this." He held out some tabs. "It's pretty good. It'll give you a nice trip and will do what you want."

"Give me a couple of those as well. How much is that?"

Max handed over the amount the guy asked for and shoved the weed and the tabs into his pocket. Heading back into the bar, he was relieved to see that the bartender who had witnessed him throwing his drink across the table was nowhere in sight.

Max took one of the tabs from his pocket, put it into his mouth, and swallowed as he headed outside. The sooner he forgot today the better.

He steadied himself by grabbing the doorjamb on his way out and blinked as the glare of the sun stung his swollen eyes. Stumbling off in the direction that looked most familiar, he soon realized he was going the opposite way from his hotel. He turned around to walk back the other way, saw he was outside another bar, and decided to go in there instead.

"Max!"

What the fuck? Had the drugs kicked in already? That was quick. He was hearing things now?

"Max, babe, thank God."

Max staggered to the side and swung his arms wildly as someone grabbed him around the waist. "Get off me," he screamed as his arms were restrained.

"It's okay. Calm down, I've got you." Sian cupped his face, and her image faded into darkness as he slumped to the ground.

"WHAT THE hell happened to him?"

Was he dreaming? The hazy, distant voices became louder as Max regained consciousness.

"What are we going to do?" a panicked voice said. "You're supposed to be onstage in less than a half hour."

"Tony, no, you can't—"

A torrent of freezing water splashed over Max's head, and he yelped as the icy drops pierced his skin. The cold liquid flooded his mouth, and he leaned forward, choking in his fight to take a breath.

"What the actual fuck, Max?" Tony shouted. Tony grabbed his chin and forced Max to look at him, then swallowed hard. "Have you taken something? Tell me you haven't taken something. What the fuck. Your pupils are fucking huge." Tony's fingers scraped off his chin, and the wall behind him sent tremors through Max as

Tony punched it, and then Tony screamed, "What the fuck were you thinking? Why would you do this? What have you taken? Tell me what you've taken, Max."

Max coiled into a ball, his damp clothes clinging to his skin. His heart was beating fast, and the more Tony shouted at him, the worse it became. He squeezed his eyes shut and clasped his hands over his ears.

"Hey, Max." Kyle's voice was soothing, and he gently lifted Max's fingers from his ears. "You're okay. Tony's going to stop shouting now. Can you look at me?"

Max slowly opened his eyes. Kyle was smiling, and Max blinked to focus on him.

"Is it okay if I sit down here with you?" Max watched, mesmerized by Kyle's slow, smooth movements. It was strangely calming. "You know, sometimes when I'm tripping I like to draw. Here." Kyle handed him some paper and a pencil. "You want to try?"

"We haven't got time for this," Tony hissed, and Max focused on the paper, the shadows on it reminding him of something, but he couldn't quite figure out what.

"We need to calm him down. He won't be able to perform otherwise. The last thing you want is him having a bad trip, and he was freaking out back there."

"How long will it last?"

"Maybe twelve hours, I reckon. If he's taken what I think he has."

"Twelve hours? We can't put him onstage like that. What the fuck are you thinking?"

"Tony, I've played on acid before—I think that's probably what he's taken—and I don't think you even realized."

"But he's not used to it—"

"We'll be there to take care of him. It'll be okay. Our set is only thirty minutes."

"Max." Max stared at Kyle as he came closer. "Do you think you can play your bass?"

"Of course. Why wouldn't I?" He felt fine, other than being a little spaced-out. A bit drunk still, but that icy water had sobered him up a lot. "How long till we go onstage?"

"We need to go now. Think you can manage it?"

Max nodded, and Sian handed him a dry set of clothes. He changed as quickly as he could, aware of the fact that Tony didn't take his eyes off him. "I'm fine, Tony, really. I don't think it's even working. I'm just a bit drunk."

"Why did you take it? Was it Rick? Did you take it 'cause of him?" At the mention of his name, Max's stomach plummeted to depths he hadn't realized existed. A heavy despair took hold and crept up until his entire body was numb and trembling.

"There'll be plenty of time to talk about it after," Sian said, putting her arm around Max and guiding him out of the dressing room. "This gig's too important. You have to get yourself together. This affects Kyle and Tony as well, not just you. I know you're very upset about Rick, but you've got to get through this set. As soon as we're done here I'll get us the biggest tub of ice cream I can find, and we'll find someplace quiet to talk. Okay? I'm here for you. We all are."

Max nodded numbly. Had she spoken to Rick? How did she know he was upset about him? What had he said to her?

As they reached the edge of the stage, Tony still looked concerned.

"You start to feel funny during the set, you go straight over to Kyle, got it? He'll take care of you until I can get there."

"I'll be fine, Tony. Stop worrying."

"Okay." Tony nodded but didn't look convinced.

"It's time, guys," they were told. "If you want to go out whenever you are ready."

Max grabbed his bass and ran onto the stage.

Raising his hands in the air to a packed venue, Max vowed to make the most of this. If he couldn't have Rick, he'd damn well make sure he had his career.

Max turned to look at Tony as his brother took his place at the drums, and began to play his bass. The intro to "Bass-tards," one of *his* songs. Finally, he got to open a gig with one of his songs.

A COUPLE of songs later, he was feeling a bit weird—kind of spaced-out—and he kept thinking he saw things that weren't really there. Was that Rick at the back of the crowd? Max blinked, and then he was gone. He put down his guitar and stood by the microphone, searching the crowd for Rick, desperate for another glimpse of him. Tony and Kyle were playing the intro of "Black-Spot Heart" over and over, waiting for him to join in.

The crowd began to heckle, but he still couldn't see Rick. Had he imagined it? As he moved his hand to grab the microphone, the flashing lights reflected off it. It was mesmerizing. He'd never seen anything so beautiful.

Kyle shook him. "Come on, Max. You need to sing."

He took the microphone off the stand and handed it to Max.

Max looked down at the microphone and back up to the crowd. They weren't their fans. They weren't here to see them. A biker-looking guy in the front row waved his fist at him.

Slowly, Max approached him and crouched next to him, peering down and speaking calmly to him. "Listen, asshole, you heckle me once more and I'll come down there and kick your ass."

Springing to his feet, he turned his back to the crowd and raised his arms in the air. Tony and Kyle were watching him in horror, glancing at each other in a silent conversation. Max brought the microphone to his lips and turned to face the front of the stage. Biker-guy waved his fist again and threw a plastic cup of beer at him, but Max dodged it, and it sailed past him, sloshing across the stage.

He was aware that the crowd was rapidly turning against him, but he didn't care. Screw them all. He was getting hot. Unbearably hot. Max pulled his T-shirt over his head and threw it at biker-guy, and then he undid his boots and kicked them off. Then he placed his hand on his belt. "Let's see a little skin." He winked at the girl next to biker-guy. "I will if you will." That ought to piss her boyfriend off.

"Max, don't do this. You need to stop," Kyle shouted at him, but Max shoved him out of his way. He placed the microphone back in the stand and undid his belt, waiting until the cheers drowned out the angry heckling—he was back at the Torrens Club with hundreds of people screaming his name. The room was spinning a little. Steadying himself using the microphone stand, he whisked off his pants. The crowd seemed to be enjoying it. He grinned and slid off his boxers, standing onstage completely naked. Kyle and Tony were watching him and looked stunned. Max giggled and gazed out in a trance at the mass of metalheads. He was numb to emotion for the first time in months, content to stand there and watch how this played out.

Death Charm's fans pushed forward, a jumble of naked skin, black leather, and PVC. Another glass sailed past him, but this time he didn't flinch. The security guards who had been heading toward him now turned to face the crowd, trying to control the chaos.

Max's gaze was drawn to the back of the hall, which was emptying as the crowd bunched forward as they crushed toward the stage. One person was left standing there, up on the balcony. The one person he'd been searching for, and the last person he wanted to see. He was blurry, but when Max blinked, he didn't move.

Anger welled up in the pit of his stomach, and Max fought Tony and Kyle's attempts to pull him off the stage. It was all Rick's fault this was such a disaster.

He grabbed his bass guitar, lifted it high above his head, and smashed it down on an amplifier over and over again. Shards of his precious guitar flew in all directions and the strings sprung back, striking him in the face, but he didn't care, he could barely feel it, just as he didn't feel the barrage of glasses striking him.

Max collapsed, naked, down into the debris, the blood from his forehead mingling with his tears and dregs of other people's beer. The crowd began to swarm the stage, and Max felt himself being hauled to his feet and through a maze of dark, eerie tunnels, the shadows giving him the creeps.

The shadows drifted to life, floating toward him, closer and closer, terrorizing him with their deadly shapes. He swerved to avoid a shadowed sword thrust toward him, and terror threatened to take over his body. Max tried to zigzag down the path to stay out of reach of the shadows trying to attack and engulf him, trying to swallow him whole.

Max tried to scream, but no sound came out.

Suddenly the shadow-demons disappeared, and his vision was assaulted with thousands of bright, piercing lights that flashed across his vision in haphazard streaks. Were they outside? He was so hot. Someone was trying to put clothes on him, but he fought them off. He was burning up.

Tony was shouting, "We need to get him to the hospi…."

Max watched Tony's lips moving, and his voice pierced him like thousands of clusters of hypodermic needles.

He had to get away.

He sprinted—heading for the road. Roads were the quickest way to get anywhere. He'd be back at his hotel in no time. The room would be safe. Quiet. And he could take a cold bath to cool down.

CHAPTER FOURTEEN

Rick
Earlier that afternoon

"YOU DIDN'T even respect me enough to discuss it with me, or even to tell me. I'm not a fucking mind reader." Max turned and ran.

"Max, wait!"

Rick started to run after him, but found himself slowing and watching Max disappear as the enormity of their fight hit him.

He'd accused Max of being a coward because he'd hidden who he was, but then it struck him: Max had been brave enough to come out to his friends. For him. And yet he had been too scared to even tell Max the truth about his interview. If anyone was a coward, it was him, not Max. He deserved everything Max had said. And the truth stung. He wished he could turn back time until before Max spotted him, wished he hadn't lashed out at Max, that he hadn't pushed him away.

How could he have been so stupid as to think that Max couldn't have handled them talking about Rick's offer? Rick had been worried about hurting Max, about losing him. But now his actions had pushed Max away completely. The hurt on Max's face when Neil had told him the job was his would haunt him forever.

"Rick." At the sound of Neil's voice, Rick turned to face him. He was trembling, his thoughts still spinning. "Everything okay out here? We heard shouting." Neil walked up to him and frowned. "Are you okay?" Rick opened his mouth but was at a total loss of what to say. "Come on back inside. I'll make us some tea."

Rick followed Neil into the gym in a daze.

"What happened to your friend?" Neil said once they were sitting in his office with mugs of hot tea. Rick didn't even like tea, but he sipped at it anyway. It was strangely soothing.

"He left."

"Shouldn't you go after him?" Rick looked up at him. "If there's one thing I've learned over the years, it's that if Dietmar is pissed at me, he's always right, and I have been an arsehole. You should always go after them."

"But… Max isn't—"

"Rick, I heard everything. Your boyfriend's pissed at you because you didn't tell him about our arrangement."

"I didn't think he'd understand."

"That doesn't matter. Rule one of any relationship: if you're serious about them, you have to tell them everything. Even the shit stuff." Neil paused. "Especially the shit stuff. You can guarantee they'll always find out if you're hiding something. I guess the question is: is he important enough that you want to fight for him?"

Rick's shoulders slumped. "I never expected to feel this strongly for him." He rested his head in his hands, and his voice cracked as he said, "I think I might be falling in love with him. I've ruined everything. There's no way he'll want to speak to me again."

Neil raised an eyebrow. "I thought you were a fighter, Rick. Fight for him."

A COUPLE of hours later, Rick left Neil and headed back to the hotel. He had negotiated with Neil about the terms of his employment and had come away with a deal that was far better than he could have dreamed of. He would be responsible for a small stable of fighters to start with and would help with their training camps as they prepared for their fights, and would then travel with them and be ringside as their cutman.

This would be the best of both worlds. The fighters would fight a maximum of four times a year, and their training camps would be eight weeks long. He wouldn't have to be there the entire time. It would mean he would be able to spend practically half the year in Elfinbrook with Max, and the other half he would be in London, but would be able to visit with Max every couple of weeks… if Max would hear him out and still wanted to be with him, that was. His chest was heavy, and he rubbed the back of his neck as he played out Max's possible reactions in his head. He hoped that Max felt as strongly about him as he suspected he might—hoped that he would give him another chance to make this right.

It was getting close to five, and Max still hadn't returned to their room. Rick considered going to speak to Tony to find out if he had seen Max, but he knew that once Tony heard about what had happened, he would have some serious bridges to rebuild. He tried calling Max's cell, but there was no answer. He was still pissed at him. Rick didn't blame him.

He was going to have to face the consequences sooner or later. Quickly changing into something more suitable for the gig, Rick then went and knocked on Tony's door. There was no answer. Maybe they were all already at the venue.

"Rick," Sian called out. He looked behind him and saw her checking her door was locked. "Is Max ready to go? Kyle and Tony were wondering where he is. They just got to the Scarab Lounge, but he's not there."

"He's not there? Well, where is he, then?"

Sian frowned. "What do you mean, where is he? We thought he was with you."

Rick let out a frustrated growl. "We had an argument. I haven't seen him all afternoon. I thought he would've been with you?"

Sian had her cell out and tried calling Max, but he didn't answer to her, either.

"Where could he be?" Rick gripped his hair and shook his head.

"How bad was your argument? What did you do? He was really happy when I saw him earlier."

"It was awful. I've been a total jerk."

Sian narrowed her eyes but didn't press him. "In that case, my guess would be that he's in one of the bars. Where were you when you argued?"

"Belsize Park. About a half hour away."

"Rick!" Sian sighed heavily. "He could be anywhere. I just hope he had the sense to come back around here. Tell you what. We'll check the bars here in Camden and I'll keep trying his cell. We'll split up. It'll be quicker."

Rick lost count of how many bars he went into, but Max was nowhere to be seen. Finally, Sian called him.

"Did you find him?" Rick demanded.

"Yes, I found him," Sian said, and she started crying.

"Is he okay?" A cold chill rippled through his body. "Tell me he's okay."

"He's onstage."

Rick relaxed as he recognized the Purple Method song playing in the background, but not much. "Why are you crying? Are *you* okay?"

"I'm fine. Rick, he's a mess. I think you need to get down here."

Rick's heart was racing as he ran out of the bar and sprinted down Camden High Street toward the Scarab Lounge. It didn't take him long to get there. Thankfully the sidewalks were clearer than they had been earlier in the day. He was breathing hard as he had his ticket checked and went through the usual security checks.

When he reached the balcony, he couldn't believe his eyes. Max was onstage, naked, goading the crowd. He was slick with sweat, and if Rick didn't know better, he would've sworn he'd taken drugs. He looked spaced-out. Not quite focusing normally and staring at odd things like his hand and the lights.

Had he driven Max to do this? Guilt gripped him even tighter, and Rick clutched the balcony railing.

The crowd surged forward, and Rick watched in horror as they swarmed the stage. There was absolutely nothing he could do from this far back. Kyle finally managed to grab Max and dragged him off the stage and out the back, but not before Max had smashed up his bass guitar. Tony raced after them, shielding them from the glasses being thrown at them. Jesus.

Rick turned and ran back out through the entrance, and onto the sidewalk. He knew the door to backstage was a few doors up, and sure enough, farther down the street, a door flew open, and Sian, Tony, Kyle, and Max appeared.

Before Rick could get to them, Max ran out into the road, naked. Instead of crossing over, he ran down the middle of one of the lanes of traffic.

Rick willed his legs to move faster. He had to catch Max before this ended in disaster, before anything could happen to him. It was all his fault. If he had told Max the truth, none of this would be happening. Rick's heart nearly stopped as a car swerved past Max. He didn't seem to notice the traffic. It was a miracle nothing hit him. Oh God, he had to get to him soon. Rick dodged the cars as he sprinted toward him.

"Max!"

Kyle, Sian, and Tony were also running after Max, and Rick soon overtook them.

But they were all too late.

Rick's heart stopped, and he watched helplessly as Max approached the bend in the road. A car raced around the corner, not seeing him in time and striking him hard, catapulting him into the air. It didn't stop, swerving around the four of them chasing after Max and then driving away. Max tumbled to the ground in a motionless heap in the road.

"Max! No!"

Reaching him first, and without a thought to his own safety, Rick dropped to his knees next to him and curled his body around Max to keep him safe. The approaching car skidded to a stop, narrowly missing them.

"Please be okay, please be okay," Rick's panicked voice repeated as he checked him over. Max was writhing on the ground, but there was little blood. Thank goodness the car had slowed a little for the corner before hitting him. That probably saved his life.

Tony dropped to his knees beside Rick, panting hard. "Is he alive?" Tony screamed.

"He's not going to die." Rick prayed he was speaking the truth. He couldn't lose Max. He couldn't…. "Call an ambulance."

"Don't let them kill me," Max sobbed and flailed.

"No one's going to hurt you. I've got you." Rick held Max tight, cradling him in his arms and supporting his neck as Max let out a blood-curdling wail. "I won't let anyone harm you," he said. "Everything's going to be okay, I promise."

AS THEY waited for news on Max, Rick paced the hospital corridor until Sian tugged at his arm and encouraged him to sit with her. He was used to being in hospitals because of his chiropractor training, so he didn't usually mind them, but being in there because someone he cared about was hurt was a whole other thing. Surely they should've heard something by now.

"It's all my fault," he said and rested his head in his hands. "He wouldn't be here if it weren't for me."

"This is nobody's fault," Sian said.

Kyle shifted in his seat. "I honestly thought he would be okay. He must have only just taken the drugs. I didn't realize he'd taken so much. If I'd known—"

"How could you have guessed?" Sian said. "Kyle, it's not your fault either. Sure, he seemed a bit spaced-out, but no more so than you get sometimes. I thought he'd be okay too until that third song. But by then it was too late to pull him off the stage."

They sat in silence, lost in their own thoughts. Tony had been completely silent. He was sitting in one of the chairs in another row with his knees pulled up to his chest and was staring at the wall. Rick got up and moved over to sit next to him. "How are you holding up?"

Tony ignored him, not even glancing his way.

"He's going to be okay. There was no blood. That's got to be a good sign. His muscles would most likely have been relaxed from the drugs, so it's unlikely that he will have broken anything."

"My brother is in here because of you," Tony said so quietly that Rick almost missed it. Tony turned his head and stared at Rick, his face expressionless. "If you'd stayed away from him like I'd told you to, none of this would've happened. He took those drugs because of you."

"I'm sorry," Rick said, his throat tightening. "I'm so sorry."

"If you weren't in his life, we wouldn't be sitting here right now waiting to hear whether my only real family is going to make it through this." Tony clutched at his knees, his face pale, eyes bloodshot.

"Max is going to be okay. He has to be," Sian said, tearing up. "And you need to stop blaming Rick. Nobody could've predicted that Max would react this way. Yes, Rick, you've been a jerk, but you're also the best thing that ever happened to Max. None of us was there to support Max through this until it was too late. Tony, if you're going to say it's Rick's fault, then that's on all of us."

Kyle let out a sarcastic laugh. "What a total clusterfuck."

"You can say that again." Sian turned from where she was looking out the window at the glowing moon high in the sky. "But right now, looking after Max is all that's important. None of this crap matters. What's done is done. It's how we move forward that's important."

"Mr. Diaz?" A doctor approached, and they all sprang to their feet.

"Yeah," Tony said. Rick stood by Tony's side. "How is he?"

"He's been very lucky, and we expect him to make a full recovery. We've sedated him and given him something to counteract the drugs, but we'll be keeping him in for observation for the next forty-eight hours."

"Oh, thank fuck," Tony said.

"Can we see him?" Rick asked.

"Are you family?"

Tony looked around at them but avoided looking Rick in the eyes. "Yeah. We're all his family."

The doctor clearly didn't believe him, but he smiled kindly. "One at a time and don't stay long. He needs to rest."

Tony went in first, and when he came back five minutes later, his eyes were puffy and red, but he looked calmer. "He's doing okay," Tony said. "He's still pretty out of it, but he's looking better. I don't think he'll be awake much longer."

"Rick, why don't you go in next," Sian said.

"Thank you," Rick said and rushed to Max's ward. He had the bed by the window, and he looked so pale it was scary. Rick sat on the chair by his bed and gently squeezed Max's hand. Max's eyelids strained to open, and they stared at each other for a long moment. "I'm so sorry, Max," Rick said and began to cry, holding Max's hand to his cheek and sobbing—with relief that Max was okay, regret for being the reason he was lying there, and with shame for not treating Max as an equal in their relationship. He would never, ever make that mistake again—if Max could find it within himself to forgive him.

CHAPTER FIFTEEN

Max

A HEADACHE from hell hit Max as he drifted into consciousness. He groaned and blinked awake, cursing as blinding lights invaded his eyes. His mouth was uncomfortably dry, and his limbs felt as though they were weighed down, too heavy to move. This had to be the worst hangover of his life.

"Max." Rick's voice pounded through his head, and he felt his warm hand close around his, but the heat was intolerable. He winced and wriggled his fingers until Rick let go. "How are you feeling?"

Opening his eyes and taking in the clinical surroundings of the white walls and sickly green curtains around his bed, he panicked. Why wasn't he at home? What was this place? "Where am I?"

"In the hospital."

"What?" Max sat up, and his body punished him with a severity of pain he'd never felt before. Even the light sheets covering his body were unbearable against his skin, and he cried out in agony.

"You're okay, it's okay," Rick said. "The doctors said not to worry about the pain; it'll ease soon enough. How much do you remember about what happened?"

Rick helped him lie back down, and Max thought back to the previous day as his discomfort settled. Everything was hazy. Like his memories weren't his own, and yet were ingrained deep within. A jumbled mess of weird sensations and dark, terrifying images that felt too real, like he'd lived through a nightmare.

"What happened?" Max said, unsure if he wanted to hear the truth. Speaking with such a dry throat was painful. "Can I get something to drink?"

"The nurse left you some ice chips. Here." Rick helped him with them, and the coolness against the heat of his mouth felt really good. He didn't think he'd ever felt so dehydrated before. "You were hit by a car." Max relaxed back and crunched on the chips as he tried to make sense of what Rick had told him.

"How long have I been out?"

"About seventeen hours. It happened last night, and it's three in the afternoon now. How much do you remember about yesterday?"

Max thought back to the music store where he'd bought new bass strings, and then he squeezed his eyes shut as everything came flooding back: seeing Rick in the MMA gym, finding out Rick had been lying to him, and then talking to the guy in the bar and buying the drugs in the hope he could make all of it go away. He opened his eyes and stared at Rick. "You're leaving me."

"No. I'm not leaving you, Max. Please let me make this right." Rick clasped Max's hand again and brought it to his lips. His voice was desperate and pleading, and he looked to be close to tears.

Max swallowed the last of the ice chips and turned his head so he was looking at the ceiling. He was numb from the emotional roller coaster of the last twenty-four hours. It had been such a shock to find out that Rick had been lying to him when he'd trusted him completely. "How do I know you won't do that to me again?" Max asked.

"I've learned my lesson. I'll never keep anything from you again. I promise. I'll do whatever it takes to show you that you can trust me."

"Why, Rick?" Max turned to look at him again. "After everything you said yesterday… nothing's changed apart from the fact that I'm lying here. If you're feeling guilty over what happened to me, there's no need, really. You don't have to do this. Trying to force things to work between us won't make it right. Don't you think it would be better for both of us if we called it a day?"

"Is that what you want?"

Tears pricked Max's eyes. "It doesn't matter what I want. Soon we'll be living thousands of miles apart."

"If I said I'd still be living in Elfinbrook for over four months of the year, would that change your mind?" Rick's grip on his hand tightened. "I'll be back there loads, Max. With the money I'll be making, I'll even be able to get my own place in Elfinbrook. Elfinbrook's my home. Where I want to be. With you. Will you give me another chance? Please?"

Max wanted more than anything to say yes, but he was terrified of getting his heart broken. He wasn't sure he could cope with going through this pain again. It was excruciating.

"I never meant to hurt you, Max. The reason I didn't tell you was… it was because I didn't want to risk losing you. Everything was so perfect between us. I didn't know how to tell you without ruining what we had." Rick was crying now, and Max blinked furiously to stop his own tears. "I think I'm falling in love with you. I don't want to lose you. Please. Please give me another chance."

Max's heart froze, and then it was pounding in his chest, blood rushing in his ears. Rick was falling in love with him? Had he heard him right? Max's hands were tingling, and he closed his fingers around Rick's hand.

Rick looked up at him in surprise, and as the realization struck, a disbelieving smile crept onto his face. "Are you…? Does this mean…? Are we…?"

Max gave him a tired smile. "It means that I forgive you."

Rick collapsed against him, holding him tight. "Thank you. Oh my God. Thank you. I was so sure you'd say no." Max winced, his body tensing, still so sensitive to touch. The pain was easing, but he was exhausted.

The relief that everything was going to be okay with Rick was overwhelming, and fatigue washed over Max as if he hadn't slept for several days. He closed his eyes and barely heard Rick speaking to him as he drifted off, fighting the dark nightmares as sleep took him under.

THE NEXT day, Max was discharged, and Rick, Tony, Sian, and Kyle took him back to the hotel in a cab. They all looked exhausted, and he felt a spike of guilt that he'd put them through this.

"How are you feeling?" Sian asked Max.

"Much better." That wasn't even a lie. His limbs still felt heavy, and he had a lot of bruising, but the sensitivity had gone. The pain meds were doing their job. He looked sheepishly at his friends. "I'm sorry I put you all through this."

"We're just relieved you're okay," Sian said. "You don't need to apologize for anything." She stared at Max. "We're the ones who should be apologizing. We're all really sorry you didn't feel like you could talk to us about something so important."

"You could've killed yourself." Tony smacked his arm. "Pull anything like this again, and I'll kill you myself."

"Tony!" Rick reached for Max's hand.

"What?"

Tony's cell began to ring, blaring out "Someplace to Hide," and he fumbled to remove it from his pocket.

Max laughed. "Do you have a song I wrote as your ringtone?"

"Shut up," he grumbled and blushed. "I was worried." He let his cell go to voicemail and then set it to silent. "Whoever it is can wait."

Max allowed himself to relax as he held Rick's hand in public for the first time ever. It felt weird doing this out in the open without needing to hide; it was going to take some getting used to—in the best possible way. It felt so right, and Max decided there and then that he wasn't going to hide their relationship once they got back home.

When they got back to the hotel, Tony, Sian, and Kyle went to their rooms to get some sleep, and Max relaxed in bed while Rick went to get them some takeout food from Camden market. They were going to try the filled Indian puris breads that had looked and smelled delicious the other day. Rick didn't waste any time and put the parcels down on the bed when he returned.

"Mm, these are delicious," Max said as he took his first bite. "I need to learn how to make these."

"They are good. But they're not exactly healthy."

"Yeah, but you won't be fighting in the octagon anymore, though. You don't need to worry so much now about what you're eating."

Rick laughed and kissed the side of Max's head. "I still have to get in the ring with those fighters and spar with them. They're top athletes. I'll get my ass kicked if I'm not in shape."

"Remember the time you tried to cook me Philly cheesesteaks?" Max chuckled and took another bite of his puris.

"You were distracting me," Rick grumbled.

"And then your mom shouted at you for nearly burning down her kitchen again." Max laughed. "Have you told her you'll be moving out yet?"

"No, not yet. I can't wait to have my own place." He relaxed back against the wall and pulled Max closer. "If I give you a key, will you go around there and check on it for me while I'm away?"

Max stared at him. "You're gonna give me a key?"

"Don't you want one?"

Max put his puris to one side and kissed him. "Of course I want a key. Where are you gonna stay when you're in London?"

"With Neil and Dietmar. They've got a spare room. That's if Dietmar is speaking to me by then. You're lucky the riot brought him a load of publicity. Neil said the night after there were people lined up along the street, trying to get in. They had to turn half of them away."

"That's good." Max snuggled against Rick. "I'm sorry for causing problems for your friend. It is a shame we won't get to play again while we're here." He grimaced. "And I need to get another guitar."

"Don't worry about that for now. I'll help you find an even better bass guitar once we get home. We'll pay Hugh a visit as soon as we get back."

"So… we have five more days here in London now we've changed our flights. What do you want to do while we're here?"

Rick pressed his lips to Max's ear, making him shiver. "I have a few ideas. I'm sure we can find *something fun* to do."

VICTORIA MILNE discovered fiction writing relatively late in life, back in 2012, and has loved every second of the journey. Her belief that life is one big adventure to be experienced to the max has stood her in good stead, but it has resulted in rather a lot of plot bunnies that don't give her a minute's peace!

A firm believer that consensual love should come without labels and without prejudice, these themes often appear in her stories, as do Victoria's passions for martial arts, cooking, yoga, and loud music. It was no surprise when these subjects began to resonate in her writing, frequently taking center stage, and rather than fighting it she's learned to accept and enjoy that these will always be indispensable elements in her work.

Although Victoria appreciates that stories don't always have to have happy endings, hers always do—because everybody deserves to find their true love(s).

In 2016, *Love Unlocked*—the anthology in which her story "Writer's Lock" was published—was a Rainbow Award finalist. The experience fueled her desire to learn as much about the mechanics of writing as she could. In 2017 Victoria completed her training with the Society for Editors and Proofreaders and became a full-time freelance editor. Victoria has always loved reading, and still can't quite believe she's been lucky enough to not only create books of her own but also help other writers perfect theirs too!

Website: www.purplemethod.net
Facebook: fb.me/victoriamilneauthor
Twitter: @victoria_milne_

FOR

MORE

OF THE

BEST

GAY

ROMANCE

dreamspinnerpress.com

www.ingramcontent.com/pod-product-compliance
Lightning Source LLC
Chambersburg PA
CBHW070057260626
47160CB00004B/1233